CADE AT THE WALLS

THE WESTERN ADVENTURES OF CADE MCCALL
BOOK IV

ROBERT VAUGHAN

WOLFPACK
PUBLISHING
— EST 2013 —

Wolfpack Publishing
P.O. Box 620427
Las Vegas, NV 89162

ISBN: 978-1-64119-207-1

PROLOGUE

Twin Creek Ranch 1927

Cade McCall was watching as his cows were run through dipping vats of oil. This was the means used to rid them of ticks that would spread Texas fever.

"How many more?" Cade asked his son as he looked out over the herd that was enclosed in a nearby pasture.

"We've got less than 1500," Will said. "I'm a little disappointed that Stone didn't come, but maybe something came up."

Cade smiled, as he took off his hat and wiped the sweat from his brow. "He's a good boy. He'll be here."

"Pop, he's seven years older than I am, and I'm 50. When are you going to stop calling him a boy?"

Just then they looked toward the ranch house where they saw a yellow vehicle making its way down the lane.

"Well, I do believe that's him now," Cade said as he waved his hat to show the driver where they were.

The Roadster was soon bouncing across the pasture, kicking up a cloud of dust as it headed toward where Cade and Will were standing. Upon stopping, a man jumped out, and reaching into the cargo box, he pulled out a leather case.

"I'm sorry, Uncle Cade. I would have been here this morning, but I had to stop and help a gentleman get his car up and running. You're not finished yet are you?"

"Not yet," Will said. "But we decided to go ahead and start. Do you have 1500 injections?"

"That and more," Stone said. "Doctor Dalrymple mixed the serum himself, but even after we've given them the inoculation, I think we should still dip the cows just to make sure they're not infected when you ship them out of here."

"That's good," Cade said, "but I think I'll leave this work for you young fellows. I'm going back to the house."

The summer heat was bearing down, and Cade walked slowly. He should have asked Stone to drive him back to the house, but it was hard for him to admit that at 84, he couldn't do all the things he had done when he was younger.

"There you are," Molly McCall said as Cade let himself through the gate. "I was about to send out a search party to look for you. We've got company."

"I saw him. Stone's out with Will," Cade said.

"No, no. Owen's here. He had car trouble coming in from Fort Worth. He's a little frustrated, so be nice."

Molly took Cade's hand and together they walked toward the porch where they found Owen Wister sitting in the swing with a tall glass of lemonade.

Cade nodded his head, waiting for Wister to speak first.

"These roads out here. You'd think with oil everywhere, somebody would have the idea that maybe they could make it, so a man could drive without falling into a cavern. If some Indian hadn't come along, I'd still be sitting there."

"You mean Stone," Cade said. "Dr. Stone Forehead McCall."

"McCall?" Wister questioned. "I'm sure he was an Indian."

"He is, but he's still my nephew."

"Your nephew?"

"That he is."

"Now this story, I have to hear."

"You will," Cade said. "Just as soon as Molly gets me a glass of lemonade."

Dodge City, Kansas – spring, 1874

Jacob Harrison and Cade McCall were seated at their regular table in the Red House Salon, formerly known as a saloon. At one time, Cade had been the half owner of the place, but now it belonged exclusively to Jeter and Magnolia Willis.

"Do you think people will know the difference between a salon and a saloon?" Jacob asked.

"It doesn't matter," Cade said. "It's what Magnolia wanted and, so it is."

"Here you are, gentlemen," an exceptionally pretty, young woman said as she placed a steaming bowl of stew in front of each of the two men.

"Thanks, Cetti," Cade said. "Let me see. Is it beef or deer today?"

"It's neither," Cetti said. "Magnolia calls it potee, but that's not what it really is, cause it's supposed to have a lot more vegetables."

Jacob laughed. "So, Bill just cooked up some pork and added beans and potatoes."

"You'd better enjoy it while you can," Jeter said as he drew back a chair and joined the two men.

"Why do you say that? Are the porkers about to go the way of the buffalo?" Cade asked.

"No, it's not that. The end of the month, Bill and Sybil are planning on leaving."

"That's too bad," Cade said. "I know Magnolia has enjoyed having their help, especially now that there's a baby coming."

"Is Bill staying here in Dodge City, or is he heading out?" Jacob asked as he took a bite of his stew.

"They're leaving town," Jeter said as he let out a long sigh. "I think it's a big mistake. It's fine for Bill to take such risks, but to put his wife in such danger—that's just not right."

Cade lowered his head and concentrated on his food, as all three men realized what Jeter had just said. It was now almost four years since Cade's wife, Arabella, had died. She and Magnolia had been kidnapped while they served as cooks on a cattle drive that McCall and Willis had contracted to bring out of Texas. To this day, Cade blamed himself for what had happened to her.

Jacob, who was Cade's partner in a freight hauling business, cleared his throat and broke the awkward silence.

"Where are they going?"

"To the Texas Panhandle," Jeter said.

Cade jerked his head up. "You don't mean he's taking her down to the outpost Charlie Myers is trying to start."

"Yes, I do," Jeter said. "Bill says the two of them are going to start a restaurant."

"That's just asking for trouble. Wherever they put that outpost, it's a clear violation of the Medicine Lodge Treaty," Cade said. "Whatever they do is severely trespassing on Indian hunting grounds."

"Does it really bother you all that much?" Jacob asked. "Because if it does, I can back out of the contract I just signed with Charlie. I told him we'd help haul as much merchandise as he could ship."

"And where would we be taking this merchandise? As far as I can tell, he doesn't even know where he wants to put his store. Just somewhere close to the buffalo, and nobody knows where that is," Cade said.

"He won't be going by himself," Jeter said. "Tom O'Keefe's moving his blacksmith shop down, and James Hanrahan's moving his outfit down and that's at least two dozen hunters and skinners. They say he's gonna build a saloon, too."

"Of course. We don't want the buffalo hunters to be without their sauce."

"That's not all bad," Jeter said. "Those same men have been mighty good to the Red House."

"I know," Cade said, "and I'll be glad to take their money. How much do you think we'll make?"

"Charlie says he's going to ship about $50,000 worth of merchandise," Jacob said. "We could pick up a pretty penny—maybe enough to add a couple more wagons."

"That'd be good," Cade said. "We're not making much this winter, with the weather and then the agency getting less and less freight."

"Speaking of which, two wagons go out tomorrow," Jacob said, "but Dean's flat on his back. Gus says he can't move."

"I'll take it," Cade said.

"Fine. Just make sure you're back by the end of the month. That's when we move out for the Panhandle."

Indian Territory, Oklahoma:

It had been one of the coldest winters in memory with frequent blizzards making conditions even more brutal. Indian Agent John Miles watched the chiefs come in to the Cheyenne and Arapaho Agency. Never in his time at Camp

7

Supply nor since he had relocated to the Darlington agency had he seen a more pathetic sight.

The Indians had barely survived the winter, and now they were coming in for much needed rations and supplies.

"Abandon your wandering ways, learn to live in peace, and we will provide you with food and sustenance," they had been told by the government.

But the supplies had been little before the winter started and now, though the Indians were keeping their part of the bargain by staying close to the agency, some even moving into the housing that had been provided, Miles knew that he would be unable to keep up his part of the agreement.

"Ho, John," Spotted Wolf said, lifting his hand in greeting. Though John did happen to be Miles' name, Spotted Wolf greeted every white man in the same way.

There were others with him, and each of the Indians was leading a horse which they hoped to load with the provisions for their people.

"My friend," the Quaker Indian agent replied, lifting his own hand. "It is good to see thee."

"The winter has been very bad," Spotted Wolf said as he dismounted. "The women and the children are crying with hunger. We have to kill many ponies."

"It is a sad thing to kill ponies," Miles agreed. "Come inside and warm thee by the fire."

Spotted Wolf and the others followed.

Cade McCall and Gus Zordel were standing by the pot-bellied stove drinking coffee, while George Bent, the interpreter, was sitting behind a desk.

"I didn't expect to see you, Spotted Wolf," Cade said as he scrambled to find enough cups, and then began to pour coffee for the Indians. He watched as each one added generous amounts of sugar to the strong black coffee. "How is Quiet Stream?"

"She die. Wind Woman is now first wife."

"I'm sorry," Cade said. "And what of your children? How is Black Bird?"

"My son is well, and his sons are well. Cheyenne people cannot be broken. About my daughter, I do not know."

"Spotted Wolf, the news I have for ye is not good," Miles said interrupting Cade's conversation.

Spotted Wolf lowered his cup and looked at Miles. His eyes told the agent that, even before he explained the situation, Spotted Wolf knew what he was going to tell him.

"All the rations that we requested have not yet been delivered," Miles said. "McCall has brought two wagons."

Spotted Wolf turned to Cade. "With bad meat and bad flour."

Miles ran the back of his hand across his mouth, a nervous gesture, before he replied.

"It's not Cade's fault. He brought all that was shipped to Dodge City."

"A promise that cannot be kept, should not be made," Spotted Wolf said. "Give up the hunt for buffalo, we were told. Live in peace near the agency, we were told. You will not be hungry, you will not be cold, you will not be without clothing, we were told.

"But we did not get all that you said for the winter, and now we will not get all that you said for the spring," Spotted Wolf said. "What shall we tell our women and children when we return, and we have no food for their bellies?"

"I'm sorry," Miles said. "I'll give thee what we have."

"And how much is that?" He turned to Cade.

"Some flour, not much. Some beans and some bacon, but very little. No coffee, no sugar," Cade said.

Spotted Wolf shook his head.

"I want thee to know that I will continue to petition Secretary Delano for more rations. I will even send a personal letter to President Grant," Miles insisted. "I'm sure Washington will honor the agreement we have with thee and thy people."

"I think the great chiefs in Washington do not care if the Indian lives or dies." Spotted Wolf set his undrunk cup of coffee on the desk.

"Does thee not want thy coffee?"

"I cannot drink coffee if there is no coffee for my people. We will find food for our people."

"Spotted Wolf, I beg of thee, don't do anything yet. I know that we've not kept our promises, but please do not start raiding the settlers. The Lord is not pleased when one of His children raises a club against another."

"The buffalo are gone, our people are starving, our horses are run off by the white man, even while we try to farm this land, and the bluecoats refuse to take care of my people."

Neither Cade nor Miles commented.

"Quakers tell us that the Great Father does not want war," Spotted Wolf said. "I will not make war, but I do not speak for my brothers. The Kiowa have raised the pipe to the Cheyenne. If Bad Hand continues to kill the Comanche and the Kiowa, we will join them."

The Indians all turned and left, each one pouring the contents of their cups on the floor in an act of defiance.

"THAT DOESN'T SOUND GOOD," Gus Zordel said. "Who is this Bad Hand they are talking about?"

"Colonel Ranald Mackenzie. The Indians call him Bad Hand because he lost two fingers during the Civil War," George Bent said. "He and his 4th Cavalry have been down on the border going after the Kiowa and the Comanche, and now he's been posted at Fort Concho."

"Has anything happened?" Cade asked.

"Not anything from Mackenzie—at least not yet, but Colonel Brooke got word at Camp Supply that Colonel Buell hit a couple of Comanche bands near the Double Mountain Fork of the Brazos. The word is Chief Lone Wolf's son and his nephew were killed in one battle, and Quanah Parker's nephew was killed in the other."

"Oh, oh, they'll be on the warpath." Cade took a deep breath. "It's called revenge."

"Let us pray that thee be wrong," Miles said.

2

THE QUAHADI VILLAGE OF QUANAH PARKER:

Quanah Parker and a small band of Quahadi warriors were riding toward the Kiowa camp of Lone Wolf. He rode with a heavy heart as he was carrying the news that Bad Hand, the name the People called Colonel Ranald Mackenzie, was back in the Texas Panhandle. The story was that he was either at Fort Concho or at Fort Richardson, but it didn't matter. Mackenzie was the bluecoat the Comanche hated the most.

And Mackenzie hated Quanah Parker. It had been he who had bested Mackenzie at Blanco Canyon. The Comanche under Quanah's leadership had raided the cavalry herd, getting away with more than 60 horses, including Mackenzie's prized gray pacer. From that time on, Mackenzie had his sights set on the young war chief.

But after the Blanco Canyon raid, Mackenzie did not react the way other soldiers had done before him. He spent a year exploring the Llano Estacado, that part of the panhandle that had always served as the refuge of the People. Now, Mackenzie had learned the trails that led up the rugged canyon walls, and he had found the places where he could find the sweetest water. Never again would the People be able to evade the bluecoats as they had always done before.

Quanah had observed firsthand the devastation Mackenzie and his troops imposed upon him and his brothers. After a skirmish Mackenzie ordered the villages burned, the horses captured, and the women and children taken as hostages. In one raid, two of Quanah's wives had been forced to march to Fort Sill. It was only after the arrival of Agent Haworth at the Comanche-Kiowa Reservation, that the Governor forced the release of the prisoners.

After a devastating winter that lasted well into spring with no sign of the return of the buffalo, several of the People had vowed to give up their way of life and make the reservation their home, but Quanah could not do that. He could see that the very essence of who the People were was being destroyed.

The Comanche—the most feared warriors of the Plains, the best horsemen and the uncontested best hunters, were slowly disappearing. The white man's diseases, the white man's bullets, and the white man's killing of the buffalo were slowly decimating their number. The bands that once had tipis that stretched for miles along the rivers now had a few hundred in their encampments. If there was no nomadic life, no warring with other tribes, no killing of the buffalo, there would be no need for the *Nerm*, known as the People, to even exist.

The white man's encroachment on land promised the People had to be stopped, and he, the son of a captured white woman who had embraced the Indian culture, would be the one to stop them.

As QUANAH RODE into Lone Wolf's village, he sat tall and

13

straight in his saddle, thinking of Lone Wolf's son whose name was Tauankia, Sitting-in-the-Saddle. Tauankia had been killed by Mackenzie's men at Kickapoo Springs, and Lone Wolf had vowed he would recover his body. Lone Wolf's hatred of the white man was as great as Quanah's and he knew he could depend upon the Kiowa chief to join him in his effort to stop the incursion of the white man.

When Quanah was told where he could find Lone Wolf, the chief stepped out to meet his visitor. Quanah had heard that in his grief, Lone Wolf had burned his lodge, his wagon, his buffalo robes, and he had killed all his horses. In addition, he had cut his hair, and the distraught man now stood before him.

"Welcome, Quanah," Lone Wolf greeted when he stepped out of Kicking Bird's lodge. "I am honored to be visited by such a warrior."

"I thank you for the greeting, and I am here to share in your grieving," Quanah replied as one of the young horse-minders of the village took his horse.

"Come inside the tipi and smoke with me," Lone Wolf said.

A moment later Quanah was sitting on a blanket in front of the fire. The hole in the top of Kicking Bird's tipi drew well, allowing the smoke to travel up in a tight spiral.

Lone Wolf lit the pipe, took a puff, then passed it to Quanah. As they smoked, neither man spoke, the silence interrupted only by the soft puffs of the two men. When the smoking was done, Lone Wolf, by gesture alone, invited Quanah to speak.

"My heart is heavy for you, Lone Wolf, for the loss of your son and your nephew."

"My son had seen only fifteen summers," Lone Wolf replied.

"My nephew, too, was killed by the soldiers," Quanah said, "and now, Bad Hand is back among us."

"This I have heard."

"The white man says he will provide for us, but in the bad winter when there was no game, neither was their food for our woman and children. The white man says that we must live in peace, but the white thieves come to steal our horses," Quanah said. "They say that we can hunt only in the land that they have given us, but the white buffalo hunters with guns that can reach far, come to kill our buffalo.

"In the north, where once buffalo were as many as the blades of grass, they are no more, because the white men have killed them. Soon, I think there will be no more buffalo anywhere, and when there are no more buffalo, I fear there will be no more people," Quanah said.

"I hear your words, Quanah, and I ask if you have thought on them and if you have, have you come to an answer as to what can be done? Or is your answer the one Kicking Bird has chosen?"

"Kicking Bird has moved to the reservation?"

"He has. He does not want to avenge the death of my son. He does not want to go after the men who steal our horses. He says the white man is too strong."

"We cannot let the People die," Quanah said. "We cannot let our way of life disappear. If the buffalo are all killed, soon there will be no People. As of yet, I do not have an answer to our problem. I have come to seek your councils so that, you, too, may think on it. Perhaps, together, we will think of a way to drive out the whites so that the land which belongs to us will be free of the ones who kill our buffalo and steal our horses," Quanah said.

"Yes, you will council with other Quahadi, and I will seek the advice of the ones who have lived long and thought much, and we will find a way."

LATER, as Quanah rode back to his village, he thought of the visit he had had with Lone Wolf of the Kiowa. He had said the end of the buffalo would be the end of the People. The People would be forced to live on the Government's reservation, and the People would disappear, just as had the Caddos and the Wichitas.

And the Tonkawa. Quanah spit on the ground.

How he hated the traitorous Tonks. They not only accepted the white man's ways, they rode as scouts for the devil Mackenzie teaching the bluecoats the Indian ways.

He had to come up with a way to save their way of life. The People had roamed the plains killing the buffalo since the first band of the Penateka had come down from the north. The People had been here since before the horse. And now, the white man would take this land away from him.

No. He, Quanah Parker, the half-breed son of Peta Nocona and Nautdah, would save his land and his people. He would open his heart and his mind and work to receive a vision.

DODGE CITY:

When Cade and Gus rolled into Dodge City, it was like the circus was coming to town. Buffalo hunters were everywhere.

After the Atchison, Topeka and Santa Fe Railroad had reached Dodge City in 1872, and after the eastern markets had perfected the method of turning hides into quality leather, the Kansas plains had been inundated with buffalo hunters. In a three-year period, more than five million animals had been killed, with each hide bringing between two and five dollars apiece.

Buffalo hunting was the lifeblood of the economy of Dodge City, and when it was realized that the buffalo would not be coming back to Kansas, the hunters scouted the area all the way to the Texas Panhandle where they found evidence of large herds of buffalo that were still in existence.

There was no question. They were going to Texas!

"I was getting a little worried about you," Jacob Harrison said when the two wagons pulled up in front of the freight office.

"Why is that? We made good time," Cade said.

"I know. It's just that we're losing business."

Cade jumped down and handed the reins to Dean Godsey, who took the wagon to the correl.

"I thought you said we had a contract with Charlie Myers. Did we lose that?"

"No, we didn't lose it, but look around you. Myers made a deal with all these hunters. If they'll agree to haul freight south, he'll sell it back to 'em, using Dodge prices," Jacob said.

Cade chuckled. "Actually, that's sort of ingenious."

"For him. Not for us."

CADE WENT to his room at the Dodge House where he kept his meager belongings. Jeter and Magnolia had asked him many times to move in with them, and he had considered it, but when it was time to make the decision, he backed out.

It was because of Chantal.

He loved the child as much as he could love his own flesh and blood, but when he saw her he was reminded of Arabella. Chantal had so many of her mother's features—the dark eyes and hair being the most obvious. But even at three years old, he recognized Arabella's spunkiness coming out in her personality.

Why was he, a grown man, not taking the responsibility of raising a child? Why did he leave Chantal with Magnolia and Jeter, when other widowers raised their children all the time?

He knew the answer. He was scared. What if he did something that would cause her death, just as it was his negligence that had ultimately caused Arabella's death? If that happened again, he couldn't live with himself.

But now, all he needed was a bath and a shave and he would see his little darling. He smiled as he grabbed clean clothes and walked down the hall to the bathing room.

CADE AND JETER were watching the two little girls as they played with the carved horses Cade had brought from the agency.

"You couldn't find any dolls?" Magnolia asked as she set dishes of food on the table. "I do believe you're trying to turn these two into boys."

"I don't think so," Cade said as he moved one of the horses closer to Bella. "Who's been out riding with them? Me or you?"

"That's different. Every child needs to know how to ride a horse if she's going to live out here in the wild," Magnolia said.

"When you visited the agency, did you see anybody we know?" Jeter asked.

"I saw Spotted Wolf and John Miles, of course," Cade said. "I don't envy him right now. He's trying to do what's right by the Indians, but the government is making his job mighty hard."

"I thought you just took a load of rations."

"Two wagons for 500 lodges," Cade said. "You tell me if you think that's enough food."

"What's he going to do?"

"He has no choice. He has to let them leave the reservation, and the awful thing is, there isn't a buffalo in sight that's closer than a hundred and fifty miles."

"So that means raiding and killing the stock that belongs to the settlers," Jeter said, "and they won't stop with just killing animals."

Cade nodded his head in agreement.

"And you and Jacob are going to see to it that even more buffalo are killed. Are you sure you want to take this contract to haul supplies for Charlie Myers?"

"It's going to happen whether we do it or not," Cade said. "Myers has about 50 hunters and their hide wagons lined up. He's going to load them up with his supplies and head south."

"Do you know where he's goin' to set up his store?"

"No, and I don't think he knows. He says wherever he can find good water, good grass with plenty of timber and of course close enough to the buffalo herd," Cade said.

"It sounds like you're going to be on the Canadian."

"I think Myers, for sure, will be on the Canadian," Cade said. "As soon as Harrison and McCall get our freight unloaded, we're on the way back."

"I don't believe you, Cade McCall. As soon as those hunters start bringing in hides, you'll be itchin' to get out there on the plains so you can bring back a load of your own," Jeter said.

"Well, maybe we can stay a little while."

From the Dodge City Messenger:

More Hides for Dodge City
Buffalo Hunters Follow the Herd

The commerce of Dodge City, from its inception, has been in the processing and shipping of "gold" not the yellow metal that is so elusive, but the hide of the buffalo. Of recent months though, that avocation has fallen upon difficult times due to the scarcity of the buffalo.

As it has developed, however, the buffalo have not disappeared as has been so lamented by the nay-sayers. They have merely relocated to ranges south, beyond the Arkansas, beyond the Cimarron, yes, even to the Canadian River.

In order to carry out this new endeavor the buffalo hunters must follow the herd and several enterprising businessmen in town, such as Charlie Myers, Thomas O'Keefe, William Olds, and James Hanrahan, have made plans to provide goods and services for the intrepid hunters in a place close to them.

To that end, there will soon leave Dodge City a procession of wagons, forming a train not seen since our fathers and grandfathers made those long and daring treks across the vast country to bring civilization to the West. It is anticipated that many of our citizens will be on hand for the departure to wish well those who by their endeavors, can only but benefit the economy of our fair city.

W.M.D. Lee read the article, then lay the paper aside. He was in Dodge, arranging for a shipment of supplies to two of the Lee and Reynolds trading posts, the one at Camp Supply and the one at the Cheyenne-Arapaho Agency. Charlie Myers planned to put a business down in the Texas Panhandle, to follow the buffalo hunters. Lee had accepted that Charlie Myers was his competitor, but Myers was in Dodge City, and Lee had chosen to concentrate his business in the Indian Territory near Camp Supply.

Myers, and two other Dodge City merchants, Charles Rath and Robert Wright, made their livings by procuring buffalo hides just as Lee did. While the merchants who lived in Dodge provided a market for the white hunters, W.M.D. Lee had dealt exclusively with the Indians. He had a monopoly trading with the Indians for their hides, and he didn't like the thought of sharing the southern herd with the white hunters who had decimated the herd north of the Arkansas River. If they were allowed to kill buffalo indiscriminately, as they had done on the Kansas plains, soon there would be no buffalo at all.

No. Having competition south of the Canadian was not a pleasant future to contemplate.

3

It was the end of March before the merchants were organized enough to start the trip south. At first, Jacob and Cade had thought they would only put two of their three wagons in service, but Charlie Myers had offered to pay them more money. So, it was that every man who worked for Harrison and McCall was to be on this trek: Gus Zordel, Dean Godsey, Mike Foster, Dale Matthews, Fuzzy McKnight, and Ed Keaton.

"I've got a bad feeling about this," Jeter Willis said as he strapped down the canvas covering on the final wagon. "I can't help but think about what happened to Lambdin and Morris."

"When they were killed, they were a single wagon," Jacob said. "They didn't have a chance."

"Look at all this," Cade said, as his hand swept toward the crowded street. "Right now, I count at least thirty wagons loaded and ready to go, and every one of them has a buffalo hunter who could kill a buffalo a thousand feet away if he had to."

"Buffalo stand still. Indians don't."

Cade laughed. "Didn't you hear Dirty Face Jones talking the other night? He said 'if you were born to be killed by Indians, you would be killed by Indians if you went to New York. That wouldn't make any difference'."

"And you're listening to Dirty Face?" a young man said as he walked up to Cade, extending his hand.

"Well, I'll be damned. Bat Masterson. I haven't seen you for a while. Thought you must have skipped the country," Cade said.

"I thought I might be skipping the country all together," Bat said. "See this scar." He lifted the hair off his forehead. "Had a run in with Bear Shield's band, but I got 'em back. See that one, and that one, and that one." He was pointing to various horses that were saddled and ready to go. "Those used to belong to Bear Shield, but Jim Harvey and I sort of liberated 'em and about a dozen more. Sold 'em for $1,200."

"Tell me, if you can point these horses out, don't you think Bear Shield could do the same thing?" Cade asked.

"Look at these men. Have you ever seen a rougher looking bunch of scoundrels? No Indian's going to come anywhere near us," Bat said.

"I hope to hell, you're right," Jeter said.

NEARBY, several of the hunters were standing around a man who was talking in a loud voice and waving his arms wildly. The four men walked over to see what was going on.

"I tell you, don't go," the man said. "The Comanche and Kiowa are ready to take out any white man who comes to their territory. The government told them they had the right to kill buffalo south of the Arkansas, and now you bastards have moved the dead line to the Cimarron. If you think they're going to stand for them being pushed away from the Canadian, you're crazy."

"Are we gonna listen to a breed? A breed whose got hisself a Cheyenne woman?" one of the hunter's yelled. "Amos Chapman don't want to share the booty. He wants to take all the hides from his brothers and sell 'em hisself."

"I tell you it's bad," Chapman continued. "The whites are stealing their horses and scalping settlers just to make it look like it's Indians doin' it. Look around you—do you see all the spotted ponies? Those came from the Cheyenne. Little Robe and Bull Bear lost 43 head, and a lot of 'em are going south in this train."

"Hell, we didn't steal 'em. We bought 'em fair and square from Hurricane Bill Martin."

"And where did Hurricane Bill get 'em? I'm tellin' you this is not the time to be goin' past the dead line."

Bat Masterson lifted his eyebrows. "See, he didn't say anything at all about Bear Shield. These horses belonged to Little Robe."

THE NEXT MORNING, there were thirty wagons that stretched along Front Street from the Dodge House to Fringer's Apothecary, three of which belonged to Harrison and McCall. Cade and Jacob were both mounted, and after riding up and down the length of the train, they returned to their wagons, which were the last three in the line.

Nearly everyone in town was turned out to watch the departure, almost as if it were a parade. Jeter, Magnolia, and the other employees of the Red House were standing on the front porch. When the Olds wagon headed out, Magnolia ran into the street, causing the wagons that were behind to come to a complete stop, while Sybil Olds jumped down to embrace her friend.

"I'm going to miss you, my friend," Magnolia said as tears welled in her eyes.

"No, don't cry," Sybil said as her own tears rolled down her cheeks. "When we get our restaurant set up, I want you to hitch a ride with Cade and come down to visit us. You can make some beignets for the men."

"Get back on that wagon, or else stay here," James Hanrahan said as he rode up to see what was holding up the train.

IKE AND SHORTY Shadler were at the head of the train, driving a double wagon pulled by six yokes of oxen. Buster, a big, brown Newfoundland dog, was sitting patiently on the ground by the front wheel of the first wagon. Fred Leonard, Charlie Myers' new partner, was checking the contents of the wagons. If they forgot anything, they would have to do without. The most necessary items for the hunters were ammunition and weapons, but they also would need various sundries such as coffee, bacon, flour, canned tomatoes, canned peaches, dried apples, and syrup. Axle grease and wolf poison were also kept on hand, as well as corn and grain for the animals.

James Hanrahan had five wagons loaded with beer and whiskey, enough to open his saloon. He hired the Shepherd and Billy Ogg to stay with the wagons at all times. No one knew Shepherd's full name, but James had never seen either him or Ogg take a drink, and both could handle a gun. With his wagons secure, James took charge of the train and was the self-appointed wagon master. He rode to the head of the train, stood in the stirrups and lifted his wide-brimmed white Stetson hat high so that every driver could see him.

"All right, boys, let's get 'em moving!" He brought his hat down sharply.

"Heayah!" Ike Shadler shouted, his call augmented with the loud pop of his whip. The oxen strained against their yokes and the wagons started forward. The other wagons waited their turn until the wagon just ahead started moving. Then, all the wagons were rolling, with at least a dozen men mounted and riding along side. The Shadlers' dog Buster, as well as a few others, was bounding along, barking happily, while the extra saddle horses, many of them the spotted ponies stolen from the Indians, were herded behind the train.

"Hurrah, boys, hurrah!" someone cheered from the crowd that had gathered to watch the wagons get underway, and there were many more shouts and cheers as the train rumbled down First Street, then across the bridge that spanned the Arkansas River.

Because the wagons were so heavily loaded, the train moved slowly across the monotonous terrain, with only the rhythmic sound of the fall of hoof beats and the rolling wheels to interrupt the quiet. It was quite easy to see how this treeless land was once home to millions of buffalo, gone now, many at the hands of these same men who were on this trek in search of still more buffalo. And that slaughter was evidenced by bleached bones as far as the eye could see, the only thing to break up the monotony of the sea of grass.

THE TRAIN MADE Crooked Creek the first night.

"We'll hold up here, men," James Hanrahan said, still enjoying his self-appointed role as wagon master.

"Are you'ns gonna break open a keg?" one of the men asked as he came toward one of Hanrahan's wagons.

He was met by Ogg with a rifle pointed toward him.

"Not tonight, Bermuda," Hanrahan said. "They'll be plenty of time for booze when we get to where we're going. All we need is for half you galoots to be passed out drunker 'n a skunk when old Gray Beard comes riding in here with his tomahawk a' wavin', 'n his guns a' blazin'."

"Gray Beard? Ain't he an old man? If I'm gonna be kilt, I want it to be Stone Calf or Bull Bear, or even Spotted Wolf. No sirree, no old man's gonna take me out," Bermuda Carlisle said.

No sooner than he had spoken the words, Old Sam Smith rose to his feet and without fanfare, swung his fist at Bermuda, knocking the much younger man to the ground.

"What the hell?" Bermuda called out, sitting on the ground, rubbing his chin. "Why for did you go 'n do that, Sam?"

"I wanted you to know, you're just as dead iffin the bullet comes from an old man as a young'n."

"Now you know why there won't be any imbibing on this run. If Old Sam here had a mind to, why Bermuda could've had a knife stuck through his gizzard," Hanrahan said. "Now let's circle our wagons and get the fires goin'."

WHEN THE MEAL WAS OVER, a few of the men took out their banjos, fiddles and mouth harps, and soon the sound of music floated over the open prairie. Every song they could think of was sung, without regard to whether it was a Yankee or a Rebel song. Many of the hunters had fought for the Confederacy. When they had returned home, in most cases, there was no home to go back to, and those that had returned had no way to make a living.

Listening to the music made Cade melancholy. When he got out of Camp Douglas prison, he had thought his Melinda would be waiting for him. But when he got back to Clarksville, Tennessee, he learned that she had been told he was dead. In his stead, she had married his brother, Adam.

In his mind, he saw Adam and Melinda with a passel of

kids all growing up on the family farm—the family farm that he had secured for them by robbing a dispatch from a carpet-bagger's bank.

Someday, he would like to go back, but now wasn't the time.

THE MUSICIANS HAD PUT AWAY their instruments, but no one was leaving the camp fire. These men, who spent so much of their lives isolated and alone, were anxious to connect with others.

The stories began. Many of them were tales they had heard before, but each time a story was repeated it was embellished, and the men listened as if the event had just happened. It was expected that everyone would contribute something to the evening's entertainment.

There were stories about Indian skirmishes, rustlers stealing stock and leaving men stranded miles from civilization, getting caught in a blizzard, or a flood, or a tornado, setting up a buffalo stand and killing so many animals that the gun barrel melted, as well as war stories from the War for Texas Independence, or the Mexican-American War, or from the recent War of Aggression without regard as to whether that "aggression" was Northern or Southern.

Bat Masterson's stories always seemed to be the best with each one having a twist that no one saw coming. Most folks knew he was telling tall tales, but no one minded. They just enjoyed them. He had just finished yet another story, when he looked around.

"It seems to me like we've heard something from every-body around this camp fire except for two men," Bat said. "And I know for a fact, they've got tales to tell. Do we want to hear from Billy Dixon and Cade McCall?"

There was a rousing cheer clamoring for Billy and Cade to talk.

At last Billy stood up.

"Well gents, I'm afraid I don't have much to tell. I'm a long way from West Virginia where I was born," Billy said. "I've been a wood chopper and a bullwhacker, and I had a little stint at bustin' shave tails just before I became a scout."

"Bustin' shave tails? You mean like second lieutenants?" one of the others asked.

Old Sam Smith laughed. "Nah, they just call second lieutenants shave tails 'cause they're as new to the army as them mules that gets their tails shaved when they first come in."

"And as dumb, too, has been my notice," Billy said. "But none of it compares to what I'm doin' now. There's nothin' better than hearing a herd of wooly buffalos when they're on the move and they're coming your way. The excitement is something I can't describe, but every one of you knows the feeling. I'm a buffalo hunter, and that's all I want to be." When he was finished, he sat down.

"Folks, Billy's being a little too modest," Bat said. "I skinned for Billy a couple of years ago, and he's the best shot I've ever seen. He can hit a buffalo a mile away."

"A mile, huh? Billy might be a crack shot, but that's a little too tall for any of us to believe, even coming from you, Bat," Fred Leonard said.

"He can do it. I know he can," Bat said.

"He can do it, doesn't mean he has," Fred continued.

Everyone laughed as they turned their attention to Cade.

"All right, McCall. Can you top that? Can you take out a buffalo at a mile and a half?"

Cade felt an instant affinity for Billy Dixon. Even though he had not known him before this trek, he knew he was going to like him.

"My story isn't much different from Billy's. I'm just not as good a shot," Cade said. "I'm afraid I don't have a story."

"What do you mean, you don't have a story? I worked on the railroad with you, and you told my brother and me you jumped ship in South America. Was that a lie?" Bat asked

"Well, no, that did happen," Cade said.

"Then tell us about it," Hanrahan said.

"You were a sailor?" Gus Zordel asked.

Cade paused for a moment. "I was, but not by choice."

"What do you mean, not by choice? How in the hell do you get to be a sailor without sayin' you want to be one?" Bermuda Carlisle asked.

"It's what happens when you're shanghaied," Cade said. "Usually, somebody knocks you out, then drags you to a ship, and when you wake up you're out to sea and there's nothing you can do about it. You're a sailor."

"Did that happen to you? I mean did somebody knock you out?"

Cade smiled.

"Why are you a smilin'? This shanghaiing—it don't seem like somethin' to laugh about."

"I was shanghaied, because a very beautiful young woman coaxed me into her web. And while I was with her, she gave me something to drink that knocked me out."

"Damn! That's why I stay away from women," Mike Welch said.

"You stay away from women, cause you're not only a buffalo skinner, you're a buffalo stinker," Hanrahan said.

"Maybe so," Welch said, "but Cade go on with your story. Did you find the women that done that to you? I would've strung her up from a tall tree if she'd done somethin' like that to me."

"He found her all right," Jacob said, a big smile crossing his face.

"And what did he do to her?"

"He married her."

"What? That can't be true," Fred Leonard said.

"It's true," Cade said. "I married her, and all things considered, it was the best thing that ever happened to me."

"Then what are you doing out here in the middle of nowhere? Why aren't you with your woman?"

Cade looked at the fire without answering the question.

"Because things happen," Bat said. "Cade's wife died."

"Killed by some Indian, I bet," Bermuda said.

"No, it was a buffalo hunter," Cade said. He stood abruptly and walked outside the circle of men.

4

CADE WALKED DOWN TO THE CREEK AND SAT ON THE BANK FOR a long time. His emotions had run the gamut this evening. First all the war stories had put him back at Franklin and then at Camp Douglas where he had been taken after he was captured.

And then there was Melinda. He thought his heart would never heal when he lost her, but he had been able to walk away from her. When he had fallen in love with Arabella, he hadn't even thought about Melinda.

Where was he now? Tonight, he had spoken openly about Arabella without feeling a sense of anger, bitterness, or even the self-condemnation he had felt since she had died. The woman he had loved, and the woman he had married, was also the beautiful woman who had set him up to be shanghaied. And tonight, he had been able to smile when he told of the situation.

It was a good feeling to be able to think of her again without falling into depression. It was time to move on. Maybe he would find another woman to love. A woman to help him raise Chantal.

But no. That wasn't right. He had promised Arabella he would take care of Chantal, but right now she was better off where she was. Magnolia and Jeter were her parents and Bella was her sister. If he took her away it would be devastating to the child.

When he got back to Dodge City he would arrange for Jeter and Magnolia to have legal guardianship for Chantal. Because he was Arabella's husband, he was legally her father, and he would always be, but he would not pull her away from the only family she had ever known. At least, not now.

Cade made his way back to where his bedroll was laid out. The embers of the fire were dying down and the only person he saw was Ogg, keeping watch over the whiskey.

As he crawled under the buffalo robe, Cade made a decision. From listening to some of the hunters, especially Billy Dixon, he was convinced that the main herd of buffalo was to the south. He would sell Jacob his part in the freight company and go out onto the plains and hunt buffalo. Whatever he made, he would arrange for the money to be given to Chantal.

He closed his eyes, and the howling of the wolves and the yelping of the coyotes soon put him to sleep. But not for long. He sat up having been awakened by a nightmare. It was not seeing Arabella as she lay dying, or him lying under a pile of dead bodies at Franklin, or escaping from General Lopez in Paraguay, all frequent visions in his nightmares. Tonight, a band of Indians were chasing him as he ran through a herd of buffalo.

SEVERAL MILES south of the wagon train Mean To His Horses and nine warriors were on a war party.

"Mean To His Horses, do you not wonder why Quanah Parker did not come with us?" Wild Horse asked. "He is the greatest of all Comanche warriors. With him we would find the white men who stole our horses."

"If you do not wish to ride with me, you may go back to the women and the children of the village," Mean To His Horses said, stung by Wild Horse's suggestion that Quanah Parker was the greatest of all Comanche fighters.

"No, I will ride with you," Wild Horse said. "It is good that I can ride with a warrior as great as Mean To His Horses."

They had been riding for three days without finding anyone to make war against, but on this, the morning of the fourth day, they smelled smoke and cooking meat. Mean To His Horses smiled, and held up his hand.

"Soon, I think, our knives will spill the blood of the white enemy. And we will eat their food," Mean To His Horses said rubbing his stomach in anticipation.

"THEY AIN'T HARDLY NOTHIN' what tastes no better'n fried strips of buffalo," Gentry Potter said. Potter was the hunter, and he had two skinners with him. The wagon, sitting behind them, had about 50 hides, the result of their activities for the last several days. The paucity of hides was because the main herd had not yet come this far north.

"Yeah," Al Kinder said. "If you ask me, it's a shame we have to leave all them carcasses out there to just rot away, when they's near a thousand pounds o' food with each one of 'em."

"It ain't the food we're after," Felix Werth said. "It's the hides. So far, we ain't got but close to 50 hides, on account of we ain't found the main herd yet, just little bands here 'n there. But we'll find 'em soon, 'n when we do, 'n get the hides back to Dodge, they'll bring in $2.00 apiece."

"It might be that we won't have to take 'em all the way back to Dodge," Potter said.

"What are you talkin' about? If we don't take 'em to Dodge City, where will we take 'em? You ain't talkin' about Lee, are you? 'Cause from all I hear, Lee, he don't take hides from nobody but the Injuns."

"No, I ain't talkin' about Lee. But I've heard tell that some of them Dodge City traders are think'n about buildin' a place down on the Canadian where we can take the hides."

"Maybe so, but they ain't done it yet," Werth said.

"Maybe not yet, but soon. 'N when they do get it built, 'n we won't have to be wastin' time takin' the hides back, why, I wouldn't be surprised if we didn't take out a thousand of 'em. 'N that'll be at least $2,000," Potter said. "Two thousand dollars' worth of hides, 'n you're a' worryin' about the meat?"

"No, I was just commentin' is all. It do seem a shame."

"It ain't exactly like we're a' wastin' it," Potter said. "I mean, we been eatin' buffalo ever since we come out, ain't we?"

"Yeah," Kinder said. "I reckon we have. But just a little bit of it. Most of it, we've been a' leavin' behind 'n when we do that, why there ain't nothin' it can do but rot."

"So, what if it does rot? It don't mean nothin' to me," Potter said. "Not as long as we get them hides offen' 'em."

"What's that?" Kinder asked.

"What's what? What are you talkin' about?"

"I he'erd somethin' sounded like horses."

"Maybe another hunter," Potter suggested. "If it is, he might know where the main herd is. We ain't seen nothin' but . . ."

"Injuns!" Kinder shouted.

Potter grabbed his Sharps .50, the buffalo gun he used when hunting, but realized almost as soon as he reached for it, that he hadn't loaded it yet. Not one of the skinners was armed, and all three men stood there in terror as the Indians charged, their lances lowered and pointed right at them.

"Ain't we goin to run?" Werth asked.

"Better to get it over with, boys," Potter said. "Just hope that they kill us fast."

None of the lance thrusts was fatal, though all three men went down grievously wounded.

Mean To His Horses and the other Indians yelled out in the excitement and thrill of taking an enemy, and leaping down from their horses, they charged the helpless men with raised tomahawks.

Potter saw an Indian raise a war club, which was actually a hatchet, and he saw the beginning of the swing. That was his last conscious thought, because the blow to his head killed him instantly.

For the next several minutes the Indians hacked and slashed at the bodies of the hunters, then they set fire to the wagon, before taking the staked horses and leading them away. Behind them lay the scalped and mutilated bodies of their victims.

WHEN MEAN to His Horses and the others returned to the village they were carrying large chunks of meat from the more recently killed buffalo the white hunters had left in the field.

"Meat!" Mean To His Horses shouted triumphantly as he rode into the village.

Wild Horse displayed the scalp of one of the white hunters.

"We found the white hunters and we killed them," Wild Horse bragged.

"Did you find the men who stole our horses?" Quanah asked. Forty-three horses had been stolen, and beyond the loss of mobility, was the loss of face, for to the Comanche, horses were the symbol of their power and prestige.

"Are you not pleased that we have brought back meat for the People?" Mean To His Horses asked.

"I am pleased."

Mean To His Horses laughed rather jeeringly. "And so now the great Quanah Parker, who did not come with us on this raid, must fill his belly, and the bellies of his wives and children with the buffalo meat that I, Mean To His Horses, have provided for him."

"It is good to have meat," Quanah said, without taking the bait put out by Mean To His Horses.

As QUANAH RETURNED to his tipi feeling a bit discomfited by having to feed his family with meat provided by one of the most self-aggrandizing and irritating warriors in the village, he happened to encounter White Eagle.

"Do not feel put out, Quanah," White Eagle said. "Mean To His Horses seeks the approval of others, and not finding it, heaps it upon himself."

Quanah had made no open display of irritation, though White Eagle had read it in him. White Eagle was like that. He was a man who could see things, and make magic happen. He was also Quanah's friend.

"We, and our wives, will eat well tonight. Think only of that."

"Yes," Quanah agreed with a smile. "Yes, I will think only of that."

5

By mid-morning of the second day, the Dodge City wagon train reached the Cimarron River, and there, it stopped. Cade and Jacob rode up to the edge of the river to find that James Hanrahan and several others were standing there, looking out at the yellow, wind-whipped current.

"This looks like a good place to ford," Hanrahan said. "The banks are low on both sides, and that sand bar in the middle would be a place for the teams to rest if they needed to."

"I don't know," Cade replied. "I'm guessing it's at least 200 feet across—maybe more. It might be better if we moved back to the main trail before we cross."

"I don't see the point in doin' that," Shorty Shadler said. "One place is as good as the other. Anyways, if the Indians are a watchin' don't ya think they'd be a watchin' where other wagon's have went?"

"We ain't seen no Indians," Bermuda Carlisle said. "I say we go where McCall says we go. He's the one that makes them runs to Camp Supply all the time."

"Yeah, but we ain't a goin' to Camp Supply," Shorty said.

"What do you think, Billy?" Jacob asked. "You've spent more time down this way than any of the rest of us."

Billy Dixon shook his head. "This is not a place where I've ever made a crossing. We all know that white sand can be treacherous and fatal."

"Well, I'm in charge, and I say we cross here," Hanrahan said. "There's a whiskey ranch at the Cimarron Crossing, and they're not takin' my whiskey."

There was murmuring among the men as more than one questioned how Hanrahan got to be the leader.

"All right. If it'll make ya feel better, I'll go across first, and you'll see it ain't no worse or no better than any place else," Hanrahan said. He started back for his wagon.

"No, you don't," Bermuda Carlisle said. "You ain't a takin' that whiskey across, till we know it can get across."

Everybody laughed at Carlisle's comment.

"All right, get me one of them Indian ponies," Hanrahan said. "Those little ponies will know how to do it."

"Here, take mine," Mike Welch said. "I got him for $50.00, and now I know why nobody bid on 'im. He's nothin' but trouble."

Hanrahan mounted the spotted pony and urged him down to the river. He balked when he got to the water, but James forced the horse to enter. He moved ahead, taking quick short steps, knowing that his safety depended upon his quickness. When he reached the sand bar, James turned to address the men on the bank.

"Nothin to it. Shepherd, you bring my wagon down and let's get this parade on the move."

Shepherd moved to the whiskey wagon that was pulled by twelve lumbering oxen.

"Hold up," Cade said. "Let's wait 'til James reaches the other side."

"Hell, McCall, you're too damned cautious," Fred Leonard said, as he turned and started back for his own wagon.

Hanrahan and the pony had reached the other side of the sand bar.

"That's not good," Billy said. "Look how that horse has his nose on the ground. Almost like he's trying to smell where he's supposed to go."

Cade took a deep breath. "Anybody got a rope?"

"I'll get one," Jacob said as he turned his horse and headed back for the train.

Watching the horse, each foot seemed to be slipping into the quivering mass of sand.

"James, turn back," Billy Dixon yelled.

Hanrahan tried to wheel the horse around, but he couldn't make the horse turn. In an instant the horse plunged forward into water that wasn't more than three feet deep. Everyone knew the horse and rider were in trouble. The Cimarron quicksand was a notorious killer, the bones of buffalo that had succumbed were often uncovered in the raging waters of a flood. Trees, wagons, cattle, horses, and yes, men, were known to have perished in this innocent looking water.

"Do something," Hanrahan yelled. "Get me out of here."

By now the horse had sunk up to its breast and the hind legs up to the stifles. The horse was straining to get loose, but the more he struggled the deeper he went.

Sand was now inching up Hanrahan's legs.

"Get out of your boots if you can and get off that horse," Cade yelled.

James struggled to get his boots off, then flung himself off the horse. When he landed he attempted to crawl toward the other bank which was now no more than 20 feet in front of him, but as he did, he began to sink farther and farther into the oozing sand. He could feel the pressure surrounding his body. He looked back toward the horse, to see that the pony's rump and the saddle were already mired in the quicksand.

"Help!" Hanrahan shouted again.

"James, I'm going to try to get this rope to you," Cade yelled as he began twirling the lariat over his head. With a fling of the noose, he tossed it forward, but it came up short.

"Damn," Cade said as he began to reel the rope in.

"Here," Jacob said. "Take this one."

Cade and Jacob exchanged ropes and Cade repeated the throw. This time it got close enough that Hanrahan could reach it. Cade let out more rope as James pulled it over his head.

"Under your arms," Cade yelled. There was barely enough space between the sand and James's armpits. He wished that he would have told James to slip out of his clothes, because the clothes as they filled with sand would act as an anchor.

When the rope was in place, Cade made a double half-hitch as he tied the rope to his saddle horn, then turned the horse and began to take up the slack in the rope.

Hanrahan let out a scream when the rope tightened around his body. He held on to the rope and inch by inch, he began to creep out of his sandy tomb. When he was back to the gravel bed near the center of the river, Cade did not slow down. He continued to pull the man across the gravel and the next prong of the river.

When James was pulled up on the bank, he lay there panting as he realized just how close to death he had come. He looked toward Cade but couldn't speak, as tears rolled down his cheeks.

"Where's that other rope?" Cade asked.

"Do you think you can get my pony?" Mike Welch asked.

"I'm going to try."

Cade watched the horse, now showing only his head and neck. As his head bobbed, Cade timed his toss, and this time his throw was true. The loop settled around the horse's neck, and Cade pulled it tight. Again, he turned his horse and slowly began to pull. In his heart, Cade knew this was hopeless. The horse was pointed away from him, and if he could move him, more than likely he would break his neck.

The horse was still sinking, and now he began to make a sound that was almost human. His eyes were filled with torture and his breath was coming in gasps.

Suddenly, Cade's horse plunged forward falling to his knees, as Cade struggled to keep from flying over his head.

Cade looked back, startled as to why the sudden lunge, then he saw why. The rope had been cut, and Mike Welch had raised his gun. In a moment, there was the report of a rifle as the struggling horse dropped his head onto the sand.

All looked in horror as red blood began to pool on the white sand.

"I had to do it," Mike said. "No man or beast deserves to suffer like that little pony was a doin'."

"You did the right thing," Cade said. "I couldn't have pulled him out."

As they were watching, the horse disappeared and even the red stain was no more. The sand around him began to settle, and soon, there was no sign of what had just transpired.

"Now what?" Fred Leonard asked, looking toward James Hanrahan.

"Well, the first thing, I'm gonna find me some new clothes." Hanrahan tried to stand but his legs wouldn't support him.

Cade and Billy Dixon, one on each side of the big man, got him to his feet and walked him back to the wagon. "You two pick the best spot to cross."

CADE AND BILLY scouted the Cimarron. They found a place about two miles east that they thought would support the wagons. But as a precaution, they sent those men who were on horseback out to collect buffalo bones. They drug them back on hides and filled up a narrow prong of the river. Then they unhitched the oxen that had been pulling Hanrahan's wagons and drove them across the river as many times as it took to make a satisfactory bed.

When they were all safely across they made camp.

"This is it, men," Charlie Myers said. "Now we're in 'No Man's Land'."

"I can't rightly say I agree with ya," Ike Shadler said. "If I was to guess, there's plenty of Indians in this place."

"But we ain't seen none yet," Bermuda Carlisle said. "I think they're scared of us. They know we got guns, and we know how to use 'em."

"I think that's the wrong attitude," Cade said. "Technically, this is their land and we're the intruders,"

"This here belongs to the United States of America," Ike said as he picked up a handful of sand. "We have as much right to be here as any Indian ever did."

"Not according to the Medicine Lodge Treaty," Bat said.

"Hell, them things are made to be broke. Didn't that paper say we couldn't go south of the Arkansas?" Ike asked. "The answer is it did, but here we are. We just have to show them bastards who's boss."

Cade raised his eyebrows. "All that is true, but none the less, we'd better be prepared for Indians to come calling."

"If they do," Billy said, "we should treat them like they are friendly. No shooting." He looked directly at Ike Shadler. "I've had many a meet up with Indians and most of the time, if you don't bother them, they don't bother you."

"Tell that to Halen Johansson and his wife," Mike Welch

said. "And he's not the only one. Them savages'd rather kill ya' than spit in your eye."

"I think Cade and Billy are right," Fred Leonard said. "We can't get bogged down fightin' Indians. We've got to get down on the Canadian and find us a place to set up before the buffalo start moving."

THE TRAIN MOVED SOUTH GOING through the breaks of the Cimarron, then to the Beaver, one of the branches of the North Canadian. To go east would take them to Camp Supply, but they continued to the Palo Duro where they found plenty of water.

"This seems like it would be a good place to stop," James Hanrahan said. "It's got water."

"But no buffalo," Bat said. "We need to be down in the Panhandle."

Billy nodded his head. "Yes, I think that's the best place. On the Canadian, we'll have water, grass, and not too far from trees. If we're going to be building, we need wood."

"Hell, let's just build a dugout, right there in that rise," Bermuda said.

"We probably will use some sod," Myers said, "but we've got to have something to hold the roof up. I say we move on tomorrow."

"You're the boss," James Hanrahan said. Since the crossing he had relinquished his wagon-master status, and no one had taken over the position, although Cade and Billy had become the de facto leaders.

AT BILLY DIXON'S SUGGESTION, the train started down Moore's Creek toward the South Canadian. On the way they passed a few camps established by buffalo hunters who had stayed out for the winter, in hopes of getting a jump when the herd began to move north.

"Hello, Billy. Me 'n Tommie 'n Dave was wonderin' when you'd get back down this way," one of the hunters said.

"Cade, this is Joe Plummer, Dave Dudley, and Tommie Wallace," Billy said, introducing the hunters. "Are you finding any buffs?"

"A few. We come up on a stand a couple o' days ago," Joe said, "but it ain't nothin' like it used to be." He looked at all the wagons that were now in sight. "Lordee, what's all this about?"

"It's the making's for a new outpost," Billy said. "You won't have to be going all the way back to Dodge for your powder and lead."

"And there'll be plenty of beer and whiskey," Hanrahan said. "I'll bet even money, my saloon will be the first thing built."

"Are you saying real whiskey 'n real beer?" Plummer asked.

"There won't be none better in a hundred miles."

"Try tellin' that to Smith 'n Jones. They say the swill they're a peddlin' is as good as it gets."

"And who are Smith 'n Jones?" Cade asked.

"They say they're buffalo hunters," Tommie said. "But they ain't took so much as one hide they kilt their selves. Just stealin' 'em from some Injun who wants to get liquored up."

"See what they're a doin' is makin' apple jack. Hunters get a swig, now and then, but most of the rotgut goes to Injuns," Dave added. "It makes 'em crazy drunk, 'n there ain't nothin' meaner than a crazy drunk Injun."

6

THE NEXT DAY THE TRAIN CAME ACROSS MOORE'S CREEK where there were two men who greeted them with ingratiating smiles.

"Howdy, boys, howdy," one of them said. He stuck his hand out. "John Smith's the name, 'n this here's m' partner, Jim Jones."

"Smith and Jones," Cade said. "We've heard about you."

"Well then I 'spect you boys have come to the right place if you'ns is all thirsty. Some o' the best apple jack you ever tasted," Smith said holding up a bottle. "Let me get a tin cup."

"Where you gettin' your apple jack from?" Shadler asked.

"Right over there," Jones said, pointing to a nearby camp that was midway up a rise. Two Indian women were bent over a trough.

"Soon as we get us a good mash from them dry apples, all we got to do is cook it up so's we can separate the alcohol from the water, 'n we got us some liquor as good as anythin' you can get in a saloon," Jones said. "Say you don't have any raisins with ya, do ya? We'd be mighty proud to trade for some good raisins. Them's what really makes it good."

"Why don't we just see what you got?" Old Man Keeler said, as he grabbed the bottle and took a drink.

"Not so fast" Welch said, as he took the bottle from Keeler.

Smith raised his hands. "No need to tussle, gents. I don't expect you got any hides to trade, so it'll be six bits a swallow."

"Six bits! Ain't that a little rich?" Shorty Shadler asked as he, too grabbed for the bottle.

CADE DIDN'T like what he was watching, but he knew no one could stop the men from drinking once they got started. Looking around he saw that Jacob Harrison, Billy Dixon and Charlie Myers were not partaking. Billy Ogg and Shepherd were still standing guard over Hanrahan's wagons while James was matching drink for drink with anyone. Cade was disappointed when he saw that his own drivers were joining the rest.

Cade did not join the abstainers, choosing instead to sit alone resting his back against a wagon wheel. Seeing the two Indian women was disturbing. He couldn't believe they were in this camp by choice. Who, if anyone, was looking for them? He recalled the months he had spent looking for Arabella and Magnolia, and it made him sick to his stomach.

Out of the corner of his eye he saw a movement behind him. Jerking his head around, he saw a child creeping toward him. The child looked to be about the age of Chantal.

Cade smiled, trying to disarm the child.

"Hi, little buddy. What's your name?"

The child didn't answer, but he moved closer. Cade could see that it was a boy.

"Is that your mama over there?" Cade asked.

The boy nodded his head.

Cade was pleased that the boy seemed to understand English.

"Do you live here all the time?"

The boy didn't answer, but his eye brows lifted, telling Cade that the answer was yes.

"Come sit beside me," Cade said patting the ground beside him.

The boy moved closer and just as he was about to sit down, the man called Jones came over and jerked him away.

"Get the hell back where you belong, boy," Jones said as he put out his foot in an attempt to kick the child.

Cade grabbed the foot, and twisting it brought the man to the ground.

"What the hell, mister?" Jones jumped to his feet and came at Cade with his hands balled in fists.

"I wouldn't do that," Cade said as he drew his pistol.

Jones stopped, raising his hands. "I wasn't gonna do nothing. It's just that kid's supposed to stay out of sight when I'm doin' business. He don't much mind like a white boy does."

FOR THE REST of the evening as the men got drunker, several fights broke out. Smith and Jones were yelling at the women to get more and more of the whiskey, as each succeeding bottle was extended by adding what Cade supposed was water. As the whiskey got weaker, the two men charged more, until now it was a dollar a cup. When one of the women, in her haste, dropped a bottle, Smith slapped her across the face and ordered her out of his sight.

She picked up the boy who was now asleep and headed for a dugout that was built into the rise behind the camp.

Cade, who had been napping by the wagon wheel, heard the exchange and followed the woman to the dugout.

The woman sheltered the child, and in a heart wrenching voice said, "No, no, don't beat."

Cade shook his head. "I'm not going to hurt you or your child. If you understand me, do you want to get away from these men?"

She shook her head.

Cade didn't know if she didn't want to go, or if she didn't understand.

She tapped her finger on her chest.

"Gentle Horse," she said. "Find Spotted Wolf. Give him." She withdrew a silver medallion that was encrusted with small turquoise stones. "Take." She thrust the medallion into Cade's hand.

"Well, well, well," Jones said as he stepped into the dugout. "You no good son-of-a-bitch. You're too good to drink my whiskey, but my woman's good enough to dip your dobber. Now get the hell out of here, before I kick your ass."

Cade made eye contact with the woman who had said her name was Gentle Horse. He nodded his head as he raised his fist containing the medallion. He hoped she knew that he would find Spotted Wolf.

CADE KNEW that most of the next day would be lost as a lot of the men were suffering from last night's revelry. Bat Masterson, however, was up early, even though he had been drinking just as much as anyone else.

"You didn't join us last night," Bat said as he came over to the fire and filled his tin cup with coffee.

"You know I can't do that anymore," Cade said. "Who knows what I'd do this time if I got on a drunken binge."

"Jacob Harrison wouldn't let you get away with signing away his business. He'd knock you cock-eyed if you did that to him," Bat said.

49

Cade smiled as he rubbed his chin.

"It seems to me like I remember Jeter doing just that when I lost the Red House for him."

"Ah yes," Bat said, "it was a sight to see when he came out to our railroad grading camp. He was fit to be tied."

"I'm glad he got the Red House back," Cade said. "That little incident taught me never to get that drunk ever again."

"If you stay around these galoots long enough, you'll be knockin' 'em down more'n you ever did before," Bat said.

"Not me. As soon as Charlie finds a spot, and we get his freight unloaded, I'm heading back to Dodge."

"You'll be back. You haven't done enough hunting to make any real money," Bat said. "Last winter I was out with Tom Nixon and I saw him shoot a hundred twenty buffalo, before breakfast. Now at $3.00 a hide—you figure it out."

"Is it true that last year Tom killed 3,200 buffalo in 35 days?" Cade asked.

"I wasn't with him until January, but if he says he killed 'em, I say he killed 'em. Say do you happen to have a can of tomatoes?"

"I'm sure there's a can in the wagon," Cade said. "Break out several cans. These men are going to need to sober up, if we're going to get this train moving."

As CADE DRANK HIS COFFEE, he saw the two Indian women off in the distance. They were starting a fire under the trough where they would cook off the apple mash. He reached into his pocket and pulled out the medallion Gentle Horse had given him. Last night, in the dark he had not inspected it closely, but now he saw that in addition to the turquoise stones, there was also the head of a wolf etched into the silver.

A wolf to be given to Spotted Wolf.

There had to be a family connection. He wished that he could tell Gentle Horse that he knew Spotted Wolf. He would make sure he got the medal, or at least he would give it to Agent Miles to pass on.

THE TRAIN finally got underway reaching the Canadian River late in the day. It had been eight days since leaving Dodge City, and everyone was excited at arriving at their destination. After camp was established, and the meal was served, the men stretched out the biggest buffalo robe they could find. With the skin side up, they staked it to the ground, and the fiddlers and the French harp players got out their instruments. Soon men were dancing either alone as in a Scottish Highland Fling or together in a promenade or allemande left that any woman back at Fat Tom's dance hall would be proud to partner.

"Well, we're here," Jacob said.

"Not quite," Charlie Myers said. "I want to make sure we've pick the best possible spot. Even though we've not been bothered by Indians so far, I'm sure they will come calling."

"Maybe that's it," James Hanrahan said. "You didn't taste that rotgut Smith and Jones were passin' off as whiskey. When them Indians get a taste of my good stuff, they'll be as quiet as little lambs."

"Sure. Whiskey and Indians," Jacob said. "What could go wrong with that?"

"Do you have any idea where you want to set up shop?" Cade asked.

"I've been talkin' to Old Man Keeler. He says he thinks the place where Kit Carson fought off 3,000 Comanche is somewhere around here," Charlie said. "Do you think that old fort is still here?"

"Not according to George Bent," Cade said. "He's the interpreter at the Cheyenne Agency and he says the fort was built by his father. He says he burned it to keep the Indians from taking it."

"Billy, have you ever seen an old fort?" Jacob asked.

"I haven't, but there's a creek called West Adobe Walls Creek about a dozen miles from here," Billy said. "That could be it."

"Then I say, we try to find that place," Charlie said. "If Kit Carson held off 3,000 Indians, it's a good enough spot for me."

Cade smiled. "According to George, Carson had two howitzers that might have helped him out."

"But did he have any Sharps fifties?" Myers asked. "Why, I'll bet Billy, here could stand off a thousand Indians all by himself."

"Let's hope I don't have to try," Billy said.

THE NEXT DAY the train followed the Canadian about a dozen miles until they reached West Adobe Walls Creek. About a mile back they saw parts of walls, some as high as five feet.

"This has to be the place," Cade said as he dismounted and picked up one of the displaced bricks. "I wonder if George's father made these."

"Nope," Old Man Keeler said as he walked up the slope. "Comancheros did it. That's what I heared. Them Mexicans —now they knows how to get along with Injuns."

"I guess so," Cade said. "They buy or trade for anything the Indians have, no matter who they had to kill to get it."

"Well, I like it," Charlie said. "It's close to water, there are trees across the river, and there's rising ground behind it. An outpost here wouldn't be hard to defend."

THE NEXT MORNING CADE, Jacob and Billy went out to shoot some wild turkeys that were roosting in some trees across the river. When they returned, they reported that they had found a spot on another stream about a mile and a half farther down. It had the same attributes as the original site except there was a broader valley that would accommodate the buildings, and the breaks of the Canadian rose behind it, making the spot easier to defend. In addition, there was a good supply of cottonwood and hackberry trees about six miles away. After Charlie Myers, James Hanrahan, William Olds and Thomas O'Keefe looked it over, they decided the new site was a better choice. The wagons were pulled up to the valley and the unloading began.

WITHIN A WEEK, everything was unloaded and lying in an orderly fashion upon the ground. Jacob and Cade left their canvas coverings in order to give more protection to the freight they had hauled.

Most of the men were busy dragging logs up from the river. James Hanrahan was the first to lay out his building, cutting sod to form walls that were three feet thick. Before a roof was even thought about, he set up a bar by putting a flint buffalo robe over two whiskey barrels. Soon everyone had stopped for a long-anticipated drink.

"If the bar's open, I think it's time we headed for Dodge," Jacob said.

"All right," Cade said, "but I think I'm going to make a little detour. With empty wagons you and the boys should make good time once you get to the Dodge-Supply Road."

"You're not coming back with us?"

"Not right now. I've got a little business to attend to. I'm going over to the Cheyenne Agency."

"Then I'm coming with you," Jacob said. "You know someone riding alone is asking for trouble."

"And what do you think would happen to our drivers if they stop at one of the whiskey ranches?" Cade asked. "No, it's better you stay with the wagons."

"All right, but I'm going to hold up at the Cimarron Crossing, and I expect you to be there in no more than six days."

"Yes, sir," Cade said effecting a sharp salute. "I'll be right behind you."

7

THE NEXT MORNING CADE WAS UP BEFORE SUNRISE. HE HAD taken a packet of salt and some hardtack and was preparing to leave when he heard footsteps coming up behind him. He expected to see Jacob, but it was Bat.

"You're up a little early, aren't you?" Cade asked.

"I was wondering if you could do something for me," Bat said.

"Sure, that is if I can."

Bat withdrew some papers from inside his vest pocket. "I want you to deliver a message for me, but I don't want anyone to know about it."

"Ah, ha. I've seen you sniffing around Frankie at the Red House, but I didn't know you missed her enough to send her a secret letter," Cade said, barely able to contain his laughter.

"It's not to a woman," Bat said, "and if you're not going to take this seriously, I'll not give it to you."

"All right, who's it going to?"

"Alonzo Moore."

"Alonzo Moore? You mean the guy who just started the Dodge City Messenger?"

"Yes. I've written a piece for him, and I'd like him to put it in the paper."

"Well now, Bat, if he publishes the story, don't you think everyone is going to find out about it?"

Bat smiled. "Yes, but you don't understand. If he publishes it, I'll want people to know. But, if I give him something and he doesn't publish it, then I don't want anyone to know that I tried, but was turned down."

Cade nodded. "Give me the secret message, and I'll carry it through the enemy lines."

Cade intended for the comment to be a joke, but Bat didn't take it that way.

"You think that's funny, but it's not. Jacob told me you're going through 'No Man's Land' by yourself," Bat said, "you know that's stupid, don't you?"

"Then why do you trust me to get this to Alonzo Moore?"

"I don't know. I just do."

CADE TRAVELED east following the Canadian until he cut across to the North Canadian, where the agency was located. When he arrived, there were several Indians milling around, many dressed in the plain black suits that were supplied by the Quakers. He saw George Bent sitting on the porch of the Lee and Reynolds outpost, and he moved toward the interpreter.

"Howdy, George, do you know if Spotted Wolf would happen to be here?" Cade asked.

"I've not seen him," George said. "But that doesn't mean he's not here. Have you checked with Miles?"

"I'm on my way there, now."

"No, he isn't here," Miles said. "Why are ye looking for him?"

"Oh, no particular reason," Cade said, not sure why he didn't share his mission with Miles.

"Ye didn't come here just to see him, did ye?"

"No, Jacob and I took some freight down to the Canadian and we're taking the empty wagons back."

"Freight? To the Canadian? Thee wouldn't have rations for the People, now would thee?"

"I'm afraid not. We were hauling for Charlie Myers and Fred Leonard," Cade said. "They're putting an outpost down in the Panhandle."

Miles furrowed his brow. "That cannot be good for my people. Surely, they do not intend to trade whiskey for hides."

Cade laughed. "I suppose they'll be trading whiskey for hides, but Indians won't be their intended customers. Several hunters spent the winter in Dodge, and since they've killed off most of the buffalo in Kansas, they decided to move their camps south."

"Oh dear," Miles said. "My poor people. Can't someone stop this? Thou knowest what a state of depredation my people are enduring. If more buffalo are slaughtered, what will they have to eat?"

"Either you do a better job of teaching them to farm, or the government had better send more rations," Cade said.

"When President Grant signed the Indian Appropriation Act, he did not intend for the buffalo to be decimated," Miles said. "According to treaty, the white man cannot hunt south of the Arkansas, and yet they encroach. First the Cimarron, and now the Canadian. They cannot go there."

"I'm afraid it's a situation of preemptive domain. The white buffalo hunters are there, and that's it," Cade said. "When I left, the buildings were going up and the bar was open."

John Miles looked at Cade, with a dire expression on his

face. "This means war. When last thee were here, thou heard Spotted Wolf say that the Kiowa had raised the pipe to the Cheyenne. The Cheyenne will accept that pipe, and no government will stop them."

"I remember hearing him say that," Cade said. "I do need to see him. If he's not here at the agency, do you know if he's on the reservation?"

"I think he is. If the white hunters cannot find buffalo, then the Indians cannot as well."

"Where does he stay?"

"Magpie will know where to find him," Miles said. "Ask her."

WHEN CADE LEFT the agency office, he went back to the Lee and Reynolds outpost looking for George Bent. Magpie was his wife.

When he walked in, he saw W.M.D Lee, himself, behind the counter. George was there as well, as several Indians were bartering for supplies. Cade did not speak Cheyenne, but he did know *hotoa* meant buffalo, *ma'aatano'e* meant gun, and *heovohkoome* meant whiskey. In the side yard, beside the store, Cade saw thousands of hides stacked up. If there were no buffalo for food, where had the Indians been getting the hides?

"McCall," Lee said as he raised his hand. "I didn't see your wagons roll in. Did you bring in more food?"

"No, I'm on my way back to Dodge," Cade said.

"If you're comin' from Camp Supply, isn't this a little out of your way?"

"It is. I'm sort of looking for somebody," Cade said.

Lee laughed. "Lost your stock, did you?"

"No, it's not that. Jacob and the boys are taking the wagons back."

"Back from where?"

"Down on the Canadian. Charlie Myers is opening up an outpost down there."

"Yeah," Lee said. "Yeah, I heard about that, though why in the hell would he put an outpost in the middle of nowhere, is beyond me."

"Haven't you heard? The buffalo hunters have moved into the panhandle, and Myers has gone there too, so he can buy hides from them," Cade said.

"You don't say." Lee turned away and disappeared in a small room in the back of the store.

"Oh, oh," George Bent said. "The boss isn't going to like that. He's pretty much got this whole area tied up, and mark my words, he'll do what he can to shut down the competition."

"It seems to me like his pile of hides is pretty high without any white hunters," Cade said. "By the way, I'm looking for Magpie. John said she may know where Spotted Wolf is. Is she around?"

"She is. My house is the biggest one on the top of the rise."

"SPOTTED WOLF not come for long time now," Magpie said. "Last time he come to get food for his people, but there was no food."

"I know I saw him when he came in. Is there a chance you'll see him anytime soon?"

"Why you want to know?"

Cade pulled out the medallion Gentle Horse had given him and held it out toward Magpie. "When you see him, will you give him this?"

Magpie looked at the medallion for a moment, then looked back at Cade. The expression on her face changed, but Cade was unable to read it.

"Where did you get this?"

"From Gentle Horse. She gave it to me and told me to find Spotted Wolf."

"No." Magpie shook her head vigorously. "Gentle Horse is dead."

"I just left a woman who gave me this medallion. She had a child about four years old and she told me to give this to Spotted Wolf. She said her name was Gentle Horse," Cade said.

"No. Gentle Horse not give you this. This is her medicine," Magpie said.

"Well, all I can say is the woman said she was Gentle Horse," Cade said. "She's in a very bad situation, and if Spotted Wolf doesn't care about her, I'll go back and get her myself."

"Where you see this woman?" Magpie asked.

"She was on Moore's Creek with some whiskey peddlers who go by the names of Smith and Jones. If that really is her medicine, I'll take it back to her when I go to rescue her," Cade said, as he extended his hand.

"No. I give to Spotted Wolf. He will go to Moore's Creek. If your Gentle Horse is not Spotted Wolf's Gentle Horse, he will kill her."

"Why? He can't do that. The woman didn't do anything."

"If she steal this from Gentle Horse, Spotted Wolf will want revenge for his daughter."

"His daughter? Yes," Cade said. "Yes, I should have known she was his daughter."

CADE WAS two days travel from the Agency when he stopped to water his horse. Dismounting he knelt beside the cool stream and dipped his canteen into the creek when he heard the buzz of a bullet snapping by. The bullet hit the water just as the sound of the shot reached him.

Cade's first thought was that he was being shot at by Indians.

"How the hell did you miss him?" someone said, the voice clearly that of a white man.

Cade grabbed the reins to his horse, and pulled him across the stream and into a little stand of trees on the other side. There he snaked his Henry rifle from the saddle sheath, jacked a round into the chamber, then lay down behind a fallen tree trunk.

"Where did the son of a bitch go?" This was a different voice from the first one he had heard.

"He went into them trees," a third voice said. The three men remained unseen in the trees on the opposite side of the creek.

"Hey, Mister!" the first voice called. "Come on out, we ain't goin' to hurt you none. We thought you was a Injun which is the only reason we shot at you."

"Yeah, come on out 'n we can do some tradin'. We got some coffee. Bet you'd like some 'o that."

None of the three had yet exposed themselves, and Cade didn't answer.

"I don't think he's a' believin' you, Stump," one of the other voices said.

"Is that right, Mister? I guess you figured us out, didn't you?"

Cade remained quiet

"Tell you what, Mister. We don't want to hurt you none. Truth is, we don't even want your money. All we want is your horse. Turn him a' loose, 'n we'll ride on out of here."

"I'd be afoot then," Cade called back, responding for the first time.

"Well, you are over there, ain't you? Now we're a' gettin' somewhere. You wouldn't have that far to go. Baker, he's got hisself a whiskey ranch no more 'n five or six miles from here. You could walk there, 'n more 'n likely he'd sell you a horse so's you could keep on to wherever it was you was a' goin'."

"You . . . you won't hurt me?" Cade called. He was playing them now, waiting to see what opportunity might present itself.

"No, I promise you, we won't hurt you. Like I said, all we're a' wantin' is your horse."

Cade stood up, doing so in a way that kept his rifle hidden behind his leg.

All three men stepped out into view. All three were holding weapons in their hands, but none of the rifles were pointed directly at him.

"What kind of gun are you packin'?" one of the men asked. This was Stump's voice.

"You ain't a' goin' to take my pistol, are you?" Cade asked, putting as much fear and uncertainty into his voice as he could.

"Throw it into the creek, then send your horse across," Stump said. "Once we're gone, you can pick up your gun again."

Cade tossed his pistol forward, but not far enough for it to fall into the creek.

"Oh, I didn't throw it far enough," he said. "Want me to pick it up 'n throw it again?"

"No, no, just leave it there 'n start your horse across."

Cade slapped his horse on the rump and it started toward the edge of the creek. He kept his eyes on Stump and saw Stump start to bring his rifle up to his shoulder.

Moving so quickly that he caught all three men by surprise, he jerked his own weapon up, squeezing the trigger even before the butt of the rifle was against his shoulder.

Stump went down, the action so unexpected that the other men were unable to react quickly enough to stop Cade from levering two more rounds into the chamber and pulling the trigger.

Even before the final echoes of the shots returned, the three men lay dead on the ground.

Cade whistled for his horse, and it returned. Mounting he rode by the three men, glanced down toward them, then continued his ride toward the Cimarron and his rendezvous with Jacob and the others.

8

CETTI MARCELLI SAT AT THE PIANO IN THE RED HOUSE SALON. A gray-haired woman sat beside her as Cetti was practicing her music.

"No, no, dear. It goes faster," Demova Fenton said. She began clapping her hands as she sang the chorus. *"Yes, we'll gather at the river, the beautiful, the beautiful river; gather with the saints at the river, that flows by the throne of God."*

"Do you think the Slater brothers are rolling over in their graves—church music in the Devil's Den?" Jeter asked.

"Jeter, don't even mention those names in this place," Magnolia said. "That's all behind us." She smiled at Cade who was sitting at the table with them. "I am very happy, today."

"I'm glad," Cade said. "I know that Arabella would be pleased that you and Jeter are now the legal guardians of Chantal."

"You did the right thing, Cade," Jeter said, "and honestly I don't know what Bella would do if you ever did separate the two girls. When one starts to talk, the other one finishes the sentence."

"I'm not going to abandon my responsibility to take care

of her, just as I promised Arabella I would, but she needs a home."

"As long as we're together, that's what she'll have, and soon she's going to have a little brother," Jeter said as he patted his wife's enlarging stomach.

"Jeter, you say that all the time. I say it's a girl," Magnolia said.

"Well whatever it is, it's going to be loved," Cade said.

The door opened, and Jacob Harrison came in.

"I thought I'd find you here," Jacob said as he pulled out a chair and sat down. "Are you ready for another run to Adobe Walls?"

"Is that what they're calling the place?" Jeter asked.

"Yes. Ed and Fuzzy got in a little while ago with no problems," Jacob said.

"Then if the boys are making the trips all right, why did you ask if I was ready for another run?" Cade asked.

"Because guess who else is moving his outfit to the Panhandle?"

"Let me think," Cade said, putting his finger to his temple. "Who would be losing money if the buffalo hunters start selling all their hides to Charlie Myers?"

Jacob laughed. "You're thinking right. Robert M. Wright and Charles Rath are moving to the Canadian."

"And they want Harrison and McCall to help move them."

"That's right, but of course Rath and Wright aren't actually going. They've hired James Langton to be in charge," Jacob said.

"When do we go?"

"They say they want to be set up ready to buy hides by the middle of May, so I'd say we'll leave by next week."

"Cade, do you have to go?" Magnolia asked speaking for the first time. "There will be Indians, and they aren't always going to be friendly."

"That reminds me," Jacob said, "Fuzzy McKnight said Spotted Wolf sent word he wants to see you. He's camped on Mulberry Creek."

"I'm glad he didn't come in to Dodge," Jeter said. "Do you remember when we had to open up the wall of Fringer's Apothecary to get him away from Kirk Jordan?"

"Of course, I remember," Cade said, "especially when your mom hid him under her bed."

"That man is still around Dodge City," Magnolia said. "He would've killed Spotted Wolf for no reason if we hadn't helped him."

"Kirk Jordan would kill any Indian he runs across, no matter what he's done. He thinks he can because some Indian killed his brother up in Nebraska," Jeter said.

CADE STARTED out the next morning at daybreak on his way to Mulberry Creek. He was sure this meeting involved Gentle Horse, and he was hopeful, Spotted Wolf had rescued her from "Smith and Jones".

John Smith and Jim Jones.

Who made up names like that to hide from the law? At least Amon Kilgore and Fred Toombs had chosen distinctive names, but in the end, what difference did it make?

Of all the people Cade had killed, and there were many, Amon Kilgore and Fred Toombs were the most despicable and that was saying something. Not those he killed in battle, not the man he killed on board the Fremad, not those he killed in Wichita, not the Slater brothers—none of those summoned up the hatred that he had for Kilgore and Toombs.

Even now, he became angry thinking about what they had done to Arabella and Magnolia. And when he had seen

Gentle Horse, everything that had happened to his wife came back to him. If Spotted Wolf hadn't killed Smith and Jones already, Cade decided he would go after them. No woman, even if she was an Indian, should have to endure what was happening to her on Moore Creek.

As he rode on, the solitude of the morning cleared his head. He couldn't go kill them. He didn't have a personal vendetta against Smith and Jones, and if he killed them because of Gentle Horse, he would be accused of being an Indian lover. That would mean the Kirk Jordans of the world would come after him.

IN THE DISTANCE, he saw an Indian encampment. He assumed it would be Spotted Wolf's, but just to be careful, he withdrew his Henry rifle and jerked a round into the chamber. As much as he wanted to trust Spotted Wolf, he would not ride into this camp without being prepared.

Looking up, he saw a rider coming toward him. When he got close enough, he saw that it was George Bent. The rifle went back in the sheath and he urged his horse to a gallop as he closed the distance between them.

"I was about to give up on you," George said. "Spotted Wolf was going to break camp today."

"Jacob just told me he wanted to meet with me, yesterday," Cade said. "What's this about?"

George smiled. "Gentle Horse. Because of you, he got his daughter back."

"I'm glad. What about Smith and Jones?"

"They won't be takin' anymore women," George said.

"Did he kill them?"

"Not yet, but he will," George said. "He'll choose the right time—the time when it'll cause the most trouble."

"I understand. I wouldn't want to be either one of those two right now," Cade said.

"Which brings me to what's gonna happen today." George stopped. "Don't even think about not goin' along with what Spotted Wolf says, or you'll be joining Smith and Jones."

"What have I let myself in for?" Cade asked.

"You'll see." George spurred his horse and rode on ahead of Cade. "Whatever Spotted Wolf tells you, you agree, if you want to walk away from here."

GEORGE LED Cade into the camp where at least a dozen lodges had been erected. Several children were dabbling in the water of Mulberry Creek while others were hiding behind mounds of sand that they were using as imaginary breastworks. Cade hoped that Gentle Horse's son was among the children.

As he ventured into the opening between the lodges, he saw two rows of men seated on the ground opposite each other. One man was singing a chant while he was keeping time on a small hand drum.

Cade listened to the rhythmic cadence: Na . . . na . . . he . . . na . . . ha . . . ha . . . ya.

George turned and explained. "The gambling song for the hands game. You'll probably be asked to join."

Cade nodded his head, then he saw Spotted Wolf rise from his place on the ground. Getting off his horse he extended his hand to the old man.

A big smile was on Spotted Wolf's face. "*Nia'ish.* Thank you," he said. "Two times, you help Spotted Wolf. I not forget. You saved me—you saved my daughter."

"What about your grandson? Is he all right?"

"Gentle Horse's boy is here. He is not my grandson. He is a white man's grandson."

Cade nodded his head not knowing what to say.

"You know Black Bird, my son." He pointed to one of the men seated on the ground. "His sons, Wild Wind and Leaning Bear. Those are my grandsons. Come. *Hamestoo'estse.* Sit down."

"It looks like you're going to learn hands right now," George Bent said. "Don't be surprised if you lose your shirt. The Cheyenne take their gamblin' seriously."

"How does the game work?"

"There are two bones—one has a string on it and the other is plain. You're supposed to guess which hand has the marked one in it."

"Then it's fifty-fifty that you're going to win," Cade said.

"Or lose," George said with a laugh. "See the bones in the middle. When one of you has all ten of the bones, the other one loses."

Spotted Wolf indicated that Cade should sit opposite Black Bird, and the game began. Cade was not sure what he had bet, but he sat down. The bones in the center were traded back and forth as first he would guess correctly and then Black Bird would win. The game went on for several hours, and Cade was getting the hang of how to anticipate which hand would be the one Black Bird used to hide the stone. Cade had nine stones. One more and he would win whatever it was he had bet on. Three more hands were played, and Black Bird won each of them.

And then the unthinkable happened. Black Bird dropped one of the stones from his hand. He was obviously angry as he rose and stomped off.

"What happened?" Cade asked as he turned to George.

"He lost. If you drop a stone, you lose automatically."

Black Bird came back leading a horse. He handed the reins to Cade.

"What?" Cade questioned. "We were betting on a horse?"

"Yeah. He said *mo'ehno'ha*. That's horse," George said. "I thought you knew."

"No, I didn't. My interpreter said I might lose my shirt. He didn't say anything about losing my horse."

WHEN THE GAME WAS OVER, and the winners had claimed their winnings, the women brought food for the men. Gentle Horse approached Cade. She was wearing a dress made of tanned deer skin.

"I'm glad you're back with your father," Cade said as he accepted the pemmican from Gentle Horse. He knew she could speak English, but she did not address him, lowering her gaze to keep from making eye contact. He shrugged his shoulders, accepting that she would not speak to him.

The men ate alone, and George told him the names of those who had been gambling: Horse Teeth, Spots on the Feathers, Walking on the Ground, Coyote, Six Feathers, Black Moon, Rolling Bull, Two Crows, and of course, Black Bird.

Black Bird was clearly agitated after having lost to Cade, and the others seemed to be teasing him.

"I think it's time for me to get back to Dodge," Cade said as he rose to his feet.

"Not so fast," George said. "You and Black Bird are going to have another go at it. He's not goin' to let a white man beat him."

"Not the hands game again," Cade said. "I don't have another three hours."

"It won't be. He's chosen the kicking game."

"Don't I have a say in this?"

"Afraid not. Here comes Gentle Horse with your moccasins."

Cade put on the moccasins and waited to see what would

happen next. Immediately Black Bird jumped up in the air, kicking sideways, knocking Cade to the ground.

"I understand this game," Cade said getting to his feet and going after Black Bird.

"No, no hands!" George yelled. "You'll lose if you touch him."

Cade and Black Bird continued kicking at one another for several minutes each one getting in some strong hits. Black Bird was more agile than Cade and soon Cade was exhausted. He staggered to his feet one more time and again Black Bird knocked him down.

"If you want to quit, just stay seated, and that ends it," George yelled.

"And what do I lose? My horse?"

"This time he'd get his horse back."

"All right, then I'm done." Cade folded his arms around his legs and looked up at a smiling Black Bird.

"Hena'haanehe" Black Bird extended his hand to help Cade to his feet. "That's enough."

Gentle Horse held Black Bird's horse and he took the reins and led him away.

"Cade McCall, you're a good man," Spotted Wolf said. "You're a friend to my people. Gentle Horse has a gift for you."

Cade looked to where Gentle Horse had been standing but she was gone. Soon she appeared with her son beside her. She was carrying something in her hand that was the stalk of the red cocklebur.

She smiled looking directly at Cade.

"Eat."

Cade took the stalk from her and took a bite. He found it to be sweet and tender.

"Thank you, this is very good."

Gentle Horse pushed her son toward Cade.

"Your son, now. His name Stone Forehead."

Cade's eyes opened wide.

"No, no, no. You can't do this," Cade said, but as he protested, all the Indians came toward him, each one holding a knife.

George chuckled. "Well, Dad, I guess you've got a son. You know this is the greatest honor they could pay you, and if you refuse, they'll kill you."

9

Dodge City, Kansas:

Cade left Mulberry Creek with the child settled in front of him. Stone Forehead, as he was named, had brought nothing with him except the deerskin pants and shirt he was wearing. The day was cool, and a drizzle was beginning to fall making Stone's hair smell like a wet dog who had rolled in the ashes of a campfire. Cade would have liked to put his horse in a fast trot to get back to Dodge as fast as possible, but without any coat, he thought Stone would be cold. Instead, Cade got his own coat from behind the saddle and put it in front of the boy to block the rain.

As they rode along, Cade tried to communicate with the child, but he said nothing in return. He couldn't help but be impressed by the stoicism of the young boy, who had neither cried, nor even protested when he was taken from his mother.

All Cade could think about was what he had seen in the camp at Moore's Creek. Jones and Smith. Those two outlaw whiskey peddlers were undoubtedly the only white men,

Stone had ever seen. Cade's mind raced. What was he going to do with this child?

He hugged the boy closer, hoping to reassure him that he would keep him safe, as he contemplated the immediate future. He couldn't take a four-year old half-breed Indian to the Dodge House to live with him, any more than he could have taken Chantal to live with him.

Magnolia. She would know what to do.

"STONE, you stay right here beside the porch," Cade said, as he dismounted and lifted the boy off the horse.

Cade stepped up onto the porch of the Willis's house, and because Stone stayed where Cade had put him, he could only be seen from the shoulders up. Cade smiled at him, trying to reassure him, but he stared at Cade with wide, brown eyes which showed neither fear, nor anxiety.

When the door was opened, Jeter's mother was standing there.

"Cade," Mary Hatley said as she embraced him. "I always worry so about you when you're gone, even when it's just for a little while. Do you have to make those trips? One of these days, you're going to run into an Indian that has an arrow with your name on it and you won't come back."

"I'll be all right," Cade said extracting himself from her embrace. "Is Magnolia here?"

"No, she's not. It's downright unchristian for her to be out and about right now," Mary said, shaking her head. "Why, she could drop that baby at any minute, but still she thinks that Red House can't run without her being there."

Cade smiled. "You know, Mary, nobody—not you, not Jeter, not me—not anybody can tell a Cajun what to do."

"I know, I know, but Jeter so wants this baby to be a boy. If anything happened . . . oh, Cade, I'm so sorry. I forgot . . ."

"It's all right. But right now, I have a favor to ask of you."

"You don't have to ask," Mary said. "Whatever it is, I'll do it for you."

"I need you to look after someone for me while I go find Jeter and Magnolia."

"Look after someone?"

Cade turned toward Stone and signaled for the boy to come up onto the porch.

"Oh, my!" Mary's eyes widened when she saw the child. "And who is this?"

"This is Stone. Actually, it's Stone Forehead, but I think Stone will be enough."

Mary furrowed her brow. "Is he an . . .?"

"Yes, he is, at least his mother is."

"Well, where is his mother? What's he doing with you?"

"He was given to me," Cade said. "And now he's mine."

"Oh, dear." Mary held her face in her hands. "Do you want me to hide him someplace?"

"No, I want you to introduce him to Chantal and Bella. I know he can speak some English, but I haven't heard him say anything since we left Mulberry Creek. Maybe the girls can make him feel more comfortable."

"All right, Cade, I hope you know what you've gotten yourself in to." Mary shook her head. "A man takin' on a child, and not just any child—an Indian. Come on—what did you say his name was?"

"Stone."

"You've got to call him something else," Mary said. "Even if we can make him look like a real boy, if you call him that everybody will know what he is."

"No. His mother, Gentle Horse, gave him the name Stone Forehead, and that will be what he will be called. Now, I need to go find Magnolia and tell her about this new development."

As Cade walked to the Red House, he thought about Mary's reaction to Stone. He hadn't been prepared for her attitude, but he supposed many in Dodge City might have the same reaction. Most had some negative experience with an Indian, either personally or through someone they knew. But how could anyone have such hate for a four-year old boy?

Mary had said he needed to look like a real boy. By that, she must have meant a haircut and new clothes. He would have Magnolia see what she could round up for him.

When Cade stepped into the Red House, Cetti was the first to see him, and she greeted him with a wide smile.

"We're all glad you're back, Cade. Let me go get Jeter. I think he's working on the books."

"I'm glad it's him who's juggling numbers and not me," Cade said as he took his usual seat.

"Well, how was your trip?" Jeter asked as he joined him a short while later.

"Interesting," Cade said.

Jeter chuckled. "That's a rather cryptic response."

"Cryptic?"

"It's one of Bat Masterson's words that I picked up. It means that it's a very short answer and you probably have more to say."

Cade nodded. "As a matter of fact, I do," he said. Cade drummed his fingers on the table for a moment before he spoke again. "I need some help."

"All right. I was just counting out the receipts. How much do you need?"

"It's not money I'm after." Cade took a deep breath while

he thought about how he was going to broach this subject. "You know how you and Magnolia are looking out for Chantal?"

The smile on Jeter's face was replaced by a look of concern. "Wait a minute, Cade. We just signed the papers for us to be her legal guardians. You haven't backed out, have you, because if you have, it will break Magnolia's heart, to say nothing of my mother and Bella. And me, too," he added.

"No, no, it's nothing like that," Cade responded quickly, putting his hand on Jeter's wrist. "In fact, it's quite the opposite."

"Opposite? What are you trying to say, Cade? I'm not following you."

"I know," Cade said, "it's going to get complicated. Can you and Magnolia go back to your house for a little while? I have something I want to show you."

Ten minutes later Cade, Jeter, and Magnolia stepped into the house and there, sitting in the middle of the floor was a number two galvanized tub filled with water. Mary was on her knees bathing Bella, and Chantal was running around the room in her underwear, having removed her clothing.

"What happened?" Magnolia asked, as she caught Chantal and attempted to pick her up.

"Don't do that," Jeter said. "I'll take care of Chantal." He started to take the child to the bedroom, when he saw Stone sitting under the table. "Mom? Who is this?"

Mary wiped her brow, getting soap in her hair. She glared at Cade. "You'll have to ask your friend."

Jeter turned to Cade. "Does this have something to do with your cryptic answer to my question? Interesting?"

"Well, yes it does." Cade went over to the table and tried

ROBERT VAUGHAN

to get Stone to come out, but he wouldn't budge. "This is Stone Forehead. He is the child of Gentle Horse who is Spotted Wolf's daughter. I think I told you about her being a captive of two outlaws that were down on Moore's Creek, and more than likely his father is one of them. She gave me her 'medicine' and I got it to Spotted Wolf. When he rescued her, he wanted to thank me, and that was what my trip to Mulberry Creek was about."

"That woman gave you her child?" Mary asked. "Why didn't you say you weren't going to take the little fella?"

"If I would have refused, I wouldn't be here," Cade said.

"All right, that's how you got him," Jeter said. "So, now what are you going to do with him?"

"Don't even ask him that, Jeter. The child is going to stay with us, of course."

"Magnolia," Cade said. "I can't . . . I mean," he made a gesture with his hands. "You already have Chantal and . . ."

"Tell me this, Cade. What else can you do with him, besides leave him with us?" Magnolia asked.

Bella was now out of the tub, and was running around the room without any clothes on. Soon both girls were circling the table, getting closer and closer to Stone and finally sitting beside him getting as close as they could.

For the first time, Cade saw Stone smile. The two little girls laughed happily.

"Look at that," Magnolia said. "They love their new brother."

"Wait a minute, Magnolia," Jeter said. "Don't get them thinking that Stone can stay."

"He will stay," Magnolia said. "He can't help what has happened to him, but now he has a home with us. Get me three cookies. I'll bet this little fellow is hungry."

Mary rose from the floor as she moved toward the

kitchen. "Jeter, he has to have a bath. The whole house will smell like . . ."

"A wet dog," Cade interjected quickly. He did not want the girls to hear the word Indian, at least not yet.

AFTER A WHILE CADE left the Willis house satisfied that Stone was in good hands. Tomorrow he would see to it that the boy got some clothes and that he got a haircut. With his hair cut shorter, and with the dark coloring of the girls, it would be hard to tell that he was not their brother.

So much had happened since returning from Adobe Walls, Cade had forgotten the promise he had made to Bat. He felt his pocket and pulled out the packet of papers that Bat had given him.

When he reached the newly built building, he read the sign painted on the door: *Dodge City Messenger, Alonzo Moore, publisher.* A bell affixed to the door jingled as he pushed it open.

"I'll be right with you," someone called from the back. A moment later a rather smallish man, with a bald head and wearing a canvas apron came up. There were black ink stains on the apron, and the man greeted Cade.

"Oh, heavens, Mr. McCall, I hope you and Mr. Harrison aren't wanting to make any changes in your ad. I just got it set," Alonzo said.

"No, the ad for the freight company is just fine," Cade said. "I'm here on a different matter."

"Oh?"

"There's a young man that I know, a very good man, and a good friend, who wants to be a writer. He's written an article that he'd like for you to publish in your paper, if you think it's good enough."

Alonzo laughed. "What do you mean good enough? I

generally publish any letter to the editor that I receive, regardless of how good it is. Of course, I'll correct the spelling, and I do remove any curse words, but other than that, I publish the letter just as it was written."

"No, this isn't a letter to the editor. My friend wants it published as an article."

Alonzo stroked his chin, and left a little smear of black ink. "In other words, he's looking for validation of his writing." It wasn't a question, it was a declarative statement.

Cade paused a moment before answering. "I suppose that's about right."

"Very well, let me see what Mr. Shakespeare has written for his debut into the world of letters."

"No, I told you, not a letter to the . . ."

Alonzo held up his hand. "A figure of speech, my good man. Merely a figure of speech."

Cade gave Alonzo the paper that Bat Masterson had given him. Cade had read it, and believed it to be quite good. But he also knew that he was no judge in the matter.

Alonzo read through the piece, reading so quickly that Cade was certain he was just going through the motions to satisfy him.

"Damn," Alonzo said. "Damn."

"Is it that bad?" Cade asked. "I thought it was good, but I have to admit that I'm not the proper judge of such a thing."

"Oh, but you are, my boy," Alonzo replied. "Any reader is the proper judge of literature, for without the reader, there would be no literature."

"Oh. But about this piece, do you think . . ."

"It's magnificent. Who, may I ask, is the author? For I intend to publish it, and I would like, also, to give the author a byline. That is, assuming I have the author's permission."

"Oh, you do, you do!" Cade said happily. "He gave me this letter for you to read, if you made the decision to publish it."

DEAR MR. MOORE

I submit herewith for your perusal, my observation of a new community, built and occupied by men of action and adventure. I have chosen Mr. Cade McCall as my personal courier, and have sworn him to secrecy as to the authorship of this piece.

Should you choose not to publish it I would appreciate that same courtesy, for I do not wish to be humiliated by a vain attempt. However, should you deem it worthy of your fine newspaper, then I would be most grateful, and proud to have the byline.

Yours truly
Bat Masterson

ALONZO READ THE LETTER, then laughed. "I think you can tell your young friend that his writing is, indeed, worthy of publication."

A MESSAGE to the Readers of the Dodge City Messenger:

A short time previous I wrote in this newspaper an article about a wagon train departing Dodge City, the purpose of which was to follow the buffalo. One of the participants in that operation was the brother of our own Ed Masterson. This young man, known by his friends as Bat, has already established himself as an excellent marksman and proficient buffalo hunter.

He is also, as I have so recently learned, a most talented writer, and I am proud to include, in this edition, an article that readers will find most informative and interesting.

Birth of a Town
By
W. B. "Bat" Masterson

As did the Mayflower when, *just over 250 years ago it braved the Atlantic Ocean to bring courageous settlers to start a new settlement, so too did 33 wagons under the leadership of Jim Hanrahan brave the wilds to begin a new settlement.*

These "wagon pilgrims" departed the town of Dodge City, which fears not the Indian, and proceeded south, including a hazardous crossing of the Cimarron River into Indian Territory. The crossing accomplished, the adventurous group went even farther south into that part of Texas where the Comanche, Kiowa, and Cheyenne reign.

With little concern or fear of the war-like savages who indeed have the new settlement surrounded, the brave merchants and intrepid buffalo hunters have built the village of Adobe Walls, known by the residents as the Walls. And it is not by a stretch that one would call it a village, rather than a mere encampment, for there are present among the new businesses thus established, a blacksmith, a store selling groceries and various items of clothing as well as guns and ammunition, a restaurant and a saloon, all being substantially built structures, making use of sod and adobe bricks.

The reader may well ask: "What is the economic enterprise that has given birth to the Walls, and what supplies the source of income by which the merchants may prosper?" The answer to that question is the same that has, for some time now, oiled the economic engine of Dodge City. Adobe Walls will prosper from the hide of the buffalo, for Adobe Walls both supports, and is supported by, the buffalo hunter.

And why, you may ask, is the scribe who pens these words, at the Walls? Is it merely to observe, and report upon the activities of the brave men, and one woman who have made this their new home? That would be partially correct, for it is my intention to, from time to time, write my observations of the activity here conducted, but my primary reason is the same as the motive that propels all other residents of this new community. I am a buffalo hunter, and I intend to make my fortune through the procurement, and selling of buffalo hides.

The Quahadi Village of Quanah Parker:

James McAllister was driving a six-mule team and two wagons as it rolled into Quanah Parker's encampment. W.M.D. Lee, the sutler at Camp Supply, and Amos Chapman, his interpreter, led their horses alongside as dogs and children announce their arrival.

Quanah Parker, the accepted leader of the band, came out to meet the wagon.

"Ho, Lee," Quanah said, recognizing the sutler from Camp Supply. "We have few hides to trade. The great herd has not yet begun the migration."

"I know, it is early," Lee said, "but I have brought you something that may help. Come let me show you." He lifted the canvas cover of the small trailing wagon that was loaded with kegs of lead and powder and several cases of fixed ammunition.

A smile crossed Quanah's face. "It is good that you come to us with this much ammunition. I do not think the Quaker agent would like it if he saw this load."

Lee chuckled. "How are the People going to bring robes to me, if there is no ammunition?"

"If only more of the People had guns, we could bring you many thousands of robes. Thirty thousand, fifty thousand, maybe a hundred thousand," Quanah said as he exaggerated the possible numbers. "That would be much money for our friend."

"That it would." Lee walked to the big wagon. "Have a look." Parting the back cover, he exposed case after case of the newest Spencer carbines, Winchester rifles and .45 caliber Colts.

Like a child, Quanah ripped back the wooden top that covered the rifles and lifted one to his shoulder.

"You know that some merchants from Dodge City have built a settlement on the Canadian," Lee said. "Their intention is to provide a trading post for buffalo skins. I trust that with this gift, the Quahadi robes will only be traded to Lee and Reynolds."

"Yes, sir," Quanah said as he saluted, just as he had seen the soldiers do.

"No, no, Quanah. You don't have to do that. I am not a bluecoat. I am your friend."

DODGE CITY:

"I had no idea Bat could write like that," Jacob Harrison said as he put aside a copy of *The Messenger*. He and Cade were entering the Red House Salon.

"I don't know why you should be so surprised," Cade said. "He's always scribbling something in that notebook of his."

"Something he won't let anyone read," Jacob said.

"Yeah, and the words he uses," Jeter said as he joined the conversation. "Half the time I don't even know what the words mean." He smiled. "But I sure like hearing them. How many copies of the paper are you taking down to Adobe Walls?"

"I've got at least two dozen all packed in a gutta-percha bag," Cade said. "That way if we have trouble getting across the river someplace, they'll stay dry."

Jeter's expression changed to a more serious nature. "When will you be moving out?"

"James Langton is ready to go now, but you know Charles Rath. He keeps finding more and more stuff to take down, but he doesn't want to hire another wagon," Jacob said, "so he keeps piling the extra stuff onto the wagons he already has hired."

"James Langton? Aren't Rath and Wright going?" Jeter asked.

"No. It will be up to James to build the new store," Jacob said.

"Cade, is there any way you could stay behind? Send another driver in your stead?"

"This is a big shipment," Cade said. "Every wagon we have will be on this run. Why do you ask?"

"It's the boy. I don't know."

"What's wrong?"

"It's Mom. She can't get past the fact that Stone's an Indian. She thinks I should be more upset than I am that he's in our house," Jeter said. "She reminded me that it was Pa who found me hidden under the floor of our cabin back in Texas. She thinks I should remember that it was Indians who killed my real ma and pa."

"How old were you?" Jacob asked.

"About Stone's age and I hate to admit it, but except for the name Willis, I can't remember anything about my life before Titus and Mary Hatley took me in."

"I hope that's how it is with Stone, especially what he had to go through at the whiskey camp," Cade said. "I want to come by before we leave and take him down to Dugan's Clothing and get him some new clothes. Do you think Max carries kid's clothes?"

"I don't know," Jeter said. "We don't buy clothes for the girls, 'cause Mom sews for 'em."

"At least I need to find someplace where I can buy him some boots."

"And get him a haircut. Magnolia tried to cut his hair and he ran from her."

ON THE CANADIAN RIVER:

Quanah Parker, Black Horse, Wolf Tongue, Old Owl and Silver Knife had been away from camp for several days. Thirty-six horses had been stolen and they had followed the trail as far as they could before a rainstorm washed away the tracks.

"We should go back," Black Horse said. "Our horses are in Kansas by now."

"Maybe not," Quanah said. "The trader told us the Dodge City merchants are building a trading post on the Canadian. Perhaps we should see if that is true."

"Do you think our horses are there?" Black Horse asked.

"I did not say that," Quanah said. "I want to find this trading post. I want to see for myself what the white men are doing."

"Very well," Black Horse said, "but I am going back to our encampment."

"Who will go with me to find this camp?" Quanah asked.

"I will go," Silver Knife said, "and I will kill this white man, just as Mean To His Horses did."

Quanah and Silver Knife continued for another day until they reached the Canadian where W.M.D. Lee had said the merchants were putting their trading post. It was not hard to

87

pick up the trail, even after the rain, because the ruts of many heavily loaded wagons were visible. The signs of horses, mules, and oxen were so numerous that Quanah realized there were even more white interlopers than he had expected.

The terrain was such that Quanah and Silver Knife found it easy to stay out of sight from anyone who might be on the main trail. They continued following along one of the creeks until they heard the loud banging of hammering as well as the ripping sound of sawing, which was ample evidence of the nearness of the white men.

As they got closer the sounds grew louder and louder. Quanah and Silver Knife dismounted, tied off their horses, and climbed up to a level bench near the summit of a butte, not a mile away from the activity.

From this vantage point Quanah looked down to see more white men than there were fingers on both of his hands, and Silver Knife's hands combined. They were hammering, sawing, and scurrying about, all engaged in some frenzied activity.

It was even worse that Quanah thought. This wasn't a hunters' encampment, this was a white man's town!

It appeared that the men were cutting down trees, and even digging up long strips of sod from the ground itself. At first, the reason for digging up the sod was unknown to Quanah, but when they were cut into blocks then stacked up, their purpose became clear. They were being used to construct walls.

"Silver Knife," Quanah said. "We cannot let this continue. We cannot let the white man move into our country to make towns for themselves, steal our buffalo, and destroy our land."

"But how can we stop them?" Silver Knife asked. "There are only two of us, and there are many of them."

"We will come back to this spot," Quanah said. "But we will not come alone. The buffalo belong to the People, but they also belong to the Kiowa, the Cheyenne and the Arapaho. We will fight together."

Silver Knife shook his head. "You are saying that the Comanche will fight beside his old enemy—I do not think so."

"You tell me. Who is worse, our brothers or the white man?"

DODGE CITY:

Cade was having breakfast with Jeter and Magnolia. He was anxious to observe how Stone was getting along with the girls.

"It's not going to be easy," Jeter said. "Last night, he slept under the table. No matter how much we tried he wouldn't come out."

"Do you think he can adjust?" Cade asked.

"He will," Magnolia said. "Stone just has to learn to trust us."

"Humph," Mary said. "It's us that have to learn to trust that little . . ."

"Now, Mom," Jeter interrupted. "He's a four-year-old boy, and his life has been a lot different from Bella's and Chantal's. They'll show him how to act."

"You may not want to say it, but I will. That boy's an Indian and we'll all be sorry when he grows up and scalps one of us."

"Grandmere, please," Magnolia said. "We can't have talk like that."

"Well, it's true," Mary said as she began taking dishes off the table.

"I guess we're through, here," Jeter said as he smiled

89

at Cade.

"It'll be better when he has new clothes," Magnolia said. "He seems to be a sweet boy."

"That's what I came for," Cade said. "I want to go get him some new things."

"Nonsense," Magnolia said. "I'll take him."

"I at least want to pay for them," Cade said. "After all, he is my kid."

Jeter laughed. "You need to find a good woman, and settle down. Come on. I've got to get to work."

A SHORT WHILE LATER, Magnolia and Stone left the house to walk the two blocks to Max Dugan's Clothing store to see what she could find for him. She was aware that heads were turning as townspeople noticed that she was holding the hand of a child dressed as an Indian. Mary had wanted to put a dress on Stone, but Magnolia resisted. Now, because of all the staring, she thought that perhaps Mary was right.

"Tell me, Miz Willis, just what is it that you're a' doin' with that no count Injun?"

The question came from a gruff looking man who was sitting on a barrel on the front porch of Peacock's Saloon.

"I beg your pardon?"

"You heard me. I seen you with two pretty little white girls. It don't seem right to have a filthy Injun that close to 'em." The man rose from the barrel and approached Magnolia.

"He's not dirty," Magnolia said as she pulled Stone toward the clothing store.

"Ha. You could use all the soap in Kansas on that one, 'n he'll still be dirty. There ain't no way you can get the stink off 'n of a Injun."

"That's enough, Jordan," Max Dugan said, coming out of

his store. "If you're going to harass my customers, you're going to have to move on."

"Don't worry," Jordan said, stepping back from Magnolia. "Iffen this little heathen is goin' to be here, I got no wish to be anywhere's close."

Dugan stayed out on the front porch until the unpleasant man was gone.

"I'll have to apologize for that. Kirk Jordan is a man that has no understanding of manners."

"I remember Mr. Jordan well," Magnolia said. "He's the one who wanted to kill Spotted Wolf when poor Spotted Wolf was already near-dead."

"Yes, Jordan raised a posse of Indian haters as I recall, all of them vying for the opportunity to be the one to kill him. But somehow, Spotted Wolf managed to just disappear."

"Yes, didn't he?"

"You know, Mrs. Willis, I've always suspected that you and your husband, and probably Cade McCall as well, may have had something to do with Spotted Wolf getting away from that lynch mob. And make no mistake, that was a lynch mob."

"Do you really think that?"

"I do," Dugan said, then a broad smile spread across his face. "And let me tell you something else, I couldn't be happier that Spotted Wolf got away. Now, let me help you find whatever it is you've come to buy."

"Clothes for the boy," Magnolia said.

Dugan nodded. "Yes, I thought that might be the case."

Magnolia was soon absorbed in searching for anything that might be available for Stone. She found a pair of denim trousers that seemed a bit too big, but she put them on over Stone's deerskin pants, knowing that Mary could alter them to fit him.

A shirt was another matter. Nowhere could she find

anything that even came close to fitting him, so she settled on some gingham material and some blue chambray that she knew could be sewn into shirts.

"Is that all?" Max Dugan asked when Magnolia came to the counter.

"I need some shoes. Do you have anything that might work?"

"I'm afraid not," Dugan said shaking his head. "We don't carry anything like that for children, but if you go down to Mueller's Boot Shop, he's probably got a boot last that he could use to make the boy a pair."

"Thank you, Mr. Dugan, you've been most helpful," Magnolia said as she walked up to the counter to pay for her items. "Would you mind if I left these packages while I take Stone to the barbershop?"

"Of course, I don't mind. I'll just put them under the counter until you come back."

When Magnolia and Stone stepped out of the store, about half a dozen men were waiting for them.

Instinctively, Magnolia pulled Stone close to her, allowing her skirt to cover him.

"No, no, Missy, you can't hide that Injun," Kirk Jordan said. "Crazy Jack, grab that kid. We're gonna string 'im up."

"What do you mean, string him up? Don't you dare touch this child," Magnolia said, pushing Stone behind her.

"We don't want to hurt you, but we will if we have to. No Injun is gonna be in Dodge, no matter how small he is."

The man called Crazy Jack grabbed for Stone, and pushed Magnolia to the ground. Stone started running down the street, as the other men were chasing him. The child was no match for grown men and soon one of them scooped him up under his arm. Stone was kicking and trying to get away, when Cade and Jacob came out of the Red House.

"What the hell are you doing?" Cade yelled as soon as he

saw what was happening.

"Stay out of this, McCall," Kirk Jordan said. "The Willis woman had this brat leading him by the hand. No white woman is gonna do that—not in this town, she ain't."

"She can do anything she wants to," Cade said. "Now give me the boy."

"You ain't neither one of you got a gun, McCall. 'N you may have noticed that there's six of us here and there's only two of you," Jordan said.

"There're three of us," Jeter said as he came out of the Red House, holding a pistol. "And I do have a gun. Now put the boy on the ground and walk away."

"You ain't gonna do nothin'. This here's a Injun. Can't you tell one when you see one, or are you so used to sleeping with a colored woman that it don't make no difference?" The man who spoke was Crazy Jack, a big, strong man who had established somewhat of a reputation in town for being a saloon fighter. He had once taken on three men at the same time, beating them all.

Jeter handed the pistol to Cade. "What did you say?"

"You heard what I said. Your skin might be white, but you ain't no white man, not livin' with a colored woman, 'n keepin' a Injun kid . . ."

That was as far as Crazy Jack got before Jeter caught him with a roundhouse right that knocked him flat.

Jeter's adversary was three inches taller and at least twenty pounds heavier, and he raised up on his elbows, then smiled.

"Well, now, how about this, boys? Ole' Willis here has picked hisself a fight."

"Get 'im, Crazy Jack," Jordan called out. "Get 'im good."

"Oh, I'm goin' to," Crazy Jack said as he got to his feet. "Yes, sir, I'm goin' to teach this ole' boy here a lesson that he ain't soon goin' to forget."

By now not only the group of men who had taken Stone, but several other townspeople, drawn by the prospect of a fight, had gathered around. The effect was to make a large circle, and creating a fighting ring in the middle of the street.

Crazy Jack rubbed his jaw.

"I have to say, you got a pretty good one in on me," he said. His smile grew broader. "But only 'cause I wasn't expectin' it. Let's see what you can do now that I'm ready for it."

He took a step toward Jeter and swung hard. Jeter ducked under the punch that, had it connected, would probably have ended the fight right there. Jeter sent a left jab toward Crazy Jack's head, connecting with his chin, but the big man laughed it off.

"Is that the best you can do?" Crazy Jack asked, sending another broad right-cross which, like his first attempt, missed the mark.

Jeter scored with two more left jabs, then a right-hook.

The hook snapped the big man's head back, but did nothing more. His smile grew broader, and more insolent.

He changed tactics, and instead of a round-house right cross, sent out a left jab that caught Jeter on the shoulder. Jeter felt the pain of the blow from his shoulder to the tip of his fingers.

The crowd grew in size and intensity as the onlookers began yelling their encouragement to both fighters.

Cade, who was watching Crazy Jack's supporters to make sure they didn't interfere, was glad to note that the shouts that were in support of Jeter, exceeded those who were against him by a wide margin.

"Crazy Jack is goin' to kill 'im," someone said, the tone of his voice expressing sympathy for, and not antagonism against Jeter.

"Oh, I don't know," another answered. "I've seen fights like this before. Lot's of times, the littler guy wins 'cause he's quicker."

"Yeah, well, Jeter is quicker, all right."

As the fight continued, it became evident that Jeter could connect almost at will, but no matter how well he scored, the big man shook it off, as if it were no more than being irritated by a gnat. Then Jeter managed to slip a right jab in that caught his opponent on the end of his nose. He felt the nose go under his blow, then saw blood beginning to gush from Crazy Jack's nose.

Crazy Jack continued to show his evil grin, the grin even more macabre now, because the blood was running across his teeth.

Jeter realized that Crazy Jack was hurting from the blow to the nose, because now he began guarding it, that defensive position lessening the frequency of his own swings.

"I'm tired of messin' with you, you son of a bitch, so I'm

goin' to finish you off now," The big man made a rush toward him with another wild swing.

Ducking under the swing, Jeter sent a hard-left jab into Crazy Jack's solar plexus which had the effect of taking the big man's breath away. With a whooshing sound, he bent over and covered his belly with both hands.

Jeter sent a hard, whistling right into the Adams apple, and though he didn't crush it, the effect was to drop Crazy Jack again, where he lay on the ground, struggling to breathe.

"I'll be damn," someone said. "I never thought I'd see anything like that."

Jeter looked at the others.

"Does anybody else have something to say about my wife?"

"Just that this ain't over yet," Jordan said, though the remark was more of a comment, than a challenge.

Jordan and another man helped Crazy Jack to his feet, and they walked away, and with the fight over, the rest of the crowd dispersed.

During the fight, Stone had clung to Cade's leg. Now, Cade turned his attention to the boy.

"What are you doing out by yourself?" Cade asked as he comforted Stone. "Where's Magnolia?"

"That man pushed her down," Stone said, speaking for the first time.

"Where?"

"Back there." Stone pointed down the street.

Several people were gathered in front of Dugan's store. Cade picked up Stone and began running toward the crowd.

"What is it?" Jeter asked.

"I don't know, but you'd better come with me. I don't think this is going to turn out well."

WHEN JETER and Cade reached Dugan's store, they saw Magnolia lying on the ground with a group of men standing around her. A wet spot encircled her.

Jeter knelt beside her, taking her hand in his. "Magnolia, speak to me, tell me you're all right."

Magnolia opened her eyes and smiled when she saw Jeter. "It's time. Get me out of the street."

"Where? Where do you want to go?"

"I don't care, just find a place. You don't want your baby to be born in the middle of Front Street, do you?"

"I'LL RUN FOR THE DOCTOR," Jeter said after he had taken Magnolia home.

"There's no time for that," Mary said. "Get me some water and towels. This baby is about to be born now!"

"Oh, I, uh . . ."

"You stay here with Magnolia," Cade said. "I'll get the water and towels."

A moment later Cade stepped back into the bedroom with the requested items. Jeter took them from him.

"Get those three babies out of here," Mary said. "They don't need to be in the way."

It may have been a strange reaction for him, under the circumstances, but Cade felt good that Mary had said "three" babies, including Stone in the same reference.

"Come on, let's wait in the other room," Cade said, leading the three children back into the keeping room.

"Is Mama having a baby?" Bella asked.

"Yes, she is."

"She will be our sister," Chantal said.

"How do you know it'll be a girl?" Cade asked.

"It will be a girl," Chantal insisted.

The four waited nervously until, finally, they heard the cry of a baby.

"That's her. That's our sister crying," Bella said, excitedly.

A moment later Jeter stepped out of the bedroom with a big smile on his face.

"Bella, Chantal, Stone, come meet your baby sister."

"See, I told you it'd be a girl," Chantal said with a proud grin.

"We're naming her Mary Lilajean," Jeter said. He looked over at Mary, "After my two mothers."

"So, what do you girls think about your new little sister?" Cade asked when they saw the baby.

"I think she's beautiful," Bella said reaching out to touch the baby's cheek.

"I think she's beautiful too," Chantal added.

"She's little," Stone said.

"Yes, well, babies are little," Cade replied.

He looked down at Magnolia, who was holding the baby and looking at her with a beatific smile.

"How are you feeling?" Cade asked.

"I feel wonderful. And isn't she beautiful?" Magnolia asked with a warm smile.

"Yes, she is, and that isn't just my opinion. Chantal and Bella back me up on that."

"I'm sure they're going to be very helpful with the baby," Magnolia said as Bella climbed up onto the bed. "Perhaps even a little too helpful."

"Magnolia, I owe you more than I can ever repay," Cade said. "First Chantal, then Stone, and now you have a new baby. I hope I haven't given you more than you can handle."

"Oh, don't be foolish, Cade. There are lots of women who have four children and many who have five, six, or more. In a way it's easier because the children look out for one another. I'm very happy to have them."

"Yes, the girls have truly been a blessing," Mary said.

Cade couldn't help but notice how pointedly the older woman had left out any mention of the boy.

Adobe Walls:

The first resident out to welcome the arrival of the Harrison and McCall wagons was Skeeter, the cur dog, belonging to Tom O'Keefe. He ran out to the wagon, barking happily, and turning in circles to show his excitement.

"Hello, Skeeter," Cade greeted as he slid off his horse. He squatted down to rub Skeeter behind the ears, and to let Skeeter greet him with dog kisses.

"I swear that dog would probably leave with you without ever lookin' back," Tom O'Keefe said. "Dog, don't forget who feeds you."

Cade laughed. "Damn, Tom, if I didn't know better, I'd say you were jealous."

"I am jealous," Tom replied, though his demeanor and smile showed that he wasn't serious.

"Where's James Langton?" Jacob asked. "Bob Wright said he'll take care of getting our wagons unloaded."

"I thought Rath and Wright would have rode down with you," Langton said as he approached the wagons. "But I guess they'll come when I get the store all outfitted. Pull these here wagons down in front of our place if you would. I expect y'all will be a wantin to go see what Hanrahan's got set up."

"A swig would taste pretty good about now," Jacob said.

"Say, would Masterson happen to be here?" Cade asked.

"You'll find him in the bar, no doubt playin' cards. It's a wonder that boy hasn't been shot," Langton said.

"Oh? Why is that?"

"He's got so many I.O.U.'s from them fellas—why they're gonna be huntin' a month just to pay him back."

"He's winning, then," Jacob said.

"I'd say, and what's worse, nobody can say he's cheatin'. Nobody knows how he can win so much," Langton said.

"Maybe he's just lucky," Cade said, as he pulled the gutta-percha bag out of one of the wagons.

WHEN CADE and Jacob walked into Hanrahan's it took a minute for their eyes to adjust to the lantern-lit room. The building was about twenty-five feet wide and eighty feet long with walls made of stacked sod some two feet thick. The bar that had been a buffalo hide stretched over two whiskey barrels when last Cade had seen it, was now made of rough sawn planks set on sturdy tree trunks. The tables were built of the same material, but they had tanned hides stretched across them to facilitate the playing of cards. The chairs were three-legged stools. Cade's first thought was how uncomfortable it would be to sit on those hour after hour, but no one seemed to notice.

"Cade," Bat Masterson said, raising his hand. "And Jacob, too. What news have you brought from Dodge?"

"By news, would you mean the *Messenger*?" Cade asked.

"Maybe, but that all depends. Did you bring a paper?" Bat asked, bracing himself for the response.

"No, I didn't."

"I, uh, see. Well, I thank you for not . . ."

"I brought 20!" Cade said with a wide grin.

"Twenty?"

"Now that you're a published writer, I thought you might want to share your story with your friends." Cade dropped the bundle of newspapers on the table. "At least the ones who can read."

"What are you talking about?" James Hanrahan asked. "Bat doesn't have any friends."

"Oh, yeah?" Bat said. "Well, read this and weep." Bat gave a copy of the paper to Hanrahan, then went around calling out like a paper boy. "Paper! Paper! Get your newspaper here!"

IT TOOK the better part of two days to get the Harrison and McCall wagons unloaded.

"I think we should head back to Dodge, first thing in the morning," Jacob said. "It's a shame there are such a few hides to take back."

"It can't be helped," Fred Leonard said. "The herd hasn't started moving north yet, and the hides we have are from those men who didn't come in for the winter. I'd say we have less than 2,500, but they have to start movin' soon."

"If there are any buffalo left," Cade said emphasizing the word if.

Leonard shook his head. "Don't even say that. Charlie Myers and I have too much money invested in this place to just pull up and leave. No, the buffalo are out there—they have to be."

"Has anyone gone out to look for 'em?" Jacob asked.

"Yeah, Billy Dixon and a couple of skinners went out about a week after we got here. He'll be comin' back with a report on what he's found. If it's good news, he'll have a load of hides. If it's bad news . . ., but in the meantime, load up the hides we got and take 'em back to Dodge."

"All right," Cade said, "but let's have Tom O'Keefe go over the wagons, and repack the wheels before we head back."

JACOB AND CADE were sitting at a table in the back of Myers store. Sybil Olds had come to join them.

"Tell me the news from Dodge. How is my friend, Magnolia?"

"She now has four children," Jacob said.

"Don't tell me, she had twins!" A big smile crossed Sybil's face. "Jeter has to be the happiest man alive."

"She didn't have twins," Cade said. "She had a little girl, Mary Lilajean and she almost had her in the middle of Front Street."

Sybil's eyes grew large. "You can't mean that. What happened?"

Cade told her all about having the baby, how he had come to get Stone, how Kirk Jordan had gone after the child, Jeter's fight and everything else he could think to tell Sybil.

It was obvious to Cade, that as she was the only woman in the compound, probably the only white woman in the Texas Panhandle, Sybil was lonely for a woman's companionship. He remembered the day the wagons had moved out of Dodge some two months ago, how Magnolia and Sybil had embraced. He wished it would be possible for Magnolia to come visit, but with her own new baby, and the child he had thrust upon her, it would be impossible.

"Say, Sybil, why don't you ride back to Dodge with us?" Cade asked. "You can stay with Magnolia and see the new baby. We'll be coming back by the end of the month and you could come back then."

"Never. Do you think William Olds could ever get along without me?"

Both men laughed. "It was just a thought," Cade said.

"Here you are," Tom O'Keefe said. "I'm afraid I've got some bad news for you."

"Let's hear it," Jacob said.

"It looks like you've got a split hub on one of your wheels. Both of the point bands are broke and the hub bore has been settin' on the axle skein. It just couldn't take the friction."

"Can you fix it?"

"I can put the bands back on, but the hub's still split, and it could give out anywhere along the way. It's up to you two what you want me to do."

"What do you think, Cade? Shall we risk it?"

"I don't want to be the target for a marauding band of Indians if we're hung up someplace. I say we leave the wagon here. Bring a new hub when you come back down."

"I think that's best," Tom said. "I'll finish up on the other wagons. Need to replace a king bolt, but I can do that."

"Thanks, Tom," Cade said.

Jacob cocked his head and squinted his eyes at Cade. "When *you* come back? That sounded like only one of us is going back to Dodge."

"I've been thinking. It'll only be a matter of time before the buffalo head north. I could make a lot of money in a short period of time—maybe enough to buy me a piece of land somewhere, settle down, find a wife, take care of Stone —who knows what I'll do."

"Restless, huh? As it is, you've stayed in this freighting business longer than I ever thought you would," Jacob said. "I'll tell you what. I won't be back for at least four or five weeks. Stay here and when I come back, we'll talk about what we want to do. Maybe I should move on, too."

1 2

CADE STAYED AROUND THE SETTLEMENT, WHICH WAS officially named Adobe Walls, but most of the men called it the Walls. It was interesting to watch the interaction between the men as they waited for evidence that the buffalo herd was on the move. There were six or eight men who worked the shops including William Olds who along with Sybil, cooked for the crew. Then there were the buffalo hunters. At this time there were about thirty or forty in residence. The final group was made up of the skinners.

In Cade's opinion, there was no job that was more detestable. Back after a hurricane had hit Galveston and forced the closing of the original Red House, he had spent the winter skinning cattle that had died in the flood waters. That had been during the winter, when the stink was not as great. But in Kansas, and now Texas, the heat of the summer caused the buffalo to reach the putrid stage all too quickly. These men never took a bath, but even if they did, the next day their clothes and their hands would be covered with the same filth.

But now as they waited, there was an unusual spirit of camaraderie.

They played cards, had horse races, held shooting contests, but most of all they drank. And even in their drunken stupor, there were few if any fights that broke out. It was as if these men knew that if anything happened, they could only depend on one another.

Cade was in a poker game where for once he was going to best Bat Masterson, when all at once a loud cacophony of sound started outside.

Every eye around the table opened wide as stools were pushed aside and pistols were drawn.

"What's that?" Cade asked.

"It's Tom O'Keefe wantin' to get out attention," Bat said. "Sorry old man." He flipped over Cade's cards. "You had me."

Everyone hurried out of the bar to see Billy Dixon and three other men coming toward the settlement. There were two wagons each pulled by a couple of mules.

Cade noticed that the wagons were basically empty. No buffalo hides.

"What happened, Billy?" Fred Leonard asked. "Did you find the herd?"

"Not yet," Billy said. "We saw a few old bulls movin' but they haven't joined the cows yet."

"Damn," Bat said. "I'm ready to leave this place. I want to get some buffs."

"You just want to leave, cause everybody knows your luck's turnin'," Mike Welch said. "You was about to lose that pot to McCall."

"You can go out yourselves if you want to," Billy said. "I'm gonna have Tom fix my brake roller and pick up some supplies. Then I'm headed out again."

"Where ya goin?" Welsh asked.

"I'm headin' west at least as far as Hell's Creek, maybe go on down to the old Fort Bascom Trail," Billy said.

One of the men who was with Billy shook his head. "I think you're makin' a mistake. We saw those old bulls over by Cantonment Creek, and I think we should go back east. I just got me a feelin' that's where we're a gonna see 'em first."

"Well, Brick, why don't we split up? You go east, and I'll go west. That'll widen our search."

"What about Frenchy? Does he stay with you or does he come with me?" Brick Bond asked.

"I stay with Billy," the man called Frenchy said.

"And I stay with Frenchy," the other man said.

Billy laughed. "Then it's settled. I'll be eatin' the best buffalo steak on the plains. Now who wants to be my new shooter?"

"Are you serious?" Cade asked.

"I am."

"Then I'm your new shooter."

"McCall? Aren't you in the freightin' business?"

"I'm here waitin' on a hub for one of our wagons. In the meantime, I want to kill a few buffs," Cade said.

Billy nodded his head. "You and me can be partners— fifty, fifty. We'll send our hides on to Dodge and get a dollar more than what we'd get from Fred Leonard or James Langton and with your wagons we won't be paying any freight. Is that a deal?"

"I think you've got a partner," Cade said extending his hand.

CADE OUTFITTED himself with anything he thought he would need including a new Sharps .50. At one time he had had such a gun, but he had given it to Ernst Hoffmann. He and Hoffmann had been hunting partners while Cade was searching for Arabella and Magnolia. After he had killed Kilgore and Toombs, he vowed he would never use the gun again.

For the first several days the hunting party made up of Billy and Cade and two skinners, Frenchy and an Englishman named Charlie Armitage, saw only a few clusters of old bulls. Billy led them up the Canadian until they reached White Deer Creek, then turned and followed the creek until they got to the plains. For a while they hugged the plains until coming to a creek that offered an ideal camping place. The spot had plenty of grass and wood and was close to water.

"This is where we'll make our permanent camp," Billy said. "We'll need some sort of shelter." He took out an ax and handed it to Cade. "You go chop some willows and Frenchy, you start a fire. Armitage, you come with me. There's bound to be some wild turkeys around here."

That night, Cade understood why Brick Bond had wanted Frenchy to be in his camp. Cade had never eaten a better meal cooked over a campfire.

That was wrong. The meals Arabella and Magnolia had prepared on the cattle drive were better than Frenchy's, but his food came close.

As he lay in his bedroll, Cade wondered what was ahead for him. He had told Jacob that he wanted to make enough money to buy some land. Did he really want to go back to farming like he had done in Tennessee? Or did he want to buy land in Kansas, or even here in Texas? Maybe he should go back to East Texas, Galveston, perhaps.

Cade was thirty-one years old. Except for the old men who were at Adobe Walls, most of the others were young. Billy was twenty-four, Bat was twenty-one, Billy Tyler was probably not out of his teens.

And what of the richest men in Dodge? Bob Wright was

three years older than Cade, Charles Rath seven years older and Charley Meyers not much older than that. Money was not the only gauge for success, but it was a gauge. And Cade had spent the better part of his life getting in and out of one scrape after another.

This buffalo hunt was going to be his last adventure. Cade decided he was going to become an upstanding member of the community; which community that would be, he couldn't say.

He spent a restless night, the next morning arising before daylight. He put wood on the coals that Frenchy had so carefully banked the night before, and went down to the creek to get some water for a pot of coffee.

It was then that he heard it, a distant rumble. He knew immediately what it was—the bellowing of the mating bulls that would go on both day and night until the breeding season was over. The herd was coming!

Excitedly, Cade ran back to the sleeping camp.

"Wake up!" he called to the others. "Billy, Charley, Frenchy! Wake up, the buffalo are coming!"

The news galvanized the others so that the normal morning grogginess was replaced by preparation and activity. Cade and Billy checked their big .50 caliber buffalo guns as Armitage and Frenchy made coffee, fried bacon, and then fried corn pone in the bacon grease.

After breakfast, Cade and Billy rode out about five miles from the camp.

"There!" Cade said. "There they are!" He pointed to a huge herd of buffalo, a vast, undulating landscape.

"It's like old times," Billy said with a wide grin.

"It's a magnificent sight. I've never seen anything like it," Cade said. "I almost hate to kill any of them."

"Don't look at them as buffalo, look at them as dollar signs," Billy suggested. "Let the harvesting begin." Billy jumped off his horse securing him with a ground tether.

"Yes, harvesting. That sounds a little better than killing."

Cade found a forked stick, stuck it in the ground, then lay down with the barrel of his Sharps supported by the fork as he waited for the herd to come into range. When the opportunity was presented, he drew a bead on a big bull, pulled the trigger, and the buffalo dropped in place. Not another animal was disturbed by the sudden death of one of their own, and for the next hour Cade and Billy killed buffalo as rapidly as they could load and fire.

Quahadi Village near the Canadian

Quanah Parker, Silver Knife, Wolf Tongue, and Mean To His Horses had just returned to the village with six antelope they had killed. Giving them to the women to prepare, the men moved to a spot where two of the elders were sitting. Standing Bear was greasing a sapling that had been cut to the length of an arrow. When he was finished, he handed it to Crooked Nose who meticulously pushed the wood through a round hole in a buffalo bone to straighten the wood.

"I see you did not bring in a buffalo," Standing Bear said. "It is time."

"It is time," Wolf Tongue said, "but we did not see even a shaggy old bull."

Standing Bear picked up another stick. "Why do we make arrows if you cannot find the buffalo?"

"The buffalo are afraid," Crooked Nose said. "The Great Spirit is telling them, do not move to your breeding ground. You will be no more."

"It is the white man who slaughters the buffalo," Silver Knife said. "The People have hunted the buffalo for many generations, and always the buffalo returns. To give us food, to give us clothing, to give us shelter, to give us tools, to give us anything we need."

"The white man takes only the hide, and leaves the meat and bones for the wolves," Mean To His Horses said.

"I have seen the place where the white men are building their town," Quanah Parker said to the others. "If we do not stop them, all the buffalo will be gone, and our children will go hungry."

"Our numbers are few. There are more white men than there are blades of grass," Standing Bear said. Standing Bear was a man of many, many summers, and though he was no longer a warrior, his age had made him wise, so the others listened to him.

"It is not possible that there are that many white men. I have seen their villages," Mean To His Horses replied.

"The towns you have seen are small, like our villages. But our brother, Little Robe, tells of riding on the iron horse for many days. Everywhere he saw big villages, with large stone tipis, so big that all in our villages could sit in but one of them," Standing Bear said.

"And you believe Little Robe?" Wolf Tongue asked.

"I do. Lone Wolf of the Kiowa says the same," Standing Bear said. "At the agency, I saw pictures with my own eyes."

"We must make war against them," Quanah Parker said.

"I would advise against it. The white man is very powerful," Standing Bear said. "If we make war, there will be much weeping among the women for those who are killed."

"Do not the women weep for those killed by the soldiers already?" Silver Knife asked.

Standing Bear, whose brother had been killed by Mackenzie, turned his face away.

"You are right, the People cannot face Bad Hand alone," Quanah said.

"But we are alone," Silver Knife said.

"We do not have to be alone. I have smoked the pipe with Lone Wolf. I believe that Lone Wolf would have the Kiowa join the People. And I believe the Cheyenne will also join with the People. If all will do that, we can defeat Bad Hand and drive all the whites from our land."

"But the People are the best warriors," Mean To His Horses said. "Why would we want anyone else to help?"

"Because Standing Bear is right. There is much power with the white man," Two Crows said.

"My power is greater than that of the white man."

All turned to see White Eagle, a young warrior who claimed to be a medicine man.

"How is it that your power is greater?" Wolf Tongue asked.

"Did I not tell you when the great light that appeared in the sky would go away? Did I not tell you we would go many days without rain?"

White Eagle had predicted when the Coggia Comet, then visible to the naked eye, would disappear and that a long drought would follow. His prediction was accurate, to the day.

"I am told, this you did," Quanah Parker agreed.

"That does not make your power greater than the power of the white man," Two Crows said.

"Can a white man rise into the sky and speak with the spirits?"

White Eagle asked.

"No, I do not think a white man can do this," Mean To His Horses said. "I do not think anyone can do this."

"I will do this now, so that you may see."

"I would like to see you do such a thing," Silver Knife said.

"First, you must prepare yourself," White Eagle said. "Look into the sun, and do not shut your eyes. Do not look away from the sun until I tell you to do so. This you must do, so that my power will be great."

The others, anxious to see this demonstration did as they were directed. They stared at the sun until their eyes were hurting, and everything disappeared from their vising but an overwhelming brightness.

"Now, look at me," White Eagle ordered.

All of them had been blinded by the sun, and when they looked toward White Eagle they saw nothing but a black blob in the center of the brightness, that moved according to where they looked. As they lifted their eyes, the black blob seemed to lift as well. It took several minutes before they could see again, and when they could see, White Eagle was gone.

"Where is he?" Wolf Tongue asked.

"Did you not see?" Silver Knife asked. "As I lifted my eyes, I saw him rise into the heavens."

"Yes," Mean To His Horses said. "This I saw as well."

"I do not believe he has done this," Quanah Parker said.

"But you saw, with your own eyes, as did the rest of us," Silver Knife said.

"I believe it is a trick," Wolf Tongue said.

"And I believe it is a sign." Mean To His Horses said.

"Do you think he seeks counsel with the spirits?" Silver Knife asked.

"That is what he said," Quanah Parker answered.

"With which spirit does he seek counsel?"

"I do not know. This, he will tell us," Mean To His Horses said.

"I do not think the spirits will counsel war," Silver Knife said.

"We do not need the spirits to tell us that if the buffalo are gone, our people will die," Quanah said. "And you should know this, Silver Knife, for were you not with me when we saw the village of the white buffalo hunters? The white man must die. He must be driven off our land."

"Quanah, I would think that you, more than any other, would not wish to make war with the white man," Standing Bear said. "Your mother was a white Woman."

"My mother is Comanche," Quanah Parker said. "And I hate the white man all the more for taking her from me." Quanah's mother, who was born Cynthia Ann Parker, had been kidnapped when she was very young. She adopted the ways of the People and was devastated when before she died, she and her daughter were forced to live as white.

"Let us go to our tipis and wait for White Eagle to return," Silver Knife said.

"I do not believe that he has done this," Wolf Tongue said, as they left the two old men to their work.

"How can you not believe?" Silver Knife asked. "Did you not see him with your own eyes?"

It was two days before anyone saw White Eagle again. Early in the morning, when Quanah stepped out of his tipi, he saw the medicine man sitting in the same spot where the old men had been working on the shafts for the arrows.

"Where have you been?" Quanah Parker asked.

"You saw me ascend into the sky. I was with the spirits."

"I do not believe you can do that," Quanah said.

Just then, White Eagle moved his arm quickly, and an arrow appeared in his hand.

"You will see, I have much medicine," White Eagle said.

"Did you speak with the spirits?" Silver Knife asked as he came running toward the two men.

"I did."

"Who were the spirits?"

"Buffalo Hump, Iron Jacket," White Eagle paused for a

moment and stared directly at Quanah. "And I spoke with Peta Nocona."

Quanah gasped. "You spoke with my father?"

"Yes."

"And what did Peta Nocona say?"

"Your father says that you have made him proud. He says that you are a good warrior."

"And what of the others? What do they say?" Silver Knife urged.

White Eagle smiled as more began to gather around him. "They say that all the buffalo are being killed, and the meat is left to rot. Their hearts are wounded by this. It is their counsel that we go to war and kill the white men who do this."

"Yeeai!" Wolf Tongue and Mean To His Horses shouted.

Quanah Parker, too, felt a surge of excitement.

"I do not think this is a good thing," Two Crows said to Standing Bear, who was not celebrating White Eagle's announcement.

"Nor do I," Standing Bear replied. "But the blood runs hot in the veins of the young, and they seek the thrill and glory of war."

"Many of the People will die," Two Crows said.

Standing Bear did not dispute Two Crow's observation.

LATER IN THE DAY, Mean To His Horses came to Quanah Parker's tipi. Following the proper ritual of not entering the tipi of another until invited, Mean To His Horses stood outside and called for Quanah.

"Quanah, it is I, Mean To His Horses! I would speak with you!"

A moment later the tipi flap was pushed aside, and Quanah appeared.

"What do you want?

"We have heard that the spirits have counseled us to go to war," Mean To His Horses said.

"This is what White Eagle has said."

"Then let us go. Let us make war upon the white man."

"We shall do so, when we are ready. We must prepare," Quanah said.

"White Eagle says let us go to war now! Today! We will find the white buffalo hunters and we will kill them."

"We must not launch the arrow before it is notched into the bowstring."

"If you will not lead us, then I, Mean To His Horses, will find warriors who will follow me, and I will lead them into battle."

Quanah didn't answer. He was known for the power and intensity with which he could stare at someone through his gun metal gray eyes. He affixed just such a stare on Mean To His Horses now, and held it until Mean To His Horses turned away.

Soon the eager warrior was in the middle of the village, dressed and painted for war.

"Hee yah! Hee yah! Hee yah!" Mean To His Horses shouted, holding up his lance. "I am going to make war on the white buffalo hunters who have come to our land. You, who are brave of heart and filled with the wish to kill the white men who have invaded our land, ride with me. Pick up your lance, take your bow, grip your war club and come with me!

"We will find glory as we kill the white devils.

"You who are afraid, remain behind with the women and the children."

There were several shouts of excitement from the other warriors, and within a few minutes, Mean To His Horses had a raiding party assembled and ready.

Quanah watched the little band of warriors leave, and he had to admit to himself that he wished he was with him. But even though Quanah had never heard the terms, he inherently realized that small raids, such as the one Mean To His Horses would be conducting, though a satisfying tactic, was not an effective strategy. And he knew that he must plan, and implement that successful strategy.

While he was skeptical that White Eagle had ascended into the sky, he knew that those who had watched him believed in the medicine man's power. Perhaps there was a way that Quanah could harness that belief. He headed for the tipi where White Eagle stayed.

It was time to plan the next move.

13

JOE PLUMMER, DAVE DUDLEY, AND TOMMIE WALLACE WERE camped on Chicken Creek, about 25 miles down the river from Adobe Walls. Plummer was the hunter, and Dudley and Wallace were the skinners. The main herd had just arrived, and Plummer had killed a little over 100 animals so far. Only half the buffalo had been skinned, and those hides were now staked out in the sun, drying.

At the moment the three men were eating buffalo steaks.

"Well, I'll tell you what," Dudley said. "I reckon I can see why the Injuns eat buffalo all the time, seein' as it is pretty good. But I'm gettin' a might tired of it, 'n would trade you a hunnert pounds of buffalo, for one hen we could use to make us up a pot o' chicken 'n dumplins."

"This would have been better if we had some pepper to put on it," Wallace said, as he carved off a piece of meat and lifted it to his mouth.

"They prob'ly got some pepper back at the Walls," Plummer said.

"Yeah, I bet they do, and expect they's set up to buy your hides now, too." Wallace said.

"Yes, but we'll prob'ly not get as much for 'em as we'd get if we was to take 'em all the way to Dodge, our ownselves. On account of they'll have to pay the freighters to take 'em back in their wagons," Plummer said.

"Why you sellin' 'em there, then?" Dudley asked.

"Because, in the long run, I'll make more money. See, in the time it'd take to get the hides to Dodge, I could be killin' more buffalo, 'n that would more'n make up the difference."

"Yeah," Wallace said. "For me 'n Dudley too, because the more buffalo we skin, the more we'll get paid."

"Hey, Joe, you know what else they prob'ly got at the Walls? I'd be willin' to bet you just about anythin' that they got some canned peaches," Dudley said

"Oh, man, wouldn't that be good though?" Wallace asked.

"You know what?" Dudley said. "If you was to go to the Walls 'n maybe get some pepper 'n some more coffee . . ."

"And some canned peaches," Wallace added.

"We can stay here 'n keep a watch out. And maybe we can ketch up with what you've kilt."

"Well, I guess we could use a few supplies," Plummer agreed. "All right, I'll go first thing in the morning."

White Deer Creek:

The next morning, ten miles west of the Plummer, Wallace and Dudley camp, Cade, Billy, Armitage and Frenchy were just finishing their breakfast.

"We've had a good few days of shooting," Billy said. "There must be close to a 150 dead buffalo lying out there now, and we haven't even started on this day."

"I say, you two lads are going to have to reduce the number of beasts you are shooting," Armitage said, in his pronounced British accent. "I fear you are quite overtaking the capabilities that Frenchy and I have to keep up with you."

"I don't want to slow down any," Billy said. "The herd just showed up, and I don't know how long they're going to be here. The more hides we take, the more money we make."

"That may be so, but if you shoot more buffalo than we can skin, it is quite possible that some of the hides will go bad before we can get to them."

"*Oui,* and a *mal* hide is of *aucune valeur,*" Frenchy added.

"What did you say?" Billy asked.

"He said that a hide that is bad, is of no value," Cade said.

"You speak French?" Billy asked, surprised by Cade's comment.

"I've picked up a few words here and there," Cade said, thinking of Arabella and Magnolia.

"I've always thought it would be good to know another language," Billy said. He laughed. "I can understand Armitage, though, and sometimes I think he's speaking a foreign language."

"My dear boy, we British do not speak a corruption of 'American', it is Americans who speak a corruption of English," Armitage said.

"See right there. I almost know what he said," Billy teased.

"Say, I've got an idea," Cade said. "Suppose we go to Adobe Walls and see if we can hire another skinner."

"That's not a bad idea," Billy said. "That would give the boys a chance to catch up with us."

"We may as well take a load of skins in, too," Cade suggested. "We'll see if Fred Leonard will let us store them in his yard. Then if a Harrison and McCall wagon comes down, the driver can haul 'em back to Dodge. Jacob will see that we get the best price."

"You're right," Billy said. "With the herd coming through so late, Lobenstein's probably paying top dollar for hides. If Jacob could take care of 'em, we wouldn't have to go through

Rath and Company or Charlie Myers at all. Having you as a partner is gonna be just fine."

"I'm glad it's working out for both of us."

"Well, Frenchy, let's get the hides loaded," Armitage said. "The quicker we can get these lads out of here, the quicker we can get another hand to help us with the skinning."

BACK AT ADOBE WALLS, Sybil Olds was hanging up a wash she had just done, not only for her husband, but for the other six or eight men who were full time residents of Adobe Walls. She looked up to see Joe Plummer riding into the settlement.

"Hi Joe, what brings you in? Haven't found any buffalo?"

"Oh, yes, Mrs. Olds," Plummer replied. "I'm a' slayin' 'em faster'n Dave and Tommie can skin 'em. But we need a few supplies, and maybe I'll have a beer or two. Maybe pick up a few dollars playin' cards."

"There's not much going on," Sybil said. "Everybody's gone except the help and a few hunters in and out, but you can get a good meal. Bill and I have our café going, now."

"I been a hankerin' fer some good cookin'," Plummer said. "What ya' servin' today?"

"Ham, beans, greens, and cornbread. Oh, and a plum pie. I picked 'em myself."

Plummer smiled. "Yes, ma'am, I'll for sure be there," he promised. "But don't you be goin' off by yourself to pick no plums. They's Indians around."

"We haven't seen a one. I think you hunters have scared them off."

Joe shook his head. "Don't be too sure of that. We all knows they's out there. Just a' waitin'."

PLUMMER STEPPED into Hanrahan's saloon and ordered a beer. He drank half of it before he took the mug away from his lips.

"Ahhh," he said with a sigh of satisfaction. "You don't know how good that tastes."

"Oh, but I do," Hanrahan said. "Why do you think I put the saloon out here?"

"Why, to make money from the buffalo hunters, of course," Bat Masterson said, stepping up to the bar. "But, I am ready to add to your coffers. A beer, if you please."

"Hello, Bat," Plummer greeted. "Ain't you gone out yet?"

"Sure, I have," Bat said. "You saw that pile of hides out there. About a thousand of them are mine."

"Is that so," Plummer said.

"You know it's not," James Hanrahan said. "This is Bat talkin'. We all know what kind of yarns he spins."

"Maybe I don't have a thousand, but I brought in a load a couple of days ago," Bat said. "Now I'm just waitin' for enough boys to get in so I can scare up a good card game."

"Count me in for tonight," Plummer said.

THE QUAHADI VILLAGE of Quanah Parker:

"It was not wise for Mean To His Horses to take a raiding party against the white buffalo hunters," Standing Bear said to Quanah and Wolf Tongue.

"I told him so, but he would not listen to my counsel. It would be better not to do the small raids, which will only anger and awaken the white man before we are ready to go to war with him," Quanah Parker replied.

"We cannot go to war against the whites," Standing Bear said.

"Why not?" Quanah Parker asked.

"There are too many of them. There are more whites than we have bullets for all our guns."

"I can give us bullets. All the bullets we need," White Eagle said as he walked up to join.

"How will you come by so many bullets?" Wolf Tongue asked,

"I will cough them up from my belly," White Eagle promised.

"This, I must see," Standing Bear said.

White Eagle put his hands over his mouth, then began coughing and gagging. When he was through, he opened his hands to show that they were full of bullets.

"How did you do that?" Wolf Tongue asked.

"White Eagle has much magic," Quanah Parker said, a smile crossing his face. "Did we not all see him go into the sky?"

"Yes," Wolf Tongue said. "This, I saw with my own eyes."

"Do not fear to attack the white man," White Eagle said. "I will make my magic so that the bullets of the white man's guns will not harm you. And I can raise the dead."

Quanah Parker wanted to ask why it would be necessary to raise the dead, if the bullets of the white man's guns could do no harm. But Quanah Parker wanted to make war with the white man and, it was best that he let the others believe White Eagle's power, for if they believed him, his task of convincing them to go to war would be easier.

ONLY SIX INDIANS had answered Mean To His Horses' call to battle, but he wasn't worried that the number of his warriors was small. He had listened to the talk of war; he had heard Standing Bear say that it would be wrong for the People to go on the war path. But what did Standing Bear know? He was old, and his time had passed. No longer could he be with a woman, or take part in the hunt, or in battle. If there was to be war with the white buffalo hunters, Mean To His Horses must bring it about.

He knew that while the white men were many in number, the buffalo hunters who were in their camps were few, never more than three or four. Let the others talk, and let the others be swayed by the war talk of Quanah Parker and the magic of the shaman. When he came back with the scalps of the enemy hanging from his lance, he would look big in the eyes of the others.

Chicken Creek

Dave Dudley and Tommie Wallace were back in camp, waiting for Joe Plummer to return from Adobe Walls.

"I wonder how long he'll be gone," Dudley asked.

"I don't know, but to be honest, I'm sort of enjoyin' just sittin' around waitin' on 'im," Wallace said. "We've caught up with what he's done kilt, so at least we ain't skinnin' buffalo right now."

"No, but that also means we ain't makin' no money either," Dudley said.

"If the hunt keeps a goin' like it is, this here's gonna be the best year yet. "What ya gonna do with all your money, Dave?"

"I don't know," Dudley said. "Maybe, if I get enough of it, I'll see if I can find me a good woman and buy me a ranch. What about you?"

"You're goin' to go out a' lookin' for a *good* woman?" Wallace laughed. "Me? I'm gonna buy me the baddest woman in Dodge."

Dudley laughed with him.

UNSEEN BY THE SKINNERS, Mean To His Horses and the six

warriors he had gathered for his war party, were on a nearby ridge looking down toward the campsite. One of the white men was lying on the ground by the fire; the other was sitting on a box of some sort. They were drinking coffee and he heard both of them laugh.

"You laugh now, you devils. Soon your laughter will turn to begging me for mercy," Mean To His Horses said, quietly. He turned toward the warriors who were with him, and motioned them on.

"Speakin' o' bad women, have you ever been with any o' them women at Fat Tom's?" Wallace asked.

"Only to dance is all," Dudley said. "It cost too much to take any o' 'em upstairs, 'n most o' the time I don't hardly have enough money to keep a roof over my head, 'n to get me somethin' to eat." He smiled. "But I 'spect after we get back in to town, why I'll . . . uh!"

Wallace watched in shock as an arrow buried itself deep into Dudley's chest.

Neither Wallace nor Dudley had a gun close by, as neither of them was expecting danger. Their guns were a few feet away and Wallace scrambled to get one. He felt a blow in his back, concurrent with the sound of a gunshot.

Wallace turned and saw several Indians rushing toward him, shouting loudly, some of them holding war clubs over their heads. He had no way to defend himself, and with the gunshot wound to his back, he knew that he couldn't do it anyway.

"Dudley, goodbye, ole' pard," he said, just as one of the Indians brought a club down on his head.

14

Joe Plummer had spent more time at Adobe Walls than he should have, but several freight wagons from Dodge City had pulled in bringing more supplies. Both Charlie Myers and Charles Rath had come to see their respective investments, and in celebration of their being there, they had made all the drinks at James Hanrahan's free to anyone who walked in. That meant any hunter or any skinner or any freighter.

"Boys, have you looked at that pile of hides in my corral?" Charlie Myers asked. "The eastern newspapers are saying that the buffalo are gone, but they don't know what a group of determined men can do. I'm going to make a wager that you'll take at least 100,000 hides this year."

This proclamation was met by wild cheers from the men who were present.

Charlie Myers sat down at a table with Wright Mooar, a businessman who employed more than a half dozen shooters and two dozen skinners. Mooar had set up his main camp about a mile from the settlement. His shooters were sent all over the area.

"Do you think I'm exaggerating?" Myers asked.

"No, my men say the buffalo are out there. And most that they see, are young so that means the herd is not disappearing like the crowd back east is saying."

"If 100,000 are going to be killed, no matter how young they are, isn't that going to take a big chunk out of the herd?" Jacob Harrison asked as he joined Myers and Mooar.

"Jacob, why do you care? Aren't you makin' more money than ever?" Myers asked.

Jacob laughed. "That I am. I've never made so many trips as we're making this year."

"You need to invest in a couple more wagons. I could send you out every day if you wanted to make a run that often," Myers said.

"I can't make that decision without my partner agreeing," Jacob said.

"And where is your elusive partner?" Mooar asked.

Jacob laughed. "You know where he is. He's out hunting with Billy Dixon."

"I knew that," Mooar said. "One of my hunters passed by their camp at the mouth of White Deer Creek. Those two tried to hire one of Mart Galloway's skinners, but he wouldn't let him go. Mart said Billy and Cade had a pile of skins seven feet high. I expect they'll be bringin' some of 'em in fore too long."

"Then maybe I'd better hang around for a day or two or I could ride out to White Deer and see if I can convince Cade to come back to work," Jacob said.

"I wouldn't be riding out by myself," Mooar said. "Nobody's seen any Indians around, but you know they're out there. Some renegade wanting another scalp would be happy to take one from a lone rider."

"I'm surprised there hasn't been any Indian trouble,"

Myers said. "I would have thought they wouldn't want to see their commissary taken away."

"Maybe more of them have decided to go in to the reservations. One of my drivers was over at the Cheyenne Agency, and he said it was teeming with Indians," Jacob said.

"I'll bet that's not happening at Anadarko. The Comanche aren't ever goin' in," Mooar said. "They tell me they've got a young chief who's a breed that will fight till the bitter end."

"Well, in his defense, what would we be doing if everything we knew was being taken away from us?" Jacob said.

"I don't believe I heard you say that," Charlie Myers said. "They're Indians. They'll do what the government tells them to do and they'll like it."

CHICKEN CREEK:

"Dave! Tommy!" Joe Plummer called as he rode into camp. He felt guilty that he had been gone longer than he should have been. "What're you boys doin' sleeping just because I've been gone so long? Turn out, boys, turn out! I've got coffee, pepper, some more bacon, and peaches!"

Plummer held up a can of peaches.

"Peaches, boys, if you don't wake up, I'm goin' to eat 'em all by my . . ." Plummer stopped in mid-sentence. He could smell smoke, not just smoke from a campfire, but the lingering odor of something much larger than a campfire. He rode on in, feeling the hair rising on the back of his neck.

"Oh, God in heaven," he said, when he reached the campsite.

Jumping down from the wagon, he stared at the bodies of his two friends. He found Dave Dudley's blackened body next to the fire ring. Tommy Wallace had been pinned to the ground by a stake that was driven all the way through his chest, and into the ground beneath him. Both men had been scalped.

"Oh, my God, I shouldn't have left you. As God is my witness, boys, I had no idea anything like this would happen."

Plummer, fearful that the Indians were watching, cut one horse loose from the wagon and made a mad dash back to the safety of Adobe Walls.

In the Village of the Comanche:

When Mean To His Horses and the six who had gone with him returned to the village, they had the scalps of the two white men to show off to the others. They had also taken anything of value they had found at the hunter's camp, to include coffee, sugar, and a slab of bacon. And as on Mean To His Horses' earlier raid, he and the warriors who had gone with him, again returned with large chunks of buffalo, taken from the animals the white hunters had killed.

"You did not wish for me to go, but the raid was good. We returned with food, and we killed the white hunters."

"That is good, but it is only two of the white hunters," Quanah said. "I think when we make war, we should kill many."

"You talk of killing many, but it is I, Mean To His Horses, who has made two raids to kill the white man and take his food, while you stay home with the women and children. I think the time of Quanah Parker being the best warrior of the Quahadi has passed. I think that it is I, Mean to his Horses, who shall now be the warrior the others look up to." He beat his chest as a way to emphasize his words.

With a satisfied smirk, Mean To His Horses turned away and joined the six who had ridden with him. They were regaling the village with stories of their daring.

ONE OF THE INDIANS, who took particular notice of the hero status now enjoyed by Mean To His Horses, was Straight Arrow.

"Look, how others pay honor to Mean To His Horses," Quiet Dove said. Quiet Dove was a beautiful young woman.

"Would you like me to do something as brave?" Straight Arrow asked.

Quiet Dove lowered her gaze and smiled at him. "If you would be as brave, I will honor you as the others now honor Mean To His Horses."

"I will do such a thing. And not only you, but all will honor me," Straight Arrow promised.

APPROACHING THE CANADIAN RIVER:

Cade and Billy started toward Adobe Walls, with close to 400 hides on their wagon. If they sold them in Dodge City, using the Harrison and McCall wagons, these hides were worth $1,200.

"I wish we could've brought all the hides," Billy said.

"I know," Cade said, "but if we get another skinner, maybe we can send Armitage back and forth."

"Or one of us can do it," Billy said. "Twelve hundred dollars for one load of hides. That's a far cry from my first job where I got $50.00 a month."

"What were you doing?"

"I was 14 years old—my ma and pa were both dead, my sister got typhoid and died so I was all by myself. I thought I'd join the army, but they said I was too young, so I got a job as a driver in a government bull train. But what I really wanted to do was fight Indians and kill buffalo."

"I'd say you've done that, at least the killing buffalo part," Cade said.

"I have, but the fighting Indians part, I've really never done. In a way, I feel sorry for the Indians," Billy said. "You know, I was at Medicine Lodge."

"You mean for the treaty?"

"I was. I was on a bull train, hauling supplies back and forth to several forts. While we were at Fort Harker, we were told we were going to go with a party of peace commissioners to meet with some of the main tribes."

"And when was that?"

"Sometime in the fall of '67. I thought it was sort of funny that on a peace commission, we were all given our first Sharps carbines."

"Did they expect trouble?"

"Of course, they did. These were Indians—Indians who had been told over and over what the government would do, and then the treaties were broken. And now here we are, being a part of the biggest breach of that treaty there is."

"You mean hunting south of the Arkansas?" Cade asked.

Billy nodded. "I remember seeing old Satank, the chief of the Kiowas. He was riding one of the most beautiful horses I had ever seen and the outfit he was wearing was unbelievable, but the thing I remember most was the way he carried himself. There was a pride and dignity that we don't usually think about when we talk about Indians. He gave a speech about how the Indians didn't want the railroad coming through to cut off the buffalo migration, and how he didn't want the buffalo slaughtered."

"What about your gun? Did you have to use it?" Cade asked.

"No but we were ready to," Cade said, "and if any hothead would have fired his gun, we would have had an all-out war right there at the peace treaty. It was the morning of October

28, 1867. We were all in camp when out on the plains, about two miles away, a bunch of Indians, about 1,500 I'd say, came up from behind a low swell. They were dressed for battle and they were all spread out. We heard them chanting and singing, and the closer they got, the more they spread out. Then when they got about a quarter mile away, they all started firing their guns and charging at us. I thought for sure that would be the end of me."

"Well, what happened?"

"General Harney was in charge, and he came through yelling that every man get out of sight, but have his rifle ready to fire. He kept saying we had more men than they did, and that we could hold them off if we had to, but watching those Indians charge, was something to see. When they got to about 200 yards from us, they all stopped like they had had a signal, but nobody heard one. Then the General went out to meet them and asked for the chiefs to come into camp."

"And the Indians? What did they do?"

"They stayed out for about an hour. Then one of the chiefs went out and called them in. All the bucks came in and rode back and forth among our tents, checking out how prepared we were, I guess. It was not a day I'll ever forget."

"Billy, you have more stories, for somebody who's twenty-four years old than just about anyone I've ever known. I love to hear your tales," Cade said.

"Well don't sell yourself short. I've not had to get myself off a ship in Argentina after I killed a man, like you did," Billy said. "You've had your fair share of adventures, too."

"I hope this summer that the only adventure we have is making so much money we don't know what to do with it," Cade said.

"I'd go along with that," Billy said, "but now we've got to get this outfit across the Canadian."

The water was exceptionally high and moving quickly. Tree limbs, large and small, had been caught up in it and they were rushing down river so rapidly that if one of them were to hit Cade or Billy, or even one of the mules, they could be seriously hurt.

"I don't think we can cross here," Billy cautioned. "Let's try it over by Chicken Creek; the stream's a lot wider there, so it won't be as deep, and it won't be running as fast."

"You know this territory better than I do," Cade said. "Whatever you say, we'll do."

They followed the river west until they reached the mouth of Chicken Creek and here, as they had suspected, the river was wider, shallower, and not moving nearly as swiftly.

"One of us needs to wade in to test the bottom," Cade said. "We don't want to risk losing our mules the way Hanrahan lost that horse on the Cimarron."

"All right, I'll check it out," Billy said.

Billy waded out into the river and determined that the mules could cross and wouldn't have to swim more than 100 feet or so in the process. He started back toward Cade.

"I figure we'll disconnect the team, get the mules across, then connect them to the wagon by rope so we can work . . ."

"Get out of the water," Cade yelled, interrupting Billy in mid-sentence. "Somebody's coming, and they're coming hard."

Billy splashed out of the water as quickly as he could, then reached down to pull his pistol from his holster that was on the wagon seat.

"It looks like its Joe Plummer," Cade said when the rider was close enough to recognize.

"Indians!" Plummer shouted when he saw Cade and Billy. "Indians raided my camp! They kilt Dudley 'n Wallace 'n then they scalped 'em both!"

"How many were there?" Cade asked.

"I don't know," Plummer said. "The bastards done it whilst I was at the Walls for supplies. When I come back I found 'em both dead. So, I skedaddled out of there as quick as I could."

"I don't blame you," Cade said. "Are you going to the Walls?"

"I sure am. All the boys need to know what happened, cause if it can happen to Dave and Tommie, it can happen to any of us."

"We'll ride along with you," Billy said. "We're going there anyway."

"Billy, Joe is right. This can happen to any of us. I want to go back to warn Frenchy and Armitage," Cade said.

"Yes, yes you should do that," Billy agreed.

"Joe, can I use your horse? You can ride in the wagon with Billy," Cade said.

"Take 'im," Plummer said, dismounting. "I hope your skinners are all right."

"I do too," Cade said as he climbed onto Plummer's horse and headed back to the camp.

15

MEAN TO HIS HORSES HAD WON MUCH HONOR AMONG THE others by his successful attack against the white men who came to destroy all the buffalo. Straight Arrow was jealous of all the accolades being heaped upon Mean To His Horses, though there was no word in his vocabulary for jealousy. He knew only that he, too, wished to be honored by the others in the village.

To fulfill that desire, Straight Arrow had assembled eight warriors, in addition to himself, for the express purpose of finding an isolated camp of buffalo hunters.

He smiled as he pictured himself riding back into the village with the scalps of the white men he had killed, hanging from his lance. Quiet Dove and the other young women would look at him with admiration and he knew that the blankets of many of them would be open to him.

Leaving the eight warriors behind, Straight Arrow went out on his own for a scout, and found a buffalo hunting camp where two men were busy scraping some of the hides they had taken.

With a smile of triumph, Straight Arrow headed back to his men.

"I have found them."

"How many are there?" Stone Crow asked.

"*Wa hat*," Straight Arrow replied, holding up two fingers. "They are ahead on the water that the white man calls White Deer Creek."

"CADE, why are you back so soon?" Charley Armitage asked as he looked up from the hide he was scraping. "And where's Billy? And the wagon?"

"He and Joe Plummer are on their way to the Walls. Indians attacked Joe's camp. Dave Dudley and Tommie Wallace were killed."

"Monsieur Plummer got away?" Frenchy asked.

"He wasn't there when it happened. He'd gone in for supplies and he found them dead when he got back. Billy and I decided that you two needed to know what happened."

"Is Joe sure it was Indians? We all know some of the horse thieves are trying to pass themselves off as Indians. Were the horses taken?"

"Joe didn't say, but look at the one I'm riding. It's his," Cade said. "He did say both men were scalped."

"That could be the work of the thieves as well. In all the time we've been out, I've seen nothing to indicate that we might be in danger," Armitage said.

"*Mon amie*, you may be changing your song," Frenchy said as he pointed to a rise behind them.

Both Cade and Armitage looked in the direction indicated by Frenchy, and they saw half-a-dozen or more warriors, their horses lined out abreast.

"I think they may be coming for us. *Oui?*" Frenchy said.

"I think they are coming for us, yes," Armitage said.

"It looks like we're about to get busy," Cade said as he withdrew his pistol lamenting that he had left his Sharps in the wagon. "Get your guns."

The Indians began yelling at the top of their lungs as they came galloping toward the hunting camp. At the moment, only Cade was armed. He saw that he was facing nine charging Indians with only a pistol. He turned himself in such a way as to present his side to the Indians, thus reducing their target area, then he pulled the trigger three times, and three of the Indians tumbled from their saddles.

Straight Arrow was shocked to see that his attacking force had been reduced by one third almost immediately.

Involuntarily, he pulled back on the reins, checking his horse's forward momentum, but he had given nobody else orders to do the same. The remaining men forged by him, and maintaining their speed, continued on. They were headed toward the devil who was firing at them. He was standing as still as a tree.

Cade fired three more times, and three more warriors tumbled from the saddle. The remaining two, seeing how drastically their numbers had been reduced, and also that Straight Arrow wasn't with them, stopped their charge, jerked their horses around, and galloped away.

Straight Arrow was shocked by the fact that one man had so completely decimated his force of warriors, that he was unable to continue the attack. Now, as he saw his remaining two men gallop by him in retreat, he found that he was being left behind.

With a loud yell of challenge, Straight Arrow shook his fist at the white marksman, then, turning his horse, he urged it into a gallop to catch up with the two who had survived the ill-fated attack.

ON THE CANADIAN RIVER:

Billy Dixon and Joe Plummer were having their own problems. With the thought of Indians prowling about, Billy didn't want to leave the wagon behind so instead of sticking to his original plan of taking the mules across first, he left them connected to the wagon and drove on into the water, hoping for the best.

Before he was half-way across, the mules were swimming.

"This ain't good!" Plummer shouted.

"No, it isn't. Jump out."

"What?"

"Jump out of the wagon," Billy repeated. "I'm going to see what I can do about getting the mules across."

The two men leapt from the wagon and Billy made his way to the front of the team. The swift current caught the wagon and turned it over.

"Disconnect the team!" Billy called, and Plummer, working quickly, pulled the doubletree pin that connected the team to the wagon tongue. The wagon, now free, was swept downstream, tumbling over and over.

Finally, Billy and Plummer got the struggling team ashore, but one of the mules lay down on the sand, took a few deep breaths, then stopped.

"What the hell?" Plummer said. "I think this damn mule just died."

"He was a good mule," Billy said. He looked at his remaining mule that stood there with his head bowed, as if mourning the mule that had shared his toils.

"It's all right, Tobe," Billy said, patting the mule on his forehead. "I know you're going to miss him. But we all lose friends from time to time. It's a part of life."

"Hey, Billy, have you thought about this?" Plummer asked.

"We ain't mounted, we ain't armed, 'n we're at least three miles from the Walls."

"Yeah. My Big .50" is in the wagon. So is Cade's, and four hundred hides are gone." Billy put his hand on top of his head. "And the worst part, I lost my hat."

"Yeah, me too."

"We'd better get to moving," Billy said. "I don't know if there're Indians close by, but if they find us, you know we're dead."

Billy took the remaining rein that was attached to Tobe, then started walking.

"Come on, mule," he said. "At least you don't have to pull a heavy wagon."

COMANCHE VILLAGE

Straight Arrow returned to the village, not in the glory he had imagined, but in ignominy. He and the two warriors rode in with their heads bowed. As soon as they reached the village the warriors separated themselves from him. If the raid would have been successful, Strait Arrow would have gotten the glory, but with his raid unsuccessful, he now suffered the humiliation of his failure.

"Where is Red Hawk?" someone demanded, wanting to know about one of the warriors who had ridden out with Straight Arrow, but hadn't returned.

"Where are Running Deer and Brave Bull?" another asked, inquiring of two other missing participants from Straight Arrow's raid.

Demands were made as to the whereabouts of all six warriors who did not return with him.

"They were . . . killed," Straight Arrow replied, after a pause.

"Were there many among the soldiers who did this?" Quanah Parker asked. "Did you kill many soldiers?"

"There were no soldiers."

"Then it is the white buffalo hunters," Quanah Parker said. "They have come not just to take our buffalo, but to make war. How many of them were there? Why do you have no scalps on your lance?"

"There was one," Straight Arrow said.

"One? You left with eight warriors, you return with two, but you say there was but one man who stood against you?"

"Yes, but he was not like any ordinary man," Straight Arrow said. "Ask Leaping Horse, ask Bear That Walks; they will tell you. The medicine of this white man was strong."

"One man," Quanah Parker said. "You take a party of nine, but you were bested by one man. And six of our brothers lie dead, and yet you did not bring them back." Quanah Parker spat on the ground in disgust, then turned his back to Straight Arrow and walked away.

Straight Arrow looked at the others in the village. All turned their backs to him. He saw Quiet Dove, who did not turn her back. But the pity that she felt for him was reflected in her eyes.

Straight Arrow looked away from her. He would have rather had her disdain, than her pity.

As Straight Arrow returned to his tipi, he saw Mean To His Horses looking at him. The smile on Mean To His Horses' lips was one of triumph.

Adobe Walls:

Tom O'Keefe had just engineered a rear bolster stake for Bat Masterson's wagon, when he stepped outside of his blacksmith shop. Looking toward the river, he saw two men approaching. He knew all the buffalo hunters within 150 miles of Adobe Walls, but he didn't know these two. One man was leading a single mule.

"Howdy, gents," Tom called, raising his hand in greeting.

"It was Injuns!" Joe Plummer shouted as he started to run across the valley in front of the settlement. "Injuns! They kilt Tommie and Dave!"

"Hell, Joe! Billy! I didn't even recognize you," Tom O'Keefe said. "Where'd it happen? How many were there?"

By now several of the others, drawn by the commotion, came out to see what was going on.

"We weren't attacked," Billy Dixon said. "Cade and I were bringing in a load of hides, when we ran into Joe."

"But you said Wallace and Dudley were killed," Tom said.

"That's right," Joe said. "When I got back to my camp, I rode in 'specting to see my men fat and sassy, but what I found was terrible." Joe shook his head. "Poor Dave, his body was in the fire ring, blacker 'n tar, and Tommie—he had a stake drove right through him, nailin' 'im to the ground. I just hope the guys were already dead 'fore them bastards got a holt of 'em."

"We can pray that that was true," Charlie Myers said as he was one of those who had gathered around to hear what the men had to say.

"Billy, you said you and Cade were bringing in a load of hides when you ran into Joe. Where's Cade and what happened to the hides?" Jacob Harrison asked.

"Cade went back to camp to warn Armitage and Frenchy about the Indians," Billy said. He lowered his head. "And the hides. I guess I miscalculated. They're at the bottom of the river."

"Damn," Jacob said. "That's too bad."

"Losing the hides is bad, but that's not the worst of it. When we made it across one of my mules just up and died on me. The wagon started tumblin' over and over and we had to cut it loose. Cade's gonna be mighty upset."

"He'll be all right," Jacob said. "He'll know those things happen and it couldn't be helped."

"There's more. Both of our big .50s were in the wagon."

"That *is* bad," Jacob said. "That means Cade's out at the camp without a long gun."

Billy nodded his head as he started for Hanrahan's saloon.

16

Dodge City:

Cetti Marcelli loved her work at the Red House, but she particularly enjoyed her friendship with the Willis family. She spent as much time as she could, visiting with Magnolia and the children. This had been a particularly stressful day, with the baby experiencing a bout of colic.

"Let me take the big kids for a walk," Cetti said, emphasizing the word big.

Magnolia with a frazzled look on her face nodded her head.

"I think that would be wonderful, and if they could be gone a long time that would be even better," Magnolia said, as she bounced the crying baby on her shoulder. "I don't know what's gotten in to Mary Lilajean."

"All right," Cetti said picking up some of the blocks that the three children had been playing with.

"But, Cetti, do be careful," Magnolia said.

"I will," Cetti said. "We'll be just fine."

Magnolia's expression changed to one of apprehension.

"You don't understand. There are those in this town who would do anything to hurt . . ." She stopped in mid-sentence.

"I know," Cetti said. "I've heard some of the talk at the Red House. I won't let anything happen to him."

Cetti, Chantal, Bella, and Stone left the Willis house, and in order to avoid Front Street where all the saloons were, she took the children over the hill toward the school. Stone was especially enjoying being out of the house, and he began running so fast that Cetti had a hard time keeping up with him. Chantal and Bella were lagging behind, so out of frustration, Cetti had to slow down to encourage the girls to move faster. She could see the blue shirted child running toward Front Street.

"Come on girls, we have to catch Stone," Cetti said.

"I'm tired," Bella said. "I don't want to run."

"You have to," Cetti said. "I'll bet Chantal can run faster than you can."

"No, she can't." Bella said, as she hurried to catch her sister.

When they reached Front Street, Stone was nowhere in sight. Cetti was beginning to panic when she saw her piano teacher coming out of Fringer's Apothecary.

"Miss Fenton, have you seen a little boy, wearing a blue shirt run by this way?" Cetti asked between gasps of breath.

"No, I've not seen a little boy," Demova Fenton said.

"Oh, dear, where could he have gotten too," Cetti said. "I would be most grateful if you would stay with these two little girls while I look for him."

"These are the Willis children, aren't they?" Demova asked.

"Yes."

"And the boy you are looking for, would that be the Indian they have living with them?"

143

"He's a little boy. He's four years old," Cetti said. "Will you stay with the girls for me?"

"I suppose I can if you're not gone too long."

CETTI LEFT the girls and began running down Front Street hoping she could find Stone before something happened to him. When she got to the Red House, she ran in hoping Jeter would be there. She didn't know what she would tell him, but she had to find him.

"Is Jeter here?" she yelled from the door.

"No, is something wrong?" Pete Cahill asked.

"I was taking care of the little ones, and Stone ran away from me."

"Oh, that's bad," Pete said, throwing down his towel and coming out from behind the bar. "Where did you see him last?"

"I took them toward the school and he started running."

"No telling where he is," Pete said. "Can a few of you gents help us look for one of Jeter's kids?"

"Sure," one of the customers said. "Those little girls are as sweet as honey. Wouldn't want to see anything happen to one of them."

"It's not the girls," Pete said. "It's the boy."

"Oh no, we're not lookin' for no Indian," one of the other men said, "unless we can string him up."

"All right, the bar's closed. I'd like to ask you to leave."

"You're doing this for an Indian kid? You can just keep your damn bar closed forever as far as I'm concerned."

"Come on, Cetti. He has to be here somewhere. What was he wearing?"

"A blue shirt. He was running toward the river. You don't suppose that's where he got to?" Cetti asked.

"Well, let's look there first," Pete said.

Pete and Cetti crossed the railroad tracks and ran down Second Street heading for the river. It was then that they saw two boys about ten or twelve years old, dragging Stone toward Hog Creek. When they got there, they drug him out in the middle and began holding Stone's head under water.

Pete Cahill had never run as fast in his life.

He got to the creek and grabbed for Stone, pulling him out of the water. The child was lifeless. Pete turned him upside down and began hitting him on the back. Water began to gurgle out of Stone's mouth, and soon he began to cough and sputter.

Cetti took the child and held him in her arms. Never once did he cry.

"What were you tryin' to do?" Pete asked grabbing the two boys. "Don't you know you could have killed this boy?"

One boy shrugged his shoulders, but neither said anything.

"How would you like it if I hold your heads under the water?" Pete asked as he applied pressure to the back of their necks.

"No, no! We weren't supposed to kill 'im! Just scare 'im is all."

"Did somebody put you up to this?"

Both boys lowered their heads.

"I can just bet who's behind this," Pete said looking around.

On the bridge that crosses the Arkansas River, Kirk Jordan was leaning against the railing. When he saw Pete looking at him, he raised his hand and waved.

"Come on Cetti, let's get Stone home." Pete took the boy into his arms and Stone buried his head against his shoulder.

THE QUAHADI VILLAGE of Quanah Parker:

The others in the village continued to laud Mean To His Horses, even as they held Straight Arrow in scorn.

A hunting party had succeeded in killing four antelope which they cooked over a couple of campfires, and then distributed among all the People. After the warriors and the elders had eaten their fill, they allowed the women and children to eat.

Now the men were gathered around the remaining fire as they discussed the situation that weighed heavily upon all of them.

"Perhaps the soldiers will drive the white men away," Black Horse suggested.

"What makes you think they would do that?" Wild Horse asked.

"The Medicine Lodge Treaty gave this land to us."

"The white men do not have to follow the treaty," Standing Bear said.

"Why? Because they are white," Mean To His Horses said derisively.

"No," Standing Bear said. "The treaty was signed seven summers ago, but the People did not ratify it by our vote. Our brothers, the Kiowa, the Arapaho and the Cheyenne did not ratify it."

"What does ratify mean?" Wild Horse asked.

"It is a white man's word. It says that every man in every band should have a say if we accept what the government told us to do," Standing Bear said. "We did not vote."

"I will never do what the white man tells us to do," Wild Horse said.

"I will kill more hunters," Mean To His Horses said. "I will find them. When I see them not watching, I will swoop down like an eagle and kill them like they are old women."

"I will join you," Wild Horse said.

"And what of Straight Arrow?" Quanah asked. "Did he not lose six warriors at the hands of one man?"

"Straight Arrow had bad medicine," Mean To His Horses said. "I will bring good medicine."

"There are many white men who kill our buffalo," Quanah said. "We must find a way to kill a lot of them at the same time. Not just one or two."

"I believe you say this because you know this cannot be done so you do nothing. You bring shame upon yourself and to our band," Mean To His Horses said.

"Mean To His Horses speaks the truth," Black Horse said. "They have few men, one to kill the buffalo and one to cut off the robe and leave the meat."

"Yes," Wild Horse said. "Quanah, you say we should kill many of them, but where do we find a place where many have gathered?"

"Silver Knife and I know of such a place. We saw where the white men were building a village. It is said by the Camp Supply trader that the hunters gather there to sell their hides."

"But are there many hunters at this spot?" Wild Horse asked.

Silver Knife smiled. "Our trader trades us guns and ammunition for our buffalo robes, and he trades us whiskey. The merchants from Dodge City trade robes for whiskey, too. Yes, there will be many hunters at this place where Adobe Walls Creek enters the Canadian."

"Yes," White Eagle said, speaking for the first time. "To attack the whites at a place where many gather, and to defeat them, would show the whites that this land belongs to the People, and that they should go back beyond the Cimarron."

"But our village is small," Black Horse complained. "If there are many hunters at this place, will we not lose many warriors as well?"

"We will not be alone," White Eagle said. "My medicine will protect us."

"That may be true," Quanah said, "but we need to invite all the People to come join us. We will send runners to the Nokoni, the Kotsotekas, the Yamparikas, and even the Penateka who now plow the earth as the white man says."

"The bands of the Comancheria have never joined together. What makes you think they would come together for you, Quanah Parker?" Mean To His Horses asked.

"Because we will invite them to a Sun Dance," Quanah said.

"A Sun Dance?"

Wild Horse could not believe what Quanah Parker had just proposed. "Do you mean what you say? You want to have a Sun Dance?"

"Yes."

"No," Mean To His Horses said. "A Sun Dance is not of the People. This is a thing of the Kiowa, the Arapahos, and the Cheyenne— not of the Comanche."

"You are right, Mean To His Horses. The People have never done this. But our brothers claim the Great Power gives the whole tribe good medicine when they hold the Sun Dance. I can protect some of the People with my medicine, but a Sun Dance will give each of us the power to save himself," White Eagle said.

Quanah had not expected to have White Eagle as an ally when he had suggested the idea of the Sun Dance.

"White Eagle speaks the truth," Quanah said.

"I do not understand," Wild Horse said. "I have witnessed the Sun Dances of the Kiowa. We do not have a fetish doll to call the Great Spirit. The Cheyenne have a Sun Dance priest who has inherited the medicine bundle. Who will direct the Comanche Sun Dance?"

"Do I not have the power to summon the Great Spirit? I,

who rose to the sky to speak with our departed, will direct the Sun Dance," White Eagle said.

"It is decided. White Eagle will direct the Sun Dance. He and I will go together to the bands of the Comanche and invite all the People to gather at a place where the Sweetwater empties into the Red River," Quanah said.

17

"Is this the only buffalo gun you have?" Billy Dixon asked.

"I'm afraid so," James Langton said, "and I've promised it to George Causey when he comes in."

"Jimmy, this is our friend," Charles Rath said. "I'll tell you what. If you'll agree to sell me your hides and not send them back to Dodge on your own, you can have this gun. I know it's not a Sharps .50, but the Sharps .44 is a mighty fine gun."

"Ever the salesman, Charles," Billy said picking up the rifle. "If I do that, this gun's gonna cost me thousands of dollars."

"Then go buy one from Myers."

"You know he doesn't have one on hand."

"Then take it or leave it. After all, Jimmy's promised this gun to Causey and by rights, he can't sell it."

"You've got me over a barrel," Billy said. "Do you have anything for Cade?"

"I've got a Spencer carbine," Rath said. "It won't work as well on buffalo, but it sure will kill an Indian if one's headin' your way."

"I'll take it. Now what about a mule and a hat?"

Charles laughed. "You're in a bad way. We don't have a mule to sell, but Jimmy here, can give you a hat."

"Thanks," Billy said, his tone definitely showing he didn't mean it.

BILLY LEFT the Rath and Company store and headed for the corral to see if he could pick up either a mule or a horse. He would hate to buy a stolen horse, but at this point he would do anything to get back to the camp. There was no point in seeing if Tom O'Keefe had a wagon until he knew he had at least two animals to pull it out to the camp.

When he got to the corral, Jacob Harrison and his drivers were maneuvering one of his big Murphy wagons into the yard. There was a pile of buffalo hides 100 yards long and ten feet high waiting to be loaded.

"Billy, I thought you'd be long gone by now," Jacob said as he stepped away from his place by the wagon.

"Let me help you," Billy said as he, too, began to push the big freight wagon. Their effort was an attempt to ease the strain on the two horses pulling the back end of the wagon into position.

"I'd be gone if I had a horse and wagon."

"Oh, I forgot. Your wagon's in the river and your mule's dead."

"And our guns. Damn that Charles Rath. He wouldn't sell me a gun unless I agreed to sell our hides to him," Billy said. "Cade said you'd haul our hides back to Dodge for free."

"He said that, huh?" Jacob laughed. "Maybe I'll have to jack up the freight on these hides so it's just enough to cover your loss."

"That'd be great, but right now, I don't have a way to bring in the hides we already have."

"Maybe Harrison and McCall can help you with that. How many hides do you think you have left?"

"I'd say not more than two or three hundred," Billy said. "Since Cade doesn't have his Sharps .50, he's not doing any killin' while I'm here."

"Well, then, why don't I hitch up the wagon Tom just repaired? We'll take a team from each of the other wagons and go get your hides," Jacob said.

"I'd be much obliged if you'd do that, Jacob. Having Cade McCall as a partner has turned out to be a good investment."

"That goes for both of us."

On the Red River, West of the Kiowa-Comanche Reservation Border:

Quanah Parker and White Eagle watched as close to 1,500 tipis were being erected on the banks of the Red River.

"The People have gathered," White Eagle said. "The Nokoni, the Kotsotekas, the Yamparikas, and the Penateka. They all come to the Quahadi. Our forefathers have tried to unite Comanche bands before us, but it is you, the greatest warrior, that has caused this to happen."

"We did it together," Quanah Parker said. "The People believe your medicine."

White Eagle was forced to control a smile. "They do, don't they?"

Quanah's face contorted into a frown. "You do have good medicine?"

"We shall see. The Great Spirit will reward us because we are blowing the first puff of smoke toward the sun."

"But what of the other spirits? Those in the buffalo? The wolf? The tree? The rocks? Will those spirits leave the People?" Quanah asked.

"No, my friend. All the spirits will come to the People. The spirits will make the People victorious."

"I hope what you say is true."

FOR THE NEXT week much effort was put into making the Sun Dance a success. While it was based upon the celebrations that the Kiowa, the Cheyenne and the Arapaho held, the Comanche were not forced to conform to the strict traditions that the other tribes observed.

Much effort was spent in selecting the tree that would be used as the center pole for the Sun Lodge. The Comanche did not follow the other tribes in their treating of this pole as an enemy, thus forcing the warriors to count coup on the pole before it could be cut. They did, however, send an honored woman to cut it down, much as the other tribes did.

In erecting the pole, according to tradition, they had to fail three times. When it was finally in place, the People hoisted a freshly killed buffalo stuffed with feathers to preside over the ceremony.

Preparing the Sun Lodge was a four-day event. On the fourth day, four warriors were sent out to hide, each one covered with a shaggy buffalo skin. While they were in hiding, others went to the Sweetwater and covered their bodies, hair and faces with mud. These Mud Men as they were called rode through the village with bound willow sticks, swatting at all whom they could find.

While the Mud Men were entertaining, other warriors were sent to locate the "herd." When the disguised warriors were found they were brought back to the lodge.

Upon completion of the erecting of the lodge, White Eagle called for all who intended to participate in the Sun Dance, to go to the river and bathe. While they were at the river, the women prepared beds made of sage along the walls of the lodge. A cedar screen was built in front of the beds to conceal the dancers when they were forced to rest.

When the sun reached the noon position, those who planned to dance, sing or drum filed into the lodge. They all stomped their feet, causing the sound to reverberate throughout the encampment. When they were inside, the warriors retired behind the screens and applied paint to their bodies. When all was ready, a half-dozen older men took their places around a common drum and began to beat in unison.

The singers began to chant, each warrior having his own song. When the warrior's song was started, he emerged from behind the screen and began to recreate his most memorable feat, whether it be from a battle or from a hunt. In his mouth he had a whistle made from an eagle bone, and at the appropriate time in the song, he blew the whistle.

Unlike the other tribes, the Comanche chose not to mutilate their bodies; however, it was an honor to dance until one fainted. The thinking was that if one danced to exhaustion, visions would come to those who succumbed. But it was pointed out that the purpose of this Sun Dance was to revive the People—to enable them to exterminate the white man—not to experience visions.

On the last day, White Eagle and Quanah called all the warriors to sit around the lodge pole, while the drummers continued their rhythms. Much whiskey had been consumed and the words and the drums caused the warriors to be in a state of frenzy.

"To use the white man's word, we must ratify our revenge," Quanah said. "We must decide where we will use our medicine."

White Eagle began speaking.

"You have seen my strong medicine given to me by the Great Spirit. I can ascend into the sky and I can cough up bullets. This the Quahadi have witnessed. Did you not see that I told you when the great light in the sky would disappear, and did I now warn of the dry summer and the invasion of the grasshopper? Now I can cure the sick; I can bring the dead back to life. But my greatest gift—I can make the white man's bullets fall to the ground."

With these words, there was much excitement.

"We should go to war against the Texans."

"We should kill the soldiers who ride with Bad Hand."

"We should seek revenge for the 23 killed at Double Mountain Fork."

"We should go after our enemy the Tonkawa, who eat our people and teach the bluecoats our ways."

"We should kill the white hunters."

"We should wipe out the Texas Rangers."

Quanah Parker raised his hand to quiet the warriors.

"We speak with many tongues. We must be united. We cannot do all that you have said." Quanah paused. "Look around us; while all the Comanche have come together, we are too few to do what you say."

"Then why did we have the Sun Dance?" Wolf Tongue asked. "Did not the Great Spirit speak to White Eagle?"

"This the Great Spirit did. On the morning of the third day from this day, we will council together with the great chiefs from the Kiowa, the Cheyenne and the Arapaho. Then we will decide if the People will join our brothers and go to war against the white man."

155

DODGE CITY:

Magnolia was in the bedroom with Chantal, Bella, and Stone. Chantal and Bella were sharing a bed; Stone was sleeping on a trundle that had been put in the corner of the same room.

"Is Mary Lilajane asleep?" Chantal asked, inquiring about the baby.

"Yes. She's in her cradle."

"Does she need me to rock her to sleep?" Bella asked as she bounded out of bed.

"Hold on, Missy," Magnolia said as she grabbed her daughter. "I said she was asleep."

Bella cocked her head. "I think I hear her crying. I should go see her."

Magnolia shook her head. "I don't think so. What Mary Lilajean wants is for her sisters to go to sleep."

"Stone's not sleeping," Chantal said. "He's pretending."

"I don't care," Magnolia said. "Look how quiet he is. He's such a good boy."

"Mama, do you love Stone more than you do us?" Bella asked.

"Of course not, darling. I love all of my children equally."

"But Stone's not your children," Bella said.

"He is. He's your brother."

"That's not what *Grand-mere* says."

"Well then, I'm going to have to have a talk with *Grand-mere*. But right now, I want all of my children to go to sleep." Magnolia bent over to give the girls a kiss. She was moving toward Stone's trundle when she was interrupted by her mother-in-law's call from the next room.

"Magnolia! Get in here. We have problems!" Mary's voice was tinged with fear.

Magnolia pulled closed the blanket that hung in the doorway, in an attempt to shield the children from whatever had upset Mary. When she looked around she saw the reflection of wavering yellow light splashing against the walls.

"Grand-mère? What's going on?"

"There are a lot of men outside!" Mary said, her voice rising.

Magnolia looked through the front window and saw at least a dozen men standing there. Several of them were carrying lit torches, and their faces were bathed a demonic orange in the glow. She started toward the door.

"Don't do that! Don't go outside!" Mary grabbed Magnolia's arm.

"It will be all right," Magnolia said in a very calm voice, as she patted Mary's hand. "I'll see what they want." Opening the door, she stepped out onto the front porch.

"Good evening, gentlemen," she called out to them. "What do you want?"

"You know damn well what we want. We want that Injun brat!"

Magnolia recognized Kirk Jordan as the spokesman for the group.

"Mr. Jordan, I don't think you're going to get him." Magnolia turned toward the door.

"Wait a minute, Missy," Kirk Jordan said. "We're goin' to give you five minutes to bring that little blanket-ass nit out here 'n turn 'im over to us. 'N if you don't do that, we're goin' to burn this house down over your head. Now what do you have to say about that?"

Magnolia hurried back inside and slammed the door, leaning against it as she tried to compose herself.

"We need Jeter," Mary said. "Hurry out the back door."

"Yes, I'd better . . ." Magnolia stopped in mid-sentence. "No, I can't leave the children."

"Then I'll go get him," Mary said. "There's no way I'm going to see that child turned over to that gang of henchmen out there."

ED MASTERSON HAD JUST FINISHED TELLING a funny story, and everyone in the Red House Salon was laughing when Mary came in. Jeter, who was also laughing looked up and saw her. He was very surprised because his mother never came to the salon, and the expression on her face made it obvious that something was wrong.

Jeter rushed to her. "Mom! What is it? What's wrong?"

"Oh, Jeter, you have to come home. That Jordan man who's after Stone is down at the house with a whole bunch of men. He says they're going to burn the house down if we don't send Stone out to them."

"What?" Ed Masterson said when he heard Mary's comment. Ed turned to Herman Fringer. "Go find Charley Bassett, and you, Alonzo, run down to the Dodge House and get Evans and Cox. Tell them what's going on and round up as many men as you can. And, Pete, you step over to George Hoover's Saloon and do the same thing. Have 'em meet up here."

Masterson turned to the others in the Red House. "Those of you who have the guts to come with us, we need as many as possible. Soon as the others come, we'll go set this straight."

"I'm going now," Jeter said.

"Don't be foolish," Ed said. "There's nothing you can do by yourself. Wait for Sheriff Bassett to get here."

"I'm not going to challenge them directly, but I'm not going to leave my wife and kids alone in that house."

"I'm going back with you," Mary said.

"Mom, you'd be better off to stay here with Frankie and Cetti."

"I got here, and I can get back to that house. No matter what happens, Magnolia will need help with those four children. Can you imagine how scared she must be?"

"All right, let's go, but you're gonna have to hurry."

As JETER and Mary approached the house, Jeter could hear some of the taunts of the men out front.

"THEY AIN'T no sense in all of you burnin' up, Miz Willis. All we want is the Injun brat!"

"Send 'im out here. Hell, he won't feel nothin'. It ain't as if ya can hurt Injuns."

"We don't wanna hurt ya, but we'll do it iffn we have to. You got about a minute left, then we're goin' to commence a burnin' your house down!"

159

STEPPING up onto the back porch, Jeter jerked the door open, and when he did he saw Magnolia standing there, holding a shotgun pointed toward him.

"Magnolia, it's me!" Jeter yelled. "Don't shoot."

"Oh, Jeter!" Magnolia said, putting the shotgun down and running to him. Jeter took her in his arms and as he held her he saw Bella, Chantal, and Stone peeking out from behind the drawn quilt, their big eyes, filled with fright.

"Daddy, are those men going to burn the house down?" Bella asked as she ran toward him.

"No, Darlin', I'm not gonna let them do that," Jeter said as he caught his daughter in his arms.

"But Jeter, how can you stop them? You haven't looked out but there are so many," Magnolia said, as a sob caught in her throat. "How can they be so mean?"

Jeter smiled. "In about two minutes, we'll outnumber them, but in the meantime, you and Mom and the kids huddle by the back door just in case. Run to the Red House if anything happens."

"Jeter, no! I can't lose you!"

He kissed Magnolia on the nose. "Not to worry. We've been through rougher times than this."

"Your time's up, Missy!" a voice shouted from outside. "Don't say I didn't warn you!"

Jeter grabbed the shotgun and hurried to the front window. He saw Kirk Jordan coming toward the house. Jordan drew his hand back to throw the torch and as he did so, Jeter raised the shotgun to his shoulder and fired, shattering the glass in the window. In the light of the torch, Jeter could see a fountain of blood erupt from the large wound in the man's chest.

Jordan dropped the torch, then fell on it. Quickly his clothes began to blaze, but because the shot had been fatal, he didn't make a move.

"Come on, boys!" another man shouted. "He ain't got no shells left in that shotgun!"

"No, but our guns are loaded," Ed Masterson said, as he led a group of more than two dozen men up the street. "Drop those torches."

Startled by the sudden and unexpected appearance of so many of the townspeople, the ruffians dropped their torches.

Jeter stepped out onto the front porch.

"Looks like we got here just in the nick of time," Ed Masterson said, nodding toward Jordan's body.

"I had to shoot him," Jeter said.

"Look here, Masterson, Jordan warn't wearin' no gun, 'n he got shot anyway. That's murder, ain't it?"

"I would call it self-defense," Sheriff Bassett said, as he arrived at the scene.

"But he didn't have no gun!"

"This man had a torch and he was about to burn down this house," Ed Masterson said. "We all saw what happened. I'd say that makes it self-defense. What about, you Sheriff?"

Charley Bassett nodded his head. "The only thing left to do here, is put the fire out on Jordan's body. We don't want him burnin' up 'fore he gets to hell."

Several men began kicking dirt over Jordan's body.

"One more thing," Charley Bassett added. "If anything happens to the Willis house, or to the Red House, or to any one of them, and that includes the boy, I'll put every one of you in jail. And if I have to, I'll hang every one of you."

"You can't hang ever' one of us."

"Oh, yes, I can," Bassett said easily. "And you'll be the first once I hang, Lewis Benton. Now you all disperse, a' fore I arrest you now,"

Ed Masterson pointed to Jordan's body. "Before you go, drag him down to Eb Collar's place. There are children in this house, and they don't need to see a dead body lying out front."

Magnolia joined Jeter as they came down from the porch to stand by the gathered group of townspeople

"I can't tell you how much we appreciate what all you did for us," Jeter said.

"Yes, to be honest, it looked pretty much like you had it under control."

"Pete, it seems to me like all these men deserve a drink at the Red House," Jeter said. "Can you take care of that?"

"Come on, men." Pete Cahill said. "Drinks are on the boss."

EVERYONE FOLLOWED Cahill except Ed Masterson and the sheriff.

"What will we do if they come back?" Magnolia asked.

"I don't think you'll have to worry about that," Masterson said.

"I wish they didn't hate that poor innocent child, the way they do."

Masterson shook his head. "Now, Magnolia, I'm afraid there's nothing I, or the sheriff, or anyone else can do about that. Prejudice is a pretty deep-rooted thing in some people. And once they get this prejudice in them, well, there's not much of anything you can do to talk 'em out of it."

"I know this is your business," Charley Bassett said, "but if there's any place you can take that kid, you ought to find it."

"He's a little boy," Magnolia said. "He can't go back to his people. They gave him to Cade and if Cade takes him back, they'll more than likely kill both Cade and Stone."

"Ma'am, you just made my argument. Them people are savages, and this here boy you're protecting—why who's to say he won't turn on you, or worse one of your sweet little girls? Think about that tonight," the sheriff said. "Now, come on Masterson, let's go get us one of them drinks Cahill's passin' out and leave these people alone."

JETER AND MAGNOLIA were standing in front of their house. Jeter had his arm wrapped around his wife's waist, and he pulled her closer to him.

"What are we going to do about Stone? What if the sheriff is right?" Magnolia asked.

"I don't think anybody's going to try something like this again," Jeter said. "Jordan was the one who was always the worst, and with him gone, I don't think anyone will actually try to hurt Stone. But, it's like Ed said, people have prejudices, and there's nothing we can do about that."

"You're telling me that—an octoroon who grew up in New Orleans? My mother didn't even know her ancestor who was colored, and yet when the census taker came, we were always colored."

"And that makes me love you all the more," Jeter said as he pulled her to him and kissed her.

"We better go in," Magnolia said as she pulled back from Jeter. "What are we going to do? I'm so scared."

"Don't be. We'll wait and talk to Cade," Jeter said. "The three of us will come up with the right answer. We won't let anything happen to Stone."

19

Cade, Armitage, and Frenchy were eating buffalo steaks that Frenchy had cooked on a grate, over on open fire.

"Frenchy, you cook buffalo better than anyone I know," Cade said.

Frenchy laughed. "In the *Café Procope*, on rue de *l'Ancienne Comédie*, I cooked many wonderful things. But never, did I cook steak of the buffalo."

"That sounds like a pretty fancy restaurant," Cade said.

"*Oui*, it was."

"Why did you leave France?"

"*Monsieur Bellefleur*, who was the *manager de restaurant*, did not like it that his beautiful wife so often shared her charms." Frenchy smiled. "And what he most did not like, was that she shared her charms with me."

"Well, I'm glad she did," Cade said. "Otherwise, the Englishman and I wouldn't be enjoying this fine piece of meat out here in the middle of nowhere."

"The Frenchman has done an excellent job in the preparation of the steak, that is true," Armitage said. "But a bundle of fresh spring asparagus topped with drawn butter lying alongside the steak. Now that would be a meal."

"*Non, non, champignons,*" Frenchy insisted.

"You're both crazy as loons," Cade said. "What this steak needs is a big, baked potato, slathered with lots of butter. Or, maybe we should have grits," he added with a smile.

"Grits? My word," Armitage said.

"*Mon Dieu,*" Frenchy exclaimed.

The culinary conversation was interrupted when in the distance, they saw a wagon coming toward them.

"That looks like a Murphy wagon," Armitage said. "Surely, there is no hunter who has a sufficient number of hides to necessitate the need for such a wagon."

"That's not just any wagon; that's a Harrison and McCall wagon," Cade said as he folded his knife and put it in his pocket.

"So it is," Armitage said. "And I do believe that is Billy sitting beside your partner."

"This will be interesting," Cade said as he headed out to meet the wagon.

BILLY PROCEEDED to explain how he had lost the wagon, the hides, and the guns, and how the mule had died immediately after getting out of the river.

Cade burst out laughing.

"I didn't expect this to be your reaction," Billy said. "I thought you'd be mad."

"And what are you going to do about it? Can you get the wagon out of the river? No. Can you find the hides? No. Can you fish out the guns . . .?"

"All right, I get your point," Billy said.

"You went to bring back a skinner. Is this the best you could find?" Cade said, nodding his head in Jacob's direction.

"Look, I'm the driver," Jacob said. "In all my jobs, I've never skinned a buffalo."

"We will teach you," Armitage said. "It is a rather simple task, although it does require much strength."

"Then that let's Jacob out," Cade said. "He's as weak as a cat."

"You two stop your caterwauling," Billy said. "It may be that Armitage and Frenchy won't need any help. I didn't tell you, Cade, but there wasn't a big .50 to be had at the Walls."

"What? How are we going to kill buffalo without a gun?" Cade asked.

"Rath let me have a gun that he promised to George Causey, but it's a round barreled .44. And for you I got a Spencer carbine."

"You're right. We don't need another skinner. I can skin," Cade said.

"Boys, I hate to rain on your parade," Jacob said, "but the Harrison part of Harrison and McCall has to get back to Dodge and take care of business. And it wouldn't be a bad idea if the McCall part decided he should come back, too."

Cade let out a sigh. "I know, Jacob. You've been doing all the work, but how about this? We lost close to 400 hides in the river. Can you stay until Billy shoots that many? And then I'll go back to Dodge with you."

"All right," Jacob said. "But no more than four days."

THE THREE SKINNERS worked from sunup to sundown skinning the buffalo that Billy was killing. The skins were piling up and on the second day the number was up to 286. The carcasses as well were piling up, and Jacob brought out one of the mules to move them into a big pile. The vultures blackened the sky as they swooped down on the fresh meat, picking the meat until the bones bleached in the sun.

"Indians!" a rider yelled as he rode toward the men, causing the vultures to take flight. "Indians! Indians are comin'."

All five men raced toward the wagon that was standing nearby. When they got there, the rider stopped to tell them the news.

"Where and how many did you see?" Cade asked.

"I didn't see any of the bastards, but I seen what they done. Cheyenne Jack and Blue Billy—over by the Salt Fork—they cut off all their parts and then they scalped 'em."

"Are you headed to Adobe Walls?" Billy asked.

"I'll go tell 'em what I know, but you can't pay me enough to stay in this country. I got me a wife and kids back in Caldwell, and I'm gonna high tail it right back home." The man slapped his horse. "I've done my duty. If you men are fools enough to stay here, I can't help it," he yelled as the horse was galloping away.

"Do you know who that was?" Cade asked.

"I've never seen him before," Billy said, "and I thought I knew most of the hunters out here."

"Well, I hope he gets back to his wife and kids," Cade said.

"I don't have a wife," Jacob said, "but I'd sort of like to live long enough to get one someday. With Dudley and Wallace, these two make four men killed within the last week or so. I know I said I'd give you four days, but would you consider loading up and going back to the Walls?"

"It's up to you, Billy. It's your outfit," Cade said.

Billy nodded his head. "I think it wouldn't be a bad idea to go in. First of all, I miss my big .50, and second, I sort of smell Indian in the air. Maybe we'll stay at the Walls a couple days, then move the camp someplace else. The herd's movin'. Maybe I'll go north a little ways."

ENCAMPMENT OF CHEYENNE, Head of Washita River

Following the Sun Dance, Quanah Parker and White Eagle were disappointed that only about half the tribe agreed to go to war. Most of the Penatekas returned to the reservation; Chief Horse Back led many of the Nokonis away, and Chief Quitsquip took the Yamparika back to their agrarian ways. It was hard for Quanah to understand how raising plants for food could replace the excitement and freedom that killing the buffalo provided for the People.

Quanah was convinced that White Eagle could persuade the other southern plains tribes to join them, but just as the elderly of the Comanche had accepted the handouts from the government, the Arapahos, led by Chief Powder Face, chose to reject the call to war and they, too, returned to the agency. Likewise, Striking Eagle, chief of the Kiowas, took many of his people and returned as well.

Now as Quanah approached the lodges of the Cheyenne, he had Yellow Horse of the Arapaho, with twenty-two renegades, and Lone Wolf, of the Kiowa, with a slightly larger band of followers. All were primed for war.

"Do you think the Cheyenne will take the pipe against the white man?" White Eagle asked.

"The Cheyenne are brave warriors," Quanah said. "Let us hope that they take up the call to war, better than the People. I am sorry so many have chosen the white man's way."

White Eagle thumped his chest. "I will make good medicine. The Cheyenne will follow us."

FOLLOWING WHITE EAGLE'S PRONOUNCEMENT, Quanah selected four warriors along with the medicine man, to charge the camp of the Cheyenne. When they arrived, Crazy

Mule was holding a medicine lodge, and the warriors were seated around the fire in a great circle. Quanah and his followers rode in and out of the circle in a ceremonial raid. When that was concluded, they went back to their campsite with the other warriors, and the Cheyenne led a reciprocal charge. That evening all the Indians joined together in feasting and dancing.

When the time was right, White Eagle took his place by the fire. He wore only a breechclout and moccasins with a bright red sash tied around his waist. In his hair was the feather of a red-tipped hawk and a snake rattle hung from each ear. The older medicine men wore ceremonial masks, but the youthful face of White Eagle was uncovered.

Quanah was pleased with White Eagle's presentation. The young medicine man would surely convince the Cheyenne to join with the People and together, Quanah felt the action they took would lead to success.

White Eagle picked up some green cedar twigs and threw them into the fire. When the pungent smoke began to rise, White Eagle fanned the smoke around the circle. He symbolically, bathed in the smoke, washing his hands, his face and his chest. Getting as close to the flames as he could, he lifted his face as he began to speak.

"I am White Eagle, son of the wolf. I have strong medicine. The Great Spirit has given me unknown powers after I climbed to the stars to meet with those who have gone before. I have predicted when the great star in the sky would disappear, I have foretold when the snows would fly, and I have said when the rains would come. Now, the Great Spirit has shown me how to make a paint that will stop the white man's bullets.

"The great Chief Quanah and the Quahadis have witnessed these feats; I will protect us as we drive the whites from our land, and once again we will ride the plains following the buffalo, as our ancestors have done for many generations. If you but follow me. . ."

Upon hearing White Eagle's words, many in the circle began to murmur to one another.

"Where will we strike the white man?" White Horse asked.

"I say we ride to Texas," Lone Wolf said. "Avenge the death of my son."

"Find the man called Hurricane Bill," Little Robe said. "Find my 43 horses that he took from me."

"Ride against Bad Hand; kill the blue bellies."

"Go to Texas. Kill the *Tejanos*."

"It is decided," White Eagle said. "We will ride for Texas and seek vengeance." He lifted his arms to the sky and began to howl like a wolf as the council erupted in celebration.

"Quanah, Quanah Parker," a young warrior called as he crept toward Quanah. "The old men want to see you."

Quanah left the celebration and went to the lodge of Old Man Otter Belt where Standing Bear and Crooked Nose along with several other old men were gathered.

"You, Quanah Parker, you pretty good fighter, but young man. You not know everything. We think take the pipe to the white shooters who kill our buffalo. Run them out. Then come back, take the young warriors, then go war in Texas!"

QUANAH RETURNED to the council and reported what the old men had said.

White Eagle again rose to speak. "The old men have spoken. We will kill the white shooters where I have seen them as they gather on the Canadian. They drink much whiskey, then they sleep under the stars. We will attack when the sun first awakens; we can kill the white man like women who slumber, and their guns will stay silent. My medicine will keep harm from coming to the People."

"Those bastards," W.M.D. Lee said as he stepped into his trading post slamming the door behind him. "They're gone."

"Mules or horses?" George Bent asked.

"Horses. At least a dozen are gone, and I can bet my last dollar, they weren't run off by any Indian."

"It's probably Hurricane Bill's boys again. Ben Clark said they run off all the stock he had over at his whiskey ranch," George said.

"I think it's gonna get a lot worse," Amos Chapman said. Amos worked part time for Lee and Reynolds and part time for the army. He was both a scout and an interpreter.

"Why do you say that?" Lee asked.

"This morning Colonel Lewis got word from Colonel Davidson over at Fort Sill. He said a bunch of Penatekas come in sayin' they'd just left a big war council over on the Red River," Chapman said. "The word is they're goin' to war on the day after the next full moon."

"That doesn't mean a damn thing. Indians are always having some kind of powwow," Lee said. "They just want an excuse to get drunk."

"Maybe this does mean something," George Bent said. "Spotted Wolf and Old Whirlwind came back from this same war council. Spotted Wolf was tellin' anybody who would listen how all the young bucks are goin' on the warpath. He even said Black Bird had joined in."

"His son?" Lee questioned.

"That's right."

"I wonder what their intentions are."

"Old Whirlwind said they're goin' after stock that's been

stolen, but Spotted Wolf said they're goin' after the buffalo hunters down on the Canadian," George said.

"Hmmm. That would be Adobe Walls," Lee said, a sinister smile crossing his face.

"Now boss, you wouldn't want to see that," Chapman said. "You know what them savages do to a white man."

"I guess you're right," Lee said as he drummed his fingers on the counter. "I tell you what. Why don't you ride down there and see what's goin' on? You can tell 'em you're lookin' for my stolen stock."

"Are you listening to what we're tellin' you? These Indians want to kill ever white man south of the Kansas line and I don't know what part of me they see—Indian or white. I'm not sure I want to find out by havin' my scalp danglin' from some buck's lance," Chapman said.

"All right. I'll see if Colonel Lewis will send an escort with you," Lee said. "And maybe you'd better tell someone what the rumor is, but more'n likely, they won't pay any attention to what I say. They'll think I'm just tryin' to run them out so I can get rid of the competition."

WHEN THE BIG Murphy wagon pulled into Adobe Walls, near the end of June, Cade was surprised to see how many wagons were at the outpost. The pile of hides was ever growing, as men added to the stack.

"What you got there?" James Langton asked.

"Two hundred eighty-six fresh hides plus 306 flints," Billy said.

Langton took out a little book and began to write. "All right, Billy Dixon 592. Put 'em on the west end of the pile."

"Wait a minute. They're already on the wagon. I say we just leave 'em there," Billy said.

"Nope, we've got more'n 15,000 hides and them that got 'em here first, goes out first."

"But this is my wagon, and half these hides are mine," Cade said.

Langton looked at Billy. "Did you not tell your partner, you agreed to sell your hides to Rath in exchange for the gun?"

Cade took a deep breath. "Let's start unloading."

20

By the afternoon, more hunters had come in as the word had circulated saying four men had been killed. John Mooar rolled it with a huge load of hides.

"John," Billy said greeting the man. "Where're you coming from?"

"Wright's got us up by the middle Washita," Mooar said. "Let me tell you, all hell's about to break loose."

"Did you run into Indians?"

"Not exactly, but Mort Galloway was out on a scout, and he run across a whole passel of Indians up near the Sweetwater," Mooar said. "Mort said there must have been close to 500, maybe even more."

"Maybe they're moving to the agency. The last time I was at Darlington, the agent said more and more were coming in," Cade said.

"I don't think so—not these Indians. Mort said they had their horses lined up and they was trainin' just like soldiers. They had a big black man out front blowin' a bugle, and them Indians was doin' drills as big as you please."

"Well speaking of soldiers, look what's coming up the

creek," Billy said as he pointed toward four soldiers and a man dressed in civilian clothes coming their way.

"I wonder what they want," Jacob said.

"Tell me, does that man with them look familiar?" Cade asked. "I think it may be Amos Chapman."

"Ah, yes," John Mooar said. "Amos Chapman—the man who tried to stop us from comin' down here."

CHAPMAN DISMOUNTED and headed toward Charles Rath's store, while the soldiers rode over to the corral. Within a few minutes time, Rath and Chapman came out of the store and headed for Hanrahan's saloon.

"That's strange," Billy said. "Those two seem like they're in a big hurry to wet their whistles."

"No, I don't think so," Cade said. "Look, now they're on their way to Myers' place. What do you say? Do you think we might need a can of peaches or something? Let's go see if we can find out what this is all about?"

WHEN BILLY and Cade got to Myers store, Sybil Olds was standing behind the counter.

"Cade," she said, "I didn't know you were here at the Walls. What can I help you with?"

"Where's Charlie?" Cade asked as he looked around.

"Rath and Hanrahan just came in with some man," Sybil said. "Rath said, 'we've got to talk,' and they're all huddling in the storeroom."

THE HARRISON and McCall wagon was standing empty near the yard where the hides were stacked.

"This doesn't make any sense," Jacob said. "James Langton doesn't have an idea in hell, which of these hides belongs to whom."

Cade laughed. "To whom? Is that the college professor coming out in you?"

"Humph," Jacob said. "That's been so long ago, I don't even remember those days. Look at me now. I'd put my skill at unloading a wagon against the best of 'em."

"But what about loadin' one?" John Mooar asked. "Are you good at that, too?"

"I am," Jacob said.

"Well, then how about following me over to the back of Myers' place?" Mooar asked. "I'm loadin' up supplies to take back to the Washita where my brother's outfits are. Wright's got six shooters workin' for him, and that takes a lot of beans to keep 'em goin'."

"I would suppose you'll be loading a little ammunition, as well," Cade said.

"Well, yes, that, too," John said. "But seriously, will you help load the wagon? If I ask Fred Leonard to help me, I won't get out of here for three days, and I want to leave before daybreak if I can."

"We'll help," Jacob said. "I planned to load some hides tonight, but who knows which ones Langton will let me haul. He'll probably stand here, saying 'take this one' or 'take that one'. I don't understand how this place operates."

THAT EVENING BAT MASTERSON, Mike Welch, and Bermuda Carlisle invited the soldiers to join in for a friendly game of poker. Three of the four soldiers accepted, and their luck seemed to be running hot, as one of them won almost every time for the first four or five hands. After a game was over, someone refreshed all the drinks making certain that the soldiers' glasses were filled to the brim.

"We just can't beat you fellas," Bat Masterson said. "Maybe I'd better call it a night." He threw down his cards and stepped over to the bar where the one sober soldier was standing.

"Mind if I join you, Sergeant?" Bat asked.

"Sure. I'm Sergeant Popham," the man said, extending his hand.

"And I'm Bat Masterson."

"Well, I'll be damned. You're not the one puttin' the articles in the Messenger are you?"

A broad smile crossed Bat's face. "As a matter of fact, I have been known to pen a line or two for that publication. But I'm curious. Does the Messenger reach Camp Supply?"

"I don't know. I'll only be bivouacked there a few weeks," the sergeant said. "Then I'm supposed to go back to Fort Dodge."

"Well, then, how would you like to be the subject for my next submission?" Bat asked.

"I'd be mighty proud to have you say something about me, Mr. Masterson," Sergeant Popham said. "All the men teased me when they found out I was going to be sent on a detail to find stolen horses—especially Indian horses."

Bat drew back when he heard Popham's statement. "Is that why you're here? Looking for stolen horses?"

Popham nodded his head. "Some ponies got stole from Camp Supply. We tracked 'em for almost 30 miles, but then we lost the trail, so the scout who came with us said to come here. He said the horses are sure to be here, cause there ain't no place else to go."

"So, you're looking for stolen horses?" Bat said, raising his voice so all could hear. "Stolen Indian ponies and you think they're here?"

"What's that?" Bermuda Carlisle asked. He looked across the table at one of the soldiers. "Are you men actually here, looking for stolen Injun horses?"

"Yeah," one of the soldiers said, slurring the reply. "From what we been told 'bout half the Injun horses what's been stoled has been stoled by the buffers."

Carlisle got up from the stool and with a quick right cross, knocked the soldier to the floor.

"What the hell did you do that for?" the soldier asked, rubbing his chin and looking up at Carlisle in surprise.

"I don't like bein' accused of bein' a horse thief," Carlisle said.

"Hell, I didn't say you was. I just said it was the buffers what's stealin' 'em."

"Soldier, I am a buffalo hunter," Carlisle said angrily.

"Adams, Prosser, McGee," Popham called to them. "Come on, let's go. Let's get out of here."

"I ain't goin' nowhere, not while I'm winnin'," Prosser said.

"That's an order, soldier," Popham said.

"Take your money and go," Mike Welch said.

Sergeant Popham walked over to the table and stared sternly at the three soldiers. Reluctantly, and unsteadily, the men got to their feet and, with Popham herding them along, they left the saloon.

"WHEW," Jacob said wiping his brow on his shirt sleeves. "If I had to do this every day, I might decide I wanted to go back to teaching."

"A little refreshment will perk you right up," Billy said. "Come on, John, you owe us a beer."

"I do for all the work you did," John Mooar said, "but if you fellas don't mind, I think I'll just crawl up in the wagon and call it a night. But you tell Hanrahan to charge your drinks to my brother, and don't forget the J. That's J. Wright Mooar."

"Well if J. Wright's goin' to pay, we might as well drink the good stuff," Billy said.

John laughed. "He can afford it. He's got so many hides stacked up, I'll be haulin' back and forth for a week."

WHEN CADE, Billy, and Jacob got to Hanrahan's they were almost knocked over by four soldiers coming out of the saloon.

"Well, excuse us," Jacob said as he moved out of the way.

The sergeant marched the three privates toward the corral and with much difficulty got them onto their horses.

"Now see if you can stay with me," the sergeant said mounting his own horse. "We're getting out of here, before one of us gets killed." With that, the four galloped off.

"Wonder what that was all about?" Billy asked.

"Something's going on," Cade said. "Remember when we saw Chapman riding in with these soldiers? Just now, he wasn't with them."

"I think we're about to find out," Jacob said.

THE PATRONS of the saloon were loud and boisterous as they were declaring their indignities after being called horse thieves. Shepard was tending bar. He fomented the furor as he announced that there would be free drinks for everyone.

"I think we came at the right time," Billy said as he moved toward the bar.

"Or not," Cade said. "I think Hanrahan needs to be here before this gets out of hand. I'll go see if I can round him up."

ROBERT VAUGHAN

IN THE BACK OF MYERS' store, Cade found Hanrahan, Rath and Myers huddled around a table all listening intently to Amos Chapman. When Cade explained what was happening at the saloon, Hanrahan jumped up.

"Thanks, Cade. Chapman, you come with me, and men, let's just keep this little secret between the four of us. Is that agreed?"

"I think that's right," Charlie Myers said. "It could all blow over, and then where would we be?"

Cade followed Hanrahan and Chapman as they hurried toward the saloon. As they ran past John Mooar's wagon, Hanrahan stopped.

"Look, Amos, if they come after you, you come out here and hide in this wagon. Somehow, I'll keep 'em from getting' you."

"What's going on?" Cade asked.

"Nothin', McCall. Nothin'. Just pretend you didn't hear anything," Hanrahan said.

"I don't have to pretend. I didn't hear anything."

"That's good. That's good."

Hanrahan was clearly anxious about something, but Cade couldn't figure out what it might be. He didn't think that an impending brawl at his saloon was enough to provoke this kind of agitation. Cade's instinct was to go crawl in the Harrison and McCall wagon and ride this out, but his curiosity got the better of him. He followed Hanrahan and Chapman into the bar.

"THERE HE IS," Billy Tyler yelled. "He's the one that told them bluebellies they was stoled horses here. Let's get him." Billy Tyler dove for Chapman, but James Hanrahan pulled Chapman behind the bar.

"Now what's this all about?" Hanrahan asked, raising his

180

hand. "You all know Amos Chapman. He scouts for the army."

"Sure, he does," Mike Welch said, "and how'd he know to tell 'em to look for stolen horses here?"

"Cause he's a no-good spy," Bermuda Carlisle said. "He ain't no scout; he's spyin' for the army."

"Or worse, for the Injuns; he's a half-breed son of a bitch. How do we know it ain't the Injuns he's spyin' for?" Billy Tyler asked.

"Seems to me like we might ought to have us a little necktie party tonight," Carlisle suggested.

"Yeah. Let's hang 'im from the stockade down at the corral." Tyler said.

"I think I should be going down to Rath's place," Chapman said as he headed for the door. "But I'll be back after all this calms down."

Cade saw Hanrahan dart his eyes in the opposite direction from Rath's store. Chapman nodded, and Cade knew he was heading for John Mooar's wagon.

"ALL RIGHT, boys, now that that's over, how about all of you stepping up to the bar for a drink, on the house? Who's gonna be first?"

With a cheer, all the patrons in the saloon pushed forward, with beer sloshing out of their mugs, in an attempt to be the first one to get a free drink.

Soon they had forgotten about Amos Chapman and his charge of horse stealing, but after a few hours someone brought it up that he hadn't come back to the saloon. To a man, they all filed out, but Amos Chapman seemed to have disappeared.

THE NEXT MORNING, Cade and Jacob were sleeping under their wagon when John Mooar awakened them.

"You are not gonna believe this," John Mooar said. "Last night that half-breed snuck into my wagon. He didn't know I was sleepin' there and I almost shot him, but what he told me —if it's true, we're all goners."

"What'd he say?" Cade asked as he sat up.

"He said he was sent here by W.M.D. Lee at the trading post at the Cheyenne Agency. Some of the peaceful Indians who live there have been tellin' that a whole bunch of Indians are ready to go on the warpath. And guess where they're a comin'?"

"Here?" Cade asked.

"Yes, that's it. Chapman said they plan to take out ever white man they can find, especially those that are killin' their buffalo."

"Do you believe him?" Jacob asked.

"Sure I do," Mooar said. "That explains all them bucks trainin' with a bugler. You know, the ones Mort Galloway saw over on the Sweetwater."

"Did he give you any idea when this might take place?" Cade asked.

"That's the scary part. He told me the day. It'll be the first morning after the full moon."

"Damn, that's three days from now," Jacob said.

"And Rath and Myers know," Cade said.

"And Hanrahan, too. They all know." Mooar said.

"But they aren't going to tell us," Cade said. "That's the secret they're going to keep just between themselves."

"Now that we know, what should we do?" Jacob asked. "Should we leave or stay?"

"I have a favor to ask," John Mooar said. "If the Indians are coming from the Sweetwater, they'll be passing my brother's camp, and if they're gonna kill ever white man they can find, they'll all be dead. Since your wagon isn't loaded, would you mind going back with me to bring 'em in?"

"Sure," Jacob said. "We can do that."

"If you don't mind, Jacob, I'd like to stay here," Cade said. "I want to keep my eyes and ears open and just see what I can find out."

CHAPTER 21

THE QUAHADI VILLAGE OF QUANAH PARKER:

"The Great Spirit has spoken," White Eagle said. "My brothers, The Great Spirit will give you power. We will kill the white hunters, and The Great Spirit will bring back the buffalo."

"That is good," Quanah said. "The Great Spirit will protect his chosen people. And now Silver Knife and Wolf Tongue have brought good news. They have watched the white men who stay by the Canadian. They drink much whiskey. Then they sleep without tipis until the sun rises high in the sky."

"But they have bullets that go a long way," Mean To His Horses said.

"If Mean To His Horses is afraid, he can stay behind," Quanah suggested.

"I am not afraid!" Mean To His Horses insisted.

"Do not worry, my brothers," White Eagle said. "I will cast my medicine upon you; the bullets of the white men cannot harm you. And I will make my medicine upon the white men; when we attack, all white men will be asleep. I say we will club them like sleeping children."

"The whites will leave our land!" Quanah said, thrusting his fist high into the air. "And the People will once again be masters of the plains."

"Ayee, this is so!" Wild Horse shouted, and all the other Comanche, Kiowa, and Cheyenne cheered loudly.

"But first we much prepare."

ADOBE WALLS:

When Cade awakened, he was surprised to see that the Harrison and McCall wagon and the Mooar wagon were standing down by the river, with the animals still in their harnesses. He was bothered that he had not heard them approach. If Indians were going to attack, he would have to be aware of anything that went on around him.

Everyone at the Walls seemed to be going about their usual activities—playing cards, having horse races, target shooting, and of course drinking whiskey.

None of the three shopkeepers had breathed a word to anyone of the impending attack by the Indians, and Cade had kept his council. If he told someone, and then nothing did happen, he would be ridiculed for spreading the tale of Amos Chapman; a tale from a man who had tried to convince the hunters not to come in the first place.

He had tried to introduce into the saloon's conversation, the possibility that the hunters may want to leave, but to a man, everyone was against the idea. The men could see the handwriting on the wall. They knew that if they exterminated the herd, the days of buffalo hunting would soon be over. They also knew what they had done to the herd north of the Cimarron.

But this season, the summer of 1874, was shaping up to be the best season ever. The herd was large, and it was close by. All the hunters were primed to kill as many buffalos as possible, and then to take their riches and move on to something else.

That very motivation had been the reason Cade had stayed at Adobe Walls when the wagon hub had split. After losing the hides in the river, his plan for making a lot of money was curtailed.

And now Cade was torn between staying to hunt with Billy, and going back to Dodge City with Jacob as he had promised. The money from the 592 hides they had brought in would barely be enough to outfit Billy again, especially if Cade took his half. He would talk to both men, but he would wait to make his decision until after "the morning after the full moon."

How he hoped what Amos Chapman had said was all a rumor.

With much on his mind, he walked down to the river to talk to Jacob.

"THIS IS REAL. The Indians are coming," Jacob said.

"How do you know?" Cade asked.

"One of Wright Mooar's camps was ambushed by a column of bucks. They were riding two by two just like they were in the cavalry."

"Was anyone killed?"

"No, not Wright's men, but they did take out at least a half-dozen Indians. They got their big .50's out and kept shooting at the lead horses. When they went down, the ones following started piling up on top of them, and that gave Philip Sisk and his crew time to get away," Jacob said. "They left a lot of money on the ground, and

Sisk wanted to go back and get his hides, but Wright said no."

"What are you going to do?" Cade asked.

"I'm heading for Dodge City this morning, and I thought you were coming with me. Have you changed your mind?"

Cade looked down, avoiding Jacob's direct gaze. "I don't know. I think I owe it to Billy to help him get an outfit put together again, and yet I owe it to you to do my part in the freighting business."

"All right, if that's how you feel," Jacob said. "You stay out, and when you get back to Dodge, we'll settle up. That is if you get back to Dodge, at all."

Cade laughed. "You really do think this raid is going to happen."

"I do, with every fiber in my being, but I sort of thought you'd want to stay." Jacob walked over to the wagon. "That's why I bargained with Wright Mooar for hauling his gear. This is for you." He pulled out a Sharps big .50 and handed it to Cade. "Now, let's hope it keeps you alive."

Cade accepted the gun, and then shook Jacob's hand. "You're the best partner I've ever had."

Jacob chuckled. "Don't say that around Jeter Willis."

CADE WATCHED as the two wagons pulled away from Adobe Walls. Close behind were several smaller wagons that were all loaded with hides. By lunchtime, Charles Rath and Charlie Myers were seen riding out on the finest horseflesh that could be found in the corral.

Had Cade made a big mistake?

COMANCHE VILLAGE NEAR THE SWEETWATER:

The smell of smoke from the campfires from the day

before, as well as the aroma of cooked meat hung in the air. The black-white soldier, who had joined the Indians, blew the bugle call for *Assembly*, and all the warriors gathered in the pre-dawn darkness.

Nobody in the village had ever seen such a magnificent procession of warriors. Close to 700 mounted men gathered in what the army would call a regimental formation. The old men who stayed behind and the women and children watched with pride as they rode from the encampment.

Quanah, with He Bear and White Eagle rode in front of the column, followed by Red Moon and Stone Calf of the Cheyenne, and Lone Wolf and Woman's Heart of the Kiowa.

"We will be victorious," White Eagle insisted. "The spirits will make us strong, and those who slaughter the buffalo and leave the meat to rot, will be gone."

The People, the Kiowa, and the Cheyenne rode leisurely across the Texas Panhandle dispatching at least four white hunters in route. The scalps were carefully dressed and attached to those bridles of the warriors who had made the kills.

They continued toward their target, each man making his own medicine as they rode. The silence was broken only by the rumble of the unshod hooves of the horses. As they followed the river through some low hills, the sound of the approaching horses frightened some of the smaller creatures who lived in the grass. One of the creatures was black, with a white stripe running down his back.

Adobe Walls

The noise from Hanrahan's was not as boisterous as usual, as Old Man Keeler had brought out his mouth harp. Several of the men were singing along as he played *Tenting Tonight on the Old Campground.*

As the evening was quite sultry, Cade had taken his beer and was sitting with his back leaned up against O'Keefe's blacksmith shop. James Hanrahan stepped outside and looked up at the sky. When he saw Cade, he came to join him.

"Why aren't you inside enjoying the music?" Hanrahan asked.

"During the war we had different words to that song," Cade said. "Dying tonight, dying tonight, dying on the old campground."

Hanrahan didn't have a comment. He slid down beside Cade, and taking out a paper and some tobacco, he rolled a cigarette and lit it. When the smoke was finished he flipped it into the dirt and watched the flickers die.

"You know, don't you?"

"Yes, I do," Cade said. "Jacob said Chapman told John Mooar the real reason he came here."

"Then why didn't you leave when the wagons pulled out of here?"

"I have to say I was torn," Cade said. "Right now, I see Billy Dixon, who is a truly honorable man, without an outfit. If I left, he would insist that I take my part of the hides we brought in, and if I did, that wouldn't leave him with enough capital to get started again."

"He could work for somebody else," Hanrahan said.

"Maybe, but I don't see it," Cade said.

"Have you told anybody what's coming in the morning?"

"No, I have not," Cade said. "Does anybody else know about this?"

Hanrahan shook his head, and once again rolled a cigarette.

"I've sunk ever' dime I got in this place. I have to stay here and defend it, and if these roughnecks knowed what's comin' you know they'd head for the high hills. A half dozen men can't hold on by themselves, that's for sure."

"How many are here now?"

"By my count, we got twenty-eight men and Sybil. That ain't very many, but it's better'n Shepard and me trying to hold off a whole passel of Indians," Hanrahan said.

"Well, it looks like the number is going to swell a little bit. Isn't that Ike Shadler's wagon pulling up over by Leonard's store?" Cade asked.

"I think so," Hanrahan said as he got up and headed for the wagon.

"James, ain't you heard," Shorty Shadler said as he jumped off the wagon. "We run into Wright Mooar's bunch on the way down and he said that half-breed Chapman told 'em Indians are on the warpath, and they're comin' this way."

"And you believed him?"

"I guess so. That's why they was a high-tailin' it to Dodge," Ike said. "And we're gonna do that, too. We're gonna unload and then take on some hides and get out of here first thing in the morning."

"What you got there?" Fred Leonard said as he came out of the store.

"For one thing, guns and ammunition," Shorty said, "and by damn, you're gonna need 'em."

"Of course, we need guns and ammunition," Hanrahan said. "You can't be runnin' no tradin' post for buffalo hunters without guns and ammunition. When you get unloaded come on up to my place and you can get a drink on me."

"We'll be there right quick," Ike said.

As he was speaking, the Shadler's big brown dog jumped out of the wagon and ran toward Cade.

"Buster," Cade said as the dog began to shower him with

kisses. "I've not seen you for a while." Cade rubbed the dog behind his ears, and soon the dog was curled up beside Cade with his head resting on his knee.

He sat there for a long time, just thinking. What would tomorrow bring? He wasn't afraid, because he had been through this before. During the war, there had been times when he had known the next day he was going into battle. But then there had been an entire army around him. Now, by Hanrahan's count, there were but twenty-eight. He assumed that number included him, but Hanrahan hadn't said.

He thought of Chantal, as he absently rubbed the dog behind his ears. If he happened to be killed tomorrow, she was too young to really understand. Besides, he had never been much of a father to her anyway. Magnolia would see to it that she was raised properly.

And then there was Stone. Again, Magnolia would take care of him.

He had his brother, Adam, and of course, Melinda, but he hadn't been a part of their lives for close to nine years. Sure, they might feel a twinge of sadness, but there would be no real loss.

The funny thing was, Jeter would probably feel the greatest sense of loss, and even that relationship had taken a turn. Jeter was settled with a prosperous business and a wonderful family. He would soon forget about Cade.

And Jacob? At this point, because of Cade, their partnership was in a state of limbo. Hadn't Jacob said, "when you get back to Dodge, we'll settle up"? That implied that the partnership was dissolving.

He watched the setting sun, and thought the red smear in the western sky was particularly pretty this evening. Would he see the sunset tomorrow evening? It was funny, in a way, because whether he was here or not, the sun would set tomorrow.

He watched some ants crawling over the leavings of Hanrahan's cigarette.

"Ha," he said, quietly. "You fellas will be here tomorrow night, won't you? Doesn't make any difference to you what's going to happen."

Cade closed his eyes and tried to push such thoughts out of his mind.

"What the hell?" he said. "Everybody's goin' to die sometime, and once you're dead, it doesn't make any difference when it happened. It'll be the same for everyone."

He heard footsteps coming his way and for a moment he was embarrassed that someone might have overheard him.

"Here you are," Billy Dixon said.

"Hi, Billy."

"How come you aren't inside singin'? Old Man Keeler's really wound up in there."

Cade laughed. "I've had a drink or two tonight, but not near enough to forget what a bad singer I am."

"I've just been talking with James Hanrahan."

"Oh?" Cade wondered if Hanrahan had told Billy about the impending Indian attack.

"It's good news. He's offered to go into partnership with us. He'll outfit us, and give us a new wagon and team, then split the profits for all the hides we can take." Billy smiled broadly. "What do you think about that?"

"Sounds good. When does he want you to head out?"

"In the morning. He's anxious to get some more hides in here," Billy said.

"Billy, I think I'm going back into Dodge."

"Are you sure you want to do that? Hell, I thought you liked buffin'. For sure, you like the money."

"I do like it, and yes, I like the money, but there's Jacob to consider. He's right, I haven't been holding up my end of the partnership."

Billy nodded. "Well, just so you know, you can come back anytime. I'm goin' to miss havin' you around. When do you think you'll be headin' out?"

"As soon as I can get away," Cade said.

"Well, then could you help me, and the boys get loaded up? The supplies Jacob brought in from White Deer are over behind Rath's place."

CHAPTER 22

THE COMANCHE, KIOWA, AND CHEYENNE WAR PARTY:
The Indians had ridden hard across the Texas Panhandle, killing any lone hunter they came across. White Eagle had kept the warriors in a state of excitement as each night he would insist that the drums come out, and everyone danced and drank whiskey.

By noon of the third day the best fighting men of all the southern plains reached the Canadian, and Quanah called a halt. There would be no drinking or dancing on this day as the warriors spread out among the trees. Each one spent the afternoon and evening preparing their medicine and grooming their horses.

Each man removed his saddle or blanket and hid them in the trees, then they hobbled the extra ponies that had carried the paraphernalia that would be needed for the attack.

White Eagle withdrew his ingredients needed to prepare his special paint. This paint was the magic that would stop the white man's bullets from penetrating the skin of the warriors. Some was red with vermilion or yellow with ochre. White Eagle spread the yellow paint all over his naked body, and then began to walk among the warriors distributing the paint to them.

When he came to one particular band of Cheyenne, a fire had been built and a small animal was roasting. When White Eagle saw the skin lying nearby, he shrieked.

"A skunk! You have killed a skunk!"

One of the Cheyenne warriors tore off a piece of the meat and offered it to White Eagle, a broad smile crossing his face.

"Here, the first bite for our prophet."

White Eagle picked up a stick and without touching the skunk got it off the spit, and flung it into the river.

"You have killed that which the spirits say is taboo! My magic will not work. I must visit the Great Spirit so that I may make atonement for what you have done!" He turned and began to run.

"I must go. I must speak to the spirits," White Eagle said when he found Quanah. "I must make atonement."

Quanah watched as White Eagle picked up a spear, and while still naked, walked away from the river going so far that Quanah could no longer see him.

It was time for Quanah to make his own medicine.

The first thing he did was to prepare his bay stallion. He used the red paint for his own symbol that he put on the hips. Then he used buckskin combined with red flannel streamers to braid a loop in the horse's mane. This handle would be used to hang onto when he would duck to escape from the white man's bullets. Next, he put on the riding bridle that had silver medallions attached. On the cheek strap he fastened a scalp from a fair-haired woman, making certain that the flowing locks were well tended. When he was satisfied that his horse was ready, he turned to his own preparations.

The bow he used was made from two buffalo rib bones and he replaced the rawhide thongs that held them together.

Then he decked his nine-foot lance with eagle feathers, making sure that the steel point was clean and sharp.

But the most important thing was his shield. It was made from the hide of a buffalo bull's neck and the pouch that was formed between the two thicknesses was stuffed with eagle feathers. Then he covered it with soft buckskin that had a fringe of feathers. In these feathers he placed his own special medicine—the claws of a bear and the bill of an eagle. He also attached one more scalp.

And then he checked his war bonnet that each of his wives had worked on. He recognized the beadwork that Weakeah had made, and he knew that Chony had attached the feathers to the tail of buckskin. He put it on his head and saw that it reached exactly to the top of his moccasin. He smiled. It was good to have wives who could do such good work.

He painted his own chest, and then put on his leggings that were made of well-tanned leather. Now he was ready to wait until the hours before sunrise, when in the light of the moon, he would lead the finest cavalcade of warriors that had ever been assembled on the southern plains.

And tomorrow the people would be victorious. The white men who hunted the buffalo would be clubbed in their sleep.

It was two o'clock in the morning, and James Hanrahan had not yet been to sleep. He stood just outside the saloon as he looked up at the moon, a full, bright, silver orb just beyond its highest point, and now descending slightly north of west.

If what Amos Chapman had said was true, the Indians would be attacking at sunrise. He could make out more than a dozen bedrolls, the occupants sleeping peacefully. He could hear their snores as they competed with the sound of an owl down in the trees by the creek. Something moved, and

Hanrahan pulled his pistol that was strapped on his leg. But the movement was caused by Tom O'Keefe's dog which was coming to greet him.

"What have I done, Skeeter?"

Hanrahan leaned down to pat the dog's head, and in the moonlight, he could see his tail wag.

"If these men die, it's my fault."

As if he understood, the dog licked Hanrahan's hand—the hand that held the pistol.

In that instant, James Hanrahan knew what he had to do. He had to alert these men to the impending danger that was about to befall them.

Hanrahan went back into his saloon, and going behind the bar, he pointed his pistol straight up and pulled the trigger.

"Here! What the hell was that?" Shepherd, his bartender, shouted.

"Was that a gunshot? Who's shooting a gun at this time of night?" Bat Masterson asked.

"You men!" Hanrahan shouted. "I need help! The ridgepole has just cracked, and if we don't get some support under it, the roof is going to come crashing down on us."

"We need to get some weight off the roof," Shepherd yelled. "Come on, Welch, come help me get rid of the sod."

"No," Hanrahan said. "Take off some sod, but only enough to lighten the load a little. If we can find somethin' to prop up the ridgepole, that'll hold it 'til morning."

BY THIS TIME Cade and Billy who were bedded down near Billy's loaded wagon were awake, as were several others who were sleeping nearby. Bat Masterson came out of the saloon and almost ran into them.

"Come on," Bat said. "Help me go down by the creek and

cut a big enough pole to use as a prop before the whole damn roof caves in."

"Wait," Hanrahan yelled. "Check the wood pile first." He handed Bat a lantern that he had just lit.

"All right, we'll check the wood pile."

The three went around the blacksmith shop where they found Tom O'Keefe's coal pile and several pieces of slab wood that he used to fire his forge.

"Why did James send us out here?" Billy asked. "None of these pieces are long enough for us to use."

Just then, Bat tripped and fell. "Well, I'll be damned. Here's a log that's just lying here. It looks to me like it might just work."

"That ridgepole is about two feet around, and this thing only looks to be about eight inches," Cade said.

"Well, let's take it back and try it," Bat said. "After all, like James said, it only has to last until morning."

Cade took a deep breath. "Yeah, we only have to last until morning."

FOR THE NEXT couple of hours, the men worked feverishly, repositioning the sod on the roof, then putting the new pole into position.

"DAMN," Andy Johnson said. He yawned and stretched. "We've been up half the night. I think I'll go back to bed."

"Me too," Billy Ogg said.

"You boys can go back to bed if you want to," Hanrahan said. "But, I feel like I owe ya somethin' for all the work you done. So, the bar's open, and drinks are free from now, until dawn."

"All right!" Johnson said. "It doesn't have to be dark for me to sleep. I can sleep anytime."

Johnson stepped up to the bar, and so did the others who had been helping with the repairs.

Cade and Billy Dixon had taken their drinks and moved outside. "Did you notice that ridgepole?" Cade asked.

"What about it?"

"There was nothing wrong with it."

"There must've been something wrong with it. I heard it crack just like everyone else did. It was so loud it sounded like a pistol shot."

"Yes, it did, didn't it?"

"Wait a minute, are you suggesting Hanrahan fired a pistol on purpose? You know he wouldn't do that. He wouldn't want to wake everybody up at two o'clock in the morning."

"Maybe not, but I still say there was nothing wrong with that ridgepole."

CHAPTER 23

Cade and Billy Dixon were throwing on a few extra supplies that James Hanrahan had suggested they might need.

"Are you going back out to White Deer?" Cade asked.

"I don't think so—too many Indians that way," Billy said. "I'm heading to the northwest."

"With the supplies you've got, you won't have to come in for the rest of the summer."

"Speaking of which, I forgot the case of shells I bought for my .44. I left them with Fred Leonard. Would you mind getting them for me, while I see what's holding up those two I sent down to the creek to get the horses?"

"Sure," Cade said as he turned to go to the store.

"Damn, look there," Billy said, pointing toward the tree line down by the creek. "It's too bad we don't have our guns ready. Looks like the buffalo are comin' to us."

Cade looked in the direction Billy was pointing. The moving objects, no more than black shadows in the early morning light, weren't moving like buffalo. They were spread out, and unlike buffalo, they stopped.

"That's strange, I've never seen buffalo do that before," Dixon said.

"Billy," Cade said in a strained, but controlled voice. "That's not buffalo, that's Indians."

Cade's words were no sooner spoken, then a single blood-curdling yell came from Billy Ogg, one of the boys who had been sent to get the horses. That yell was answered by a war whoop that was one unified sound from the oncoming warriors. The initial yell of the Indians was followed by the thunderous hoof beats of hundreds of horses, as the Indians put their quirts to their ponies and charged the hunters' camp.

"Indians! Indians!" Cade shouted at the top of his voice.

Billy joined in giving the warning. "Indians! Ever' body up! We're being attacked!"

The Indians charged, hundreds of them, more than Cade had ever seen at one time. They were well mounted on painted ponies, and armed with pistols, rifles, bows and arrows, and lances, their weapons as festooned with feathers and other embellishments as were the horses and the riders themselves.

Billy's new Sharps .44 was in the back of the wagon and he reached for it while Cade grabbed his big .50 that was lying between the blankets of his bedroll. Cade heard Billy fire, and immediately one of the riders tumbled from his horse, making that Indian the first casualty in the battle to come.

Cade's big .50 took down the second.

"We're exposed here!" Billy shouted. "We've got to get inside!"

The two men hurried back to the saloon, but the door was closed.

"James!" Cade shouted, and he pounded on the door with the butt of his rifle. "James! It's Cade and Dixon! Let us in!"

By now the Indians were shooting and bullets were hitting the ground all around Cade and Billy, as well as plunging into the adobe walls of the saloon.

"Damnit! Let us in!" Billy shouted.

After what seemed like an eternity, the door was opened, and just as it was, they saw Billy Ogg and Andy Johnson running toward them, returning from the errand they had undertaken in gathering the horses.

Ogg was so exhausted from his run that he collapsed on the floor and had to be pulled farther inside so the door could be closed. A bullet, fired by one of the Indians, buzzed through the door, so close that it made a popping sound. When it plunged into the adobe wall on the opposite side of the room, the bullet sent out a little puff of dust.

Cade looked around to see who else was in the saloon. Hanrahan was here, and of course, Billy Dixon. Shepherd and Mike Welch who had been on the roof together were scrambling to get into the bar. Bat Masterson, James McKinley, Bermuda Carlisle and the two boys who had been out rounding up the horses made up the entirety of the defense at the saloon.

Cade reckoned that there weren't more than seven guns in the place.

"Where did all these bastards come from?" Bat asked as he moved toward a window. "It looks like every Indian in Texas is out there." He fired at one of the oncoming Indians.

"Wait," Hanrahan said taking command. "Don't fire until they're 30 yards away. Then all the guns fire at once right down the middle of the sons-of-bitches."

The shooters found places around the front of the building, making holes in the chinking to be used for gun ports. They did hold their fire, as Hanrahan had said, and when the Indians were 30 yards away, they fired as a single volley. That volley split the line as effectively as if a butcher's cleaver had been used to separate the onslaught of Indians.

One group moved to the left going toward Langton's while the other half headed toward Leonard's.

"Did everybody make it inside?" Hanrahan asked.

"It's hard to say," Cade said. "Not everybody was awake, but some made it. Listen to the big .50's."

The guns on either side were indeed booming. The Indians were charging at full speed, dashing their horses against the doors to break them down. Then they would dismount and whirl the horses around and back them against the door, all in an effort to force their way inside the building.

"Thank you, Tom O'Keefe, for reinforcin' the door frames, or them bastards would be in here already," Hanrahan said.

"The Shadler brothers? Did anybody see them?" Billy Dixon asked.

"Their wagon's around back," Mike Welsh said. "We saw it when we were on the roof, but if they heard us, they didn't come out."

"Wait! Listen!" Shepherd said. "Hear that bugle?"

"The army!" Hanrahan said. "The army's coming!"

"What's that call?" Billy Dixon asked.

"That's *To Arms*," the old soldier Hanrahan said. He was smiling. "Boy's, the United States army is preparing to attack!"

"How did they know we needed help?" Cade asked.

"Could be they had scouts out followin' the Indians," James McKinley said.

The bugle sounded again.

"Here that? That there is *Charge*! Let's take a look if we

ROBERT VAUGHAN

want to see the army settin' them Injuns to skedaddlin'," Hanrahan said.

Cade and the others looked out the windows.

"Lookit that!" Welch said. "That ain't the army. That's a Injun blowin' on that bugle."

"Injun hell! That's one o' them Buffalo Soldiers!" Shepherd said. "What's he . . ."

Before he could finish his question, the attacking Indians opened fire and bullets crashed through the windows and into the door.

The Indians continued their charge all the way up to the saloon, and some began pounding on the door. Others poked pistols through the windows and fired, forcing the men to hug the walls to get out of the way of the onslaught of bullets.

The buffalo hunters fired back, and the Indians were driven away from the building. The bodies of more than a half dozen Indians were lying on the ground now, representing not just those who were killed by the Hanrahan saloon defenders, but also those who were in the other two stores.

Billy Dixon, who had faced the first charge with his new .44, saw that the bartender was using a big .50.

"Shepherd, how about trading guns with me?" Dixon called.

"Hell yes," Shepherd said, handing the big .50 over to Billy. "I figure you can do a lot more with this than I can."

Billy took the gun, then looked outside. The Indians had all withdrawn and were now bunched together, some 500 yards away.

"I'm going to kill that one with all the shiny metal on his chest," Billy said.

"I've got a quarter that says you'll miss," Hanrahan said.

Billy pulled the trigger, and the impact of the heavy bullet knocked the Indian off the back of his horse.

Billy didn't say a word; he just held his hand out, palm up.

IN THE SHADLER wagon Ike and Shorty had not been awakened until the shooting started. Ike stuck his head out through the back of the wagon.

"What the hell is going on?" Shorty asked.

"Son of a bitch! I ain't never seen nothin' like this before," Ike said. "They must be near on to a thousand Injuns out there!"

"How many?"

"Look for yourself," Ike said, and Shorty stuck his head through the back flap of the wagon.

"Damn! Where did they all come from?"

"I don't have no idea, but we sure as hell got ourselves into a spot," Ike said. "Brother, we ain't goin' to get out of here alive."

"There's shootin' comin' from all three stores," Shorty said. "Iffen we could just make it into one of those places, I think we'd be all right."

Ike shook his head. "There ain't no way we're gonna get there," Ike said.

"Wonder how come it is there didn't nobody come tell us," Shorty asked.

"How were they goin' to do that, Shorty? Like as not they was all asleep just like us when the Injuns hit. 'N what are they goin' to do? Tell us the Injuns is here? Hell, we heard 'em our ownselves."

"Maybe the Injuns won't see us back here," Shorty suggested

CHAPTER 24

THE ATTACK WAS NOT GOING AS QUANAH HAD PLANNED.

"They will all be asleep, and we can walk in and club them to death," White Eagle had promised.

Even though they had attacked early in the morning when the hunters should have been asleep, they weren't.

Two times they had charged to the bugle calls of Black Buffalo. White Eagle had promised that by playing the bugle, they would be able to steal the army's magic, but that did not happen. Quanah could see that many lay dead from the People, Kiowa, and Cheyenne. There would be much weeping by the women and children when they learned that so many were dead.

"COME WITH ME," Straight Arrow said to Wild Horse and Silver Knife.

Straight Arrow had seen a wagon that was set apart from the rest of them, and he decided to go there. If it was loaded, maybe he could find many things—perhaps guns and ammunition. He would like a white man's rifle that would shoot a big bullet a long way.

Several others got the same idea, and as Straight Arrow, Wild Horse, and Silver Knife approached the wagon, so too did several Kiowa and Cheyenne.

Straight Arrow rode faster to make certain he got there first. As soon as he reached the wagon, he leaped down, then climbed onto the back of the wagon and pulled the canvas aside. That was when he saw the open end of a shotgun, not two hand widths from his face.

WILD HORSE, who was just behind Straight Arrow, heard and saw the blast. He also saw Straight Arrow fall back with only a large red hole where his face had been.

Wild Horse fired, as did all the others who were with him. Everyone shot many times into the wagon.

Silver Knife dismounted and, slowly, approached the wagon. When he pulled the canvas aside he saw the bodies of two white men and a large brown dog. Taking his knife from his belt, he began carving away the scalp of the man who still clutched the shotgun in his hands. Wild Horse climbed into the wagon to scalp the second man, while one of the Kiowa carved a large piece of fur from the side of the dog.

Holding their trophies high and yelping loudly in victory, they hurried back, just in time to join the next attack. This time both Silver Knife and Wild Horse had the bloody scalps hanging from the ends of their spears.

Several guns, as if firing in volley, erupted as they approached the buildings, and many more Indians were unseated from the narrow blankets of rawhide that they used as saddles.

Again, the Indians were forced to retreat.

"WHO DO you reckon those fresh scalps belonged to?" James McKinley asked.

"Shadlers, maybe?" Billy Dixon asked.

"There's no way to know," Hanrahan said.

"Yes, there is," Cade said.

"How are you goin' to do that?" Shepherd asked.

Cade walked over to one of the windows and looked out through the shattered glass. When he saw that the coast was clear, he opened the door and stepped outside.

"Fred!" he called. "Fred, are you there?"

The door at Myers store cracked open, and Fred Leonard peered out.

"Are you holding up over there?" Cade asked.

"So far, we're fine."

"Are the Shadler brothers with you?"

"No," Fred replied.

Cade made the same inquiry of James Langton who was in Rath's store, and got the same response. Nobody was wounded, and the Shadler brothers weren't with them.

"That answers the question, boys," Cade said when he stepped back into the saloon. "The two scalps belonged to Ike and Shorty."

"Too bad," Billy Dixon said.

"Here they come again, boys!" James Hanrahan called as he raised his rifle to his shoulder.

"How come we didn't hear no bugle?" Ogg asked.

"Because it isn't an attack," Cade said. "Look what they're doing. They're coming for their dead."

Cade held his fire as the Indians dashed in to recover their own.

The others watched as a big Indian rode in, hanging to one side of his horse by a loop that seemed to be a part of the horse's mane. He reached down and scooped up a fallen

Indian. He rode back at a gallop, carrying the Indian under one arm.

"Lookie there," Billy Ogg said. "That black bugler feller has took him some things from the Shadler wagon."

The bugler was running from the wagon with a can of coffee under one arm, and a can of sugar under the other. Cade was about to shoot him, but someone from one of the other buildings beat him to it. The bugler fell forward, the tins of coffee and sugar rolling away from him.

"I reckon he won't be blowin' that bugle no more," Ogg said.

Another charge of Indians came, but this time they were firing at the animals that even though they had been hit, had made their way to the buildings. Then they circled around and began firing through the pickets of the stockade.

The gunfire was interspersed by the pitiful sounds of terror from the horses, mules, and even the oxen as they were mowed down by the bullets.

"Damn!" Mike Welch said. "They're killin' all the animals. Why the hell would they want to do that?"

"I expect they don't plan on any of us leaving," Hanrahan said.

"Yeah? Well I plan on seeing that a few more of the Indians don't leave as well," Billy Dixon said.

Dixon took aim again, and pulled the trigger and the big .50 roared.

"That one, for example."

"Isn't that Fred Leonard and Billy Tyler?" Andy Johnson said. "Were they in the stockade when all them animals was being kilt?"

ROBERT VAUGHAN

"They're damn fools if they were," Mike Welsh said.

Everyone watched as Leonard and Tyler raced for the door of Leonard's store.

"Maybe they were trying to save the horses," Shepherd said.

The door opened, and Leonard got inside, but Billy Tyler turned to make one last shot at an Indian that was headed toward him. That was when he went down. They all saw him drawn back inside, then the door closed.

"Bat! Billy Tyler's been hit," Fred Leonard shouted over to Hanrahan's.

"Is it bad?" Bat asked.

"Yeah, real bad. I don't think he's going to make it."

"I have to go see him," Bat said. "Billy Tyler's been my friend since I first came to Dodge."

"They'll be watching the front door," Cade cautioned.

"Then I'll go through the window."

"All right, the rest of you men, let's do a little shooting to keep the Indians busy while Bat runs over there," Cade suggested. "Bat, let us know when you start."

Bat opened the window, then stuck one leg through.

"Now!" he called, and every gun in Hanrahan's saloon opened up.

Billy dashed across the open area between the two buildings and banging on the door, was given entry.

Inside the store, Billy Tyler lay stretched out on the floor.

"He's frothing blood at the mouth," Leonard said. "I'm pretty sure he's been shot through the lungs."

"Bat?" Billy said in a strained voice, a slight smile forming on his lips. "Is that you?"

"I'm here, Billy." He took Billy's hand in his.

"Could you get me somethin' to drink? I'm powerful thirsty."

Bat looked up at Leonard, who shook his head.

"We ain't got a drop o' water in the place," Leonard said. "Truth is, we're all thirsty."

"I'll get you some water," Bat promised, and grabbing an empty bucket, he started toward the door.

"Hold on there, youngster," Old Man Keeler said.

"We need water," Bat replied.

The old man nodded. "I ain't sayin' we don't. Fact is, I'm thirsty too 'n I ain't even been shot. But I know a lot o' them Comanche 'n it could be that I ain't as likely to get shot as you are."

Keeler took the bucket and started toward the pump. Keeler's dog, Bo, ran out with him. Hooking the bail over the spout of the pump, Keeler began working the handle up and down. For a few minutes, the squeak of the handle was all that could be heard.

Then the shooting started. In all three of the buildings where the defenders had taken shelter, the Indian's gunfire was returned. Often, the loud roar of a buffalo rifle could be heard, and in every instance, another Indian was knocked off his horse.

The Indians made no effort to return fire, choosing instead to shoot at the old man who stood, unflinching, as he pumped water. The only time he stopped pumping, or showed any reaction at all, was when his dog was hit. Bo gave one little yelp, then died.

When the bucket was filled, Keeler returned to Meyer's store, even as bullets continued to fly around him.

"That's the damndest thing I ever saw," Sam Smith said.

When, safely inside, Keeler set the bucket on the floor.

"I'd sure like to kill the Injun sumbitch that kilt my dog."

Bat got a cloth from Fred Leonard, wet it, and bathed Billy Tyler's face. Then dipping a cup into the water, he lifted Billy's head and gave him a drink.

"Thanks," Billy said. "That tasted mighty good."

Billy's head fell to one side, and though his eyes remained open, they quickly became opaque.

Very gently, Bat closed Billy's eyes, then he stood up and walked over to the window that faced the saloon. Opening it, he called out.

"Cade! Cade, can you hear me?"

"I hear you," Cade called back.

"Billy just died. I'm goin' to stay over here for a while."

BACK IN THE SALOON, Cade turned to the others. "I don't know if you heard Bat, just now, but Billy Tyler's dead."

"Too bad," Billy Dixon said.

"BLACK BUFFALO IS DEAD," Quanah said. "So is Straight Arrow, and Walks On The Ground."

"White Eagle told us that the white hunters would be asleep," Mean To His Horses said. "He does not speak the truth."

"Yes," Red Moon said. "You told us that the white hunter's bullets would not hurt us, but now many are dead."

"It is not my fault," White Eagle replied. "One of your people killed my sacred totem. It is through the skunk that I can make my medicine but now, the spirits are angry."

At that moment, White Eagle's horse fell to the ground, a big hole in its forehead.

White Eagle barely managed to leap from his horse before being trapped under it.

"How is this so?" Wild Horse asked. "How is it that the white hunters can kill a horse that they cannot see?"

"The whites have very strong medicine," White Eagle said. "They can shoot today, and kill you tomorrow."

"Is the medicine of the white hunters stronger than the medicine of White Eagle, who can go into the sky to speak with the spirits?" Mean To His Horses asked. "How can this be possible? Is White Eagle's medicine polecat medicine?"

CHAPTER 25

"ANDY, GET ME SOME MORE BULLETS," BILLY DIXON SAID AS HE killed another Indian.

"We're getting' awful low," Andy Johnson said. "James, where do I find some more?"

"I'm afraid when that case is gone, we're done," James Hanrahan said.

"Well, that can't be," Cade said. "There's been a lot of shooting going on, but didn't someone say we've got 15,000 rounds of ammunition in this place?"

"That's right," Hanrahan said, "but all that ammunition is at the two stores."

"Well, then, who's going with me to one of the stores?" Cade asked.

"You can't do that," Mike Welsh said. "We all saw what happened to Billy Tyler."

"And what do you think will happen to us when they find out we don't have bullets?" Billy Dixon said. "Come on, Cade, let's get over to Rath's."

"I'm goin', too," Hanrahan said. "Cade's right. We've got to have more ammunition."

"We'll try to keep 'em busy while you boys run like hell, but keep your heads down," Carlisle cautioned.

"That's something I don't think you have to tell any of us," Billy Dixon said as he stepped through the window.

After a brief sprint across the space between the two buildings, Cade, Dixon, and Hanrahan reached a side window at Rath's store.

"Hey, inside! Open up!" Cade shouted.

A moment later the shattered window was opened, and the three climbed through to the inside.

"Langton, we need more ammunition over there," Hanrahan said.

"What calibers?"

"Lots of .50 caliber, also some .44 for pistols, and some .44-40 for rifles."

"All right, I can fix you boys right up." Leonard began filling empty flour sacks with the ammunition.

At that moment, there was a lull in the shooting and Hanrahan ran back to the saloon with the ammunition. Seeing Sybil Olds and knowing what would happen to her if she was captured by the Indians, Cade and Billy opted to stay at Rath's since there were fewer shooters to protect the store. Also, this was where the most ammunition was.

Cade walked to the front of the store where Sybil and Bill Olds were standing side by side at one of the windows. Both held carbines.

"I'll bet you don't have any beignets today," Cade said.

"Cade McCall," Sybil said flashing him a big smile. "How I wish I was still at the Red House. If we get through this, I'm heading right back to Dodge, and I'll open a shop that only serves beignets."

"You can't take her away from us," Tom O'Keefe said. "She's workin' just as hard as we are."

"Can she shoot?" Cade asked.

"Look out there," O'Keefe said, pointing. "You see those two dead Indians laying just this side of that little rise? She got both of 'em."

"That's pretty good shooting."

"Then that answers your question, doesn't it?"

Cade chuckled, and nodded. "I guess it does."

"And you're goin' to see me in action. Here they come again!" Sybil shouted as she raised her rifle.

The intense shooting in the building caused a buildup of gun smoke that burned the eyes, and choked the nostrils. Cade glanced at Sybil and saw that tears were streaming down her face, but she continued to fire.

The attacking Indians swept across the meadow, and though they no longer had a bugler to play the call for attack, they kept their battlefield integrity just as if it were a company front attack of the U.S. Cavalry.

Indian bullets crashed through the windows, breaking what little glass remained, but not one of the rounds fired by the Indians found a victim. The whites were more effective with their fire, however, and when the Indians broke off the attack and retreated from the field they left still more of their number dead or dying on the ground behind them.

WHEN THE ATTACKERS reached the hill that was far enough away from the buildings to be safe, Black Bird of the Cheyenne spoke.

"Quanah, we are running out of bullets. If we attack again, we will have to use our arrows."

"White Eagle," Mean To His Horses called.

Because White Eagle was shorter and fatter than all the others, he was never an imposing figure. He looked even more pathetic now, a totally naked man, his entire body painted a bright yellow, staring at his dead horse as if not comprehending the situation.

"White Eagle," Mean To His Horses repeated. "You say you can cough up bullets, and many say they have seen you do it. Now is the time. We need more bullets."

"I cannot," White Eagle said.

"But you must! We need bullets now."

White Eagle shook his head. "My magic has been broken."

"If White Eagle cannot cough up bullets, we will take the white hunters bullets. They have many in their houses," Red Moon said.

"I do not think we can kill them all," Black Bird said. "I think if we try to take their bullets, they will kill all of us."

"White Eagle has promised us victory. We cannot stop now," Wolf Tongue said.

"White Eagle said that he could cough up bullets, but he cannot," Black Bird said. "White Eagle told us that the white man's bullets cannot hurt us, but many lie dead on the ground, and if we attack again, many more will die."

Mean To His Horses walked over to White Eagle. He spat upon him and hit him with his quirt.

"No longer will you be called White Eagle," Mean To His Horses said. "You do not deserve such a noble name. From now and forever you will be called Isatai, because that is what you are."

"Isatai?" one of the other Indians said, and several began to laugh. "Yes, Wolf Shit is a good name for a medicine man who has no medicine."

The word spread quickly that White Eagle was now called Isatai, and the humiliated medicine man, slunk away from the battle.

AFTER THE DISGRACED White Eagle was gone, Quanah attempted to rally the spirit of the warriors.

"If cowards do not choose to run away, we will defeat the white men. I will lead another attack. The brave will come with me, the cowards will stay behind."

"I will count coup!" Black Bird shouted and, slapping his legs against the side of his horse, he charged out alone toward the adobe buildings.

"See the son of Spotted Wolf!" Quanah said. "By his bravery we will win this battle!"

"LOOK AT THAT FOOL INDIAN!" Bill Olds said. "What does he think he's doing, coming all by himself?"

"He's giving medicine to the others," Old Man Keeler said. "If he gets all the way here then back, we'll be fighting Injuns for a month o' Sundays."

"Then we'd better not let him do that," Cade said as he raised his rifle, sighted, and fired.

The lance the Indian was carrying that he intended to use to count coup, fell and stuck into the ground, its decorative feathers fluttering in the wind. The pony continued forward with the Indian still on its back, but no other shot was needed, for Cade realized the wound was fatal. The body fell not ten feet from the building.

Then, with a shock of recognition, Cade realized the Indian he had just killed was Black Bird, son of Spotted Wolf and uncle of Stone Forehead! And the horse he was riding, for a short while following the game of hands, had belonged to Cade. Even though he had killed many Indians on this day, the death of Black Bird, suddenly made him nauseous.

BY LATE AFTERNOON, the shooting by the Indians was not as

intense as it had been, and the defenders were able to go outside and walk around without drawing fire from the Indians.

"We need to bury our dead," Hanrahan said after finding the Shadler brothers bodies still in their wagon.

"Poor Buster," Cade said as he picked up the faithful dog. "He was protecting Ike and Shorty till the end."

Bat Masterson was first to take up a shovel and began to open a grave. Then another man would take the shovel, and then another, and in a short time they had a common grave for the three dead men and the two dead dogs, Buster and Old Man Keeler's dog, Bo. Wrapping Ike and Shorty and Billy each in a blanket, they lowered them into the grave. The two dogs were each put in a flour sack.

"Anybody know any words that can be said?" Hanrahan asked. "If you do, say 'em fast. I don't really feel all that good 'bout just standin' out here in the wide open like this."

"I was a preacher man once," Old Sam Smith said.

"Fine. You go ahead 'n say a few words then, but if you start in a' preachin' a sermon, you'll be preachin' to your ownself," Hanrahan cautioned.

"Ever' body bow your heads real respectful," Smith said. "Lord, you know a lot more about what kind of lives these three men lived than any of the rest of us do. Could be, in their time, they were sinnin' men. But in the time that I've know'd 'em, I ain't never heard nobody say nothin' bad about 'em. They treated ever' one honest 'n decent, 'n now they lie here, kilt by Godless heathens. And so, we're askin' that you take 'em into your bosom. Amen."

"Well, that was real good, Preacher Smith. Now lets get 'em covered up 'n back inside before the injuns starts in a' shootin' again," Welch said.

Everyone had come out for the impromptu funeral and they took a few minutes to compare notes. Then as the sun dropped below the western horizon, they all returned to their relative defensive positions.

Once back inside they prepared to spend the night. They were reasonably certain that the Indians would not attack at night, but they left a sentry in each building, the guards rotating so that all could get some rest.

Just on the other side of the open meadow, there could be hundreds of Indians waiting for dawn, so they could attack again. Cade wondered what was going to happen, and his concern wasn't just about tomorrow.

THERE WERE no Indian attacks on the second day, nor the next, but the Indians were still there. The men could see them riding back and forth, never approaching the buildings and always staying just out of range of the big .50's.

Because the Indians were no longer attacking, the defenders felt safe in leaving the buildings. Many picked up trinkets off the dead Indian bodies.

Around Black Bird's neck, Cade saw a medallion similar to the one Gentle Horse had given him to give to Spotted Wolf. Cade reached for it, intending to return it to Spotted Wolf, but what would he say?

I am the man who killed your son.

But Black Bird was Stone's uncle. Cade cut the rawhide cord that held the medallion. It had an etching of a wolf, just as had the one that had belonged to Gentle Horse, but this one did not have the turquoise stones. Cade slipped it into his pocket. Someday Stone would want to know about his people and Cade would give this to him.

Cade pulled Black Bird's body down by the river. Several of the other hunters were desecrating some of the bodies of the Indians. They said this was in retaliation for what they had seen Indians do to white men, including the Shadler brothers, but Cade did not want that to happen to Black Bird. If the Indians across the river saw him, he hoped they would come to get the body and handle his remains in the Indian tradition. That was the least he could do for Stone Forehead.

When he walked back to the compound, Billy was standing there watching him.

"Why did you do that?"

"That one bothered me," Cade said. "I knew him."

"That's not good. Come on, James has opened the few whiskey bottles that weren't hit."

"After this day, we all could use a stiff drink."

"THERE'S something else we need to address besides food and water," Bat Masterson said.

"Oh? And just what could be more important than food and water?" Fred Leonard asked.

"The stink," Bat said. "It's enough to gag us. There are dead animals everywhere you look, and they're beginning to get ripe."

"Don't forget all the dead Indians they ain't come to get yet," James McKinley said, "and I don't think they's a gonna get 'em."

"I ain't a diggin' no grave for a stinkin' Indian," Bermuda Carlisle said.

"I don't intend for us to bury them," Bat said, "but we need to move them."

"And how the hell are we gonna do that?" Mike Welch asked. "We ain't got no horses, that's for damned sure."

"May I offer a possible remedy to that problem?" Armitage asked.

"If you have an idea let's hear it," Cade said.

"When I fought in India, I saw the Shudra moving

deceased water buffalo using nothing but skins and ropes. We have the hides and the ropes readily available, and I'm certain we can provide enough muscle to get the job done."

"Sometime you Brits come up with a good idea," Langton said. "Let's get started."

SOON THEY HAD some of the largest hides selected; then they attached ropes to them. Working together, they rolled the animal carcasses onto the hides, then dragged them as far away from the buildings as they could. For those that had been killed in the stockade, several men dug a long trench and the animals were rolled into it and then covered with dirt.

When they were finished with the animals they drug 13 Indian bodies down by the river and deposited under a chinaberry tree.

"Now if anybody comes to get 'em, we'll just plug 'em where they stand, and we won't have to drag the dead bodies away," Carlisle said.

"You know them bastards have been watchin' ever move we made," Billy Ogg said. "I'm so tired, I don't care if they kill us or not."

"I wouldn't say that if I were you," Cade said. "How many buffalo hunters do we know?"

"A lot," Ogg said.

"And with the storekeepers included, there were only 28 of us here. Now, what do you think has happened to all those others who didn't come in to the Walls?"

"Probably dead." Ogg lowered his head.

"Well maybe not," Tom O'Keefe said. "Lookie what's coming across the river."

Everybody looked toward the river and they saw two wagons coming toward them. A loud cheer went up.

"It's people!" Fred Leonard yelled as he threw his hat into the air.

"Yes, but more importantly, its horses," Bat Masterson said.

The wagons belonged to a big German named George Bellfield, who barely spoke English. But he could see the results of the battle. With much gesturing, and using the few words he knew, he was able to tell them he had come up from the south and that he had not run into any Indians.

Very soon after Bellfield's arrival, Jim and Bob Cator, two brothers from England, came in from their camp that was north of Adobe Walls. They, too, reported that they had not seen any Indians.

With these two reports, the hunters were encouraged that perhaps others were still in their camps. A skinner for the Cator brothers, decided to ride to as many camps as he could find and spread the word as to what had happened at the Walls.

The mood of the settlement was immediately uplifted, especially when throughout the afternoon, more and more wagons rolled in. Even though the Indians were still within sight, with the additional men in camp, and with their horses, there was a euphoric release of tension.

There were about 20 Indians congregated on the bluff, but none had attempted to come forward again, not even to claim their dead.

"Cade, how far away would you say those Indians are?" Billy Dixon asked.

"I don't know, but if I had to guess, I'd say it's close to a mile," Cade said.

"Do you think we could hit one of 'em?"

Cade laughed. "If one of us did, it would sure scare the hell out of 'em."

"And if we only came close, it would still ruffle their

feathers," Billy said.

"All right. Why not?"

QUANAH, Mean To His Horses, Wild Horse, Red Moon, He Bear, and another dozen Indians sat on their horses observing what was going on at the settlement.

"More and more white hunters are coming," He Bear said. "Soon there will be as many whites as we have warriors."

"And they have more bullets than there are stars in the sky," Wild Horse said.

"If Woman's Heart had not taken the Kiowa away, we would be putting the white man's food in our bellies and putting their bullets in our guns," Mean To His Horses said.

"We should attack again," Wild Horse said.

Quanah shook his head. "It is not to be. Look around, now we are few, and we have no bullets."

"Perhaps it is you who should have stayed with the women and children," Mean To His Horses suggested with a sneer. "I am a man of great courage. If it had been I who led this attack, every white hunter would be dead, and the buffalo would roam the plains again."

"Your words are not from courage, but from foolishness," Quanah said.

"I say we should take up the knife," Mean To His Horses said. "Then we will see who has the courage."

Quanah was not watching Mean To His Horses as he spoke. Instead, Quanah's eyes were fixed upon the building in the middle; the building which he knew had the largest number of defenders. And as he watched, he saw two puffs of smoke, as two guns were fired.

"We will fight, and the winner shall be the new . . . uh. . ." Mean To His Horses grunted.

Quanah heard the two low, heavy thumps that had come

from the big guns.

Quanah looked over quickly and saw that both Mean To His Horses, and Wild Horse were on the ground. Both had huge, bleeding holes in their bodies; Mean To His Horses had been hit in the stomach and Wild Horse had been hit in the chest. The rest of the group scurried to take cover on the other side of the butte.

"The white man's guns can bounce off the rocks and hit Quanah in the back and now they kill Mean To His Horses and Wild Horse from a place our eyes cannot see. If they can kill from that far, we cannot defeat them," Red Moon said. "The war is over, and we are going back to our women and children."

Quanah did not try to stop Red Moon, as he rode down to join the Cheyenne who were awaiting his instructions. Quanah watched as the band turned and headed for the Washita.

"What will we do now?" He Bear asked. "The Cheyenne and the Kiowa have deserted us."

"The People have lost many warriors, and my heart is heavy. Let us wrap Mean To His Horses and Wild Horse in their blankets and put them with the others who have joined the Great Spirits. When that is done, we will gather our wounded and go home."

"Isatai misled us," Silver Knife said, bitterly.

"No, I was the leader, not White Eagle," Quanah said, refusing to use the derisive name the others had given the medicine man. "It is I who misled you, and it is I who will lead The People to slaughter the white man. We may have lost this battle, but the war has just begun."

BY THE FIFTH day after the attack, the white hunters were no longer concerned that they would be overrun, but they weren't yet aware that the Indians had withdrawn. As a precaution, they had cut port holes in the walls and cutting a hole in the roof, they had erected sod lookout enclosures that could be accessed from the two stores. They kept a sentry posted on the roof at all times to keep watch.

"How long you been up there, Bill?" Tom O'Keefe called up to William Olds who was currently on guard.

"Oh, I don't know; a couple of hours I guess."

"Why don't you come on back down and I'll take a turn," O'Keefe said. "No sense getting' yourself all tired out and fallin' asleep up there. It don't seem all that likely to me that they's goin' to be any more of 'em comin' at us. Seems to me like them bastards pretty much learned their lesson."

"I reckon they have at that." Olds chuckled. "And Sybil done her part in sendin' some o' them heathens to hell."

Olds started down the ladder.

"That she did," Sam Smith said. "A woman who can shoot like that, you for sure don't want to make her mad."

The others laughed at Smith's comment, but their laughter was interrupted by the loud roar of a big .50.

Olds fell the rest of the way, landing face up on the floor beneath the ladder. The top of his head had been blown off, and the rifle that landed beside him, was still smoking.

"Bill!" Sybil shouted, rushing to her husband. She fell to her knees beside him, crying piteously.

Cade and the others stood by, watching helplessly as the widow grieved.

They buried Olds next to the other three men who had fallen, about sixty feet from where he had died.

OVER THE NEXT FEW DAYS, more and more hunters came in as the word was spread about the attack. By now there were more than 100 men gathered at the Walls.

"I don't understand why Charlie Myers hasn't come to see if we're still here," Fred Leonard said. "You'd think he'd want to check on his investment, even if he didn't care about us."

"Don't be so hard on Charlie," Billy Dixon said. "We don't even know if they got through or not."

"Since we have transportation now, I think several of us should load up and go back to Dodge ourselves," Cade said.

"I'm for that," Billy said. "About 25 men should go just in case the Indians attack us on the way, and of course Sybil should go."

"No," Sybil Olds said. "I'm not goin'. My husband lost his life here, tryin' to save this place, and I don't think he'd want me to just up and leave all that we worked for. I've got his big .50 and I can take care of myself."

"I'm not trying to meddle in your business," Bat Masterson said, "but I think you should go."

"Well, I'm not." Sybil walked out of the store and went out to Bill's grave. She sat down and wrapped her arms around her knees, and there she sat in the sun while the departing wagons were loaded.

As a precaution the three wagons, moved west away from the freight road. The thinking was that if the Indians were watching, they would more than likely think they would take the main route.

On the second day out, they made it to San Francisco Creek, where they knew a hunter called Dublin had a camp. When they got there, they found three dead bodies, all of whom had been scalped and mutilated. They buried them where they lay.

"A way of life is over," Billy Dixon said.

"You won't try to go back out?" Cade asked.

"No. I think I've killed my last buffalo."

Dodge City

One of the outlying buffalo hunters had ridden back to Dodge to spread the news about Adobe Walls, and when the wagons rolled in, there were many people in the streets cheering for them. Once they returned, they learned that about 50 townspeople had taken wagons to rescue them, but since they had stayed off the main route they had missed seeing them.

"You should have come back with me," Jacob Harrison said, as he took a seat at the Red House Salon.

"And miss all the excitement? No way," Cade said. "But I will say I sure am glad you got that big .50 for me."

"Is it true what they're saying? Did you and Billy really hit Indians a mile away?" Jeter Willis asked.

"I don't think it was a mile, but it was a long way." Cade said. "But I will say this. We didn't have one skirmish after those two shots were fired."

"You showed them that nobody can mess with a big .50," Jacob said. "Have you given any more thought to what you're going to do now that you're out of the freighting business?"

"I've thought about it, but I haven't come to any conclusion," Cade said.

"You can always come back to work at the Red House," Jeter said.

Cade shook his head. "I didn't work here when I owned half the place, so I don't see myself working here now. I may go to Tennessee."

"What? Why would you go there?" Jeter asked.

Cade contemplated the question. It had been nine years since last he had seen his brother. Initially he had stayed away because of Melinda, the girl he had planned to marry. He had been captured by the Yankees after the Battle of Franklin, and it had been reported that he was dead. When he returned home, he even found his marker in the family cemetery. And he found that Melinda had married his brother, Adam.

At first, Cade wanted nothing more than to be gone, to put that all behind him, but much had happened in the last nine years, and he realized that any residual pain or resentment was gone.

"I want to see my brother," Cade said, answering the question Jeter had asked several seconds earlier.

"Well, that's reason enough," Jeter said.

"What about you, Jacob? You're out of the freighting business, too, now that the Mooar brothers bought our wagons, and hired our people," Cade said.

"You're both going to be surprised when you find out what I want to do," Jacob said as a big smile crossed his face.

"All right, you have our attention. What is it?" Jeter asked.

"I'm going to Texas."

"Texas?" both Jeter and Cade asked together.

"Didn't Cade just get out of there with barely the skin on his back? And now you want to go again?" Jeter asked.

Jacob laughed. "I didn't say I wanted to go back to Adobe Walls. Texas is a big state."

"You're tellin' me," Jeter said. "I was born and raised there, but you won't get me to go back."

"You can't say that," Cade said. "Texas was good to us. You wouldn't have Magnolia if you hadn't been in Texas."

"Which, by the way, you haven't seen her yet," Jeter said.

"Well, you two run along," Jacob said. "I need to clear out my things from the office. You won't leave before I see you again, Cade."

"Oh no, it will be a few days before I go."

WHEN CADE and Jeter walked in the door, Magnolia let out a little squeal of joy and running to him threw her arms around him.

"Now that's a greeting a man could get used to, pretty lady," Cade said as he returned her hug. "There was a time there, when I didn't think I'd get back."

"Then don't ever leave again," Magnolia said as she kissed him on the cheek.

"It's too late," Jeter said. "He's already making plans to go off again."

"Oh?" Magnolia's eyebrows lifted. "And where would you be planning to go?"

"Tennessee. I want to go back and see my brother," Cade said, "and I think I'll take Stone with me."

"You'll take Stone?" Jeter questioned.

"Yes. I think he might enjoy a train ride."

Magnolia lowered her head. "Cade, there's more going on here than you know about. Jeter had to kill a man because of Stone."

"What? What happened?"

"You remember Kirk Jordan—the man who tried to get Spotted Wolf at the apothecary."

"Of course, I remember him."

"He organized a bunch of hoodlums and they tried to burn our house down," Jeter said.

"They wanted to hang a four-year old boy, whose only crime is that he is half Indian," Magnolia said, her eyes brimming with tears.

"Then for sure, I'm taking Stone back to Tennessee. Neither the girls nor Stone needs to put up with that again," Cade said.

CHAPTER 26

C<small>ADE AND</small> S<small>TONE STOOD ON THE DEPOT PLATFORM AT</small> D<small>ODGE</small> City waiting for the train, its whistle already announcing its arrival. Jeter, Magnolia and the two little girls were waiting with them.

"You are so lucky, Stone," Chantal said. "I've never ridden on a train."

"I haven't either, Bella said.

Chantal laughed. "You didn't have to say that. If I haven't ridden on a train that means you haven't, because we do everything together."

"Will the train fall over?" Stone asked.

"Fall over? No, I don't think so," Cade said. "The train will go very fast, as fast as the fastest horse. I think you'll like it."

"Here it is!" Chantal announced.

The train moved swiftly into the station, the big driver wheels pounding by with steam streaming around them. The engineer was leaning out the side window of the cab and when the children waved at him, he flashed a big grin and waved back at them.

The train stopped with a hiss of steam and the squeal of

231

steel on steel as the brake shoes clamped down onto the wheels. They waited as first the conductor, then the arriving passengers stepped down.

The conductor, looking very official in his dark blue uniform and the shiny brass shield, opened the cover to his watch, examined it importantly, then snapped the cover shut. After that, he walked up to the front of the train. The fireman had left the cab and climbed up onto the tender to pull a big spout down from the tank, so he could take on water.

"Bye, Daddy," Chantal said, holding up her arms. Cade lifted her, and gave her a hug, and because Bella held up her arms, he did the same thing with her.

"Bye, Stone, you be a good boy now," Magnolia said. She squatted down to kiss him, but Stone turned his head away.

Magnolia laughed. "You're going to have to learn to let people show you some affection," she said. "Someday, I'm sure you will."

Cade and Jeter shook hands. "I'm going to miss you, my brother," Jeter said. "And the money you gave us, I'm going to set that aside, so Chantal will get an education."

"It's for you, but you do with it whatever you want."

"Don't forget us," Magnolia said as she embraced him.

Cade smiled. "That's not going to happen."

"I hate it that you're going so far away." A tear ran down Magnolia's cheek.

"Don't do that," Cade said as he wiped her tear away with his finger. "It's hard enough to leave as it is"

"Then don't do it!"

"Board!" the conductor shouted.

"That's us, Stone. We have to go."

STONE HELD BACK until Cade reached out to take his hand.

Although he was initially hesitant, Cade was glad to see that the boy climbed onto the train.

They took a seat half way down on the side of the car that faced the depot. When they were situated, Cade saw that the two girls had come up to wave at them, and call goodbye.

Stone returned the waves, but he didn't call back to them.

A few moments after they boarded, the train began to move. There were a few jerks as the slack was taken up between the cars before settling into a smooth acceleration. Cade saw that Stone was holding tightly onto the window, but if he was frightened, he didn't say anything. But by the end of the day, Stone seemed to be enjoying his ride on the train.

Stone went to sleep quickly, but sleep eluded Cade. He would be seeing Melinda for the first time in nine years, and he was wondering how she would react. But the real question was, how would he react?

He thought of the last time he had seen her as a single woman, when she had been the woman he was going to marry.

The moon, reflecting on the surface of the Cumberland River, sent forth little slivers of silver, to compete with the golden flashes of hundreds of fire flies. Cade and Melinda were sitting on a blanket that had been spread out on the bank of the river.

"Papa said he would help us buy some of Mr. Byrd's land," *Melinda said.*

Cade picked up a rock and tossed it into the river. The concentric circles working out from the rock disturbed the moon silver. He didn't answer Melinda's comment.

"I know, I know, you're too proud to accept anything from papa, but remember, it'll be my farm too. I mean, if we are husband and wife, won't it?"

"Melinda, maybe we should wait," Cade finally said.

"Wait? What do you mean, wait? Wait for what?"

"There's a war on."

"I know there's a war on, but what does that have to do with us?"

"It has everything to do with us, Melinda." He pointed to the river. "Right now, the Yankees control this river. Why, they could put a gunboat right out there and start shelling Clarksville, and there wouldn't be anything we could do about it.

"It's up to us. I can't just sit by and let the Yankees take over everything I've ever known . . . everything I've ever loved."

"I thought you loved me."

"I do. When I said, everything I've ever loved, I'm talking about you."

"So, what you are saying is, you don't want to marry me."

"Yes, I do want to marry you, more than anything in the world. But Melinda, I can't do it now. I can't go off to war and leave a wife behind me. Why, there'd only be half of me, and half of you. If you love me, you will wait for me. We'll get married when the war is over, and I've come back home. Cade smiled, then put his finger under her chin. "Why, I'll even let your papa help us out in buying the farm."

THE TRAIN WHISTLE interrupted Cade's musings about the past, and he began thinking of his future. Did he really want to be back in Tennessee? He guessed he would take up farming, but would Adam want him around either Melinda or the farm?

Late the next afternoon, Stone was sitting next to the window, looking at the countryside as it passed by. For the entire trip his conversation had been limited only to when communication was required. He asked to go to the toilet, he asked when they were going to eat, and he asked where he was to sleep. But other than that, he said very little.

"WE'RE ALMOST THERE," Cade said when the train left Memphis.

"Cade, am I going to stay here?" Stone asked.

"I think so," Cade said, pleased to answer his question.

"Will people like me in Tennessee?"

Cade pulled the boy close to him. "Of course, they're going to like you. Everybody likes good little boys like you are."

"Then why did they try to burn our house down?"

"Stone, that man was a very mean man. That's not going to happen in Tennessee."

"Do the people in Tennessee like Indians?"

"Of course, they do, but you know what? You're a very special person. You have one foot in the Indian world and one foot in the white man's world. You can be either one, but it's better if you're both, because then you can have all the good things about being an Indian and all the good things about being a white man."

Stone smiled. "All right. When I am in Tennessee, I will be white, and when I am in Kansas, I will be Indian."

THE TRAIN SLOWED as it approached Clarksville, and Cade gathered up the few things he had brought with them. The telegram he had sent Adam had been vague about the nature of this trip, and he had not mentioned that he was bringing Stone. He hoped that what he had told Stone about Indians being liked in Tennessee would be true.

ANY QUESTION as to whether his brother had received the telegram was answered when the train pulled into the station in Clarksville, Tennessee. The man standing on the depot platform was a little older and perhaps a little heavier than

Cade remembered but it was clearly Adam McCall. There were also three children standing with him—two boys and a girl.

The exchange of letters between the two brothers had been so infrequent over the years that Cade was surprised to see the children. He knew about two of them; he was unaware that there was a third.

When the train came to a full stop, Cade stood up, stepped out into the aisle and invited Stone to come, too. They had changed trains a few times on the trip, and had detrained even more times, so Stone was familiar with the procedure. Cade mentioned nothing to Stone about his brother waiting for them until they were on the platform. Then it was Adam who spoke first.

"Cade! Over here!" Adam called, raising his hand, though the signal wasn't necessary.

"Come, Stone. I want you to meet my brother," Cade said.

When they reach the small group, Cade and Adam shook hands, heartily.

"I can't tell you how happy Mellie and I were to get your telegram saying that you were coming for a visit," Adam said.

"Mellie?"

Adam chuckled. "That's what I've been calling Melinda for some time now. I don't think she liked it that much when I first started, but she's come around to it."

"Daddy, is this Uncle Cade?" the oldest boy asked pulling on Adam's shirt.

"It sure is, CG," Adam replied. "Cade, meet your nephews, this is Cade Gordon, we call him CG. He's eight."

"Going on nine," CG said, quickly, extending his hand. "Daddy says I'm named after you."

"So you are," Cade replied. Smiling, he accepted the proffered handshake.

"It's supposed to be ladies first," the little girl said.

Adam chuckled. "Oh, and you think you're a lady, do you?"

"I'm a girl, and girls grow up to be ladies."

"Well, you're right about that," Adam replied. "This is your niece, Margaret Ann. She's named for Mama, and she's six."

Margaret curtsied, and Adam dipped his head.

"And this is James Lee. He's five."

"So, you have three, do you? I should've known that, I'm sure we've communicated at least once or twice in the last five years."

Adam laughed. "I have four. Susanna Marie is only three years old, so I left her at home with Mellie. Oh, and I might as well tell you now, you'll find out soon enough, Mellie is pregnant, so we're soon to have five."

"That's, uh, quite a family you've got," Cade said.

"Yes, it is," Adam said with a happy smile. He looked at Stone, who had been following it all with a face devoid of all expression.

"And who is this little fellow with you?" Adam asked.

"This is Stone Forehead."

The smile on Adam's face was replaced by an expression of curious surprise.

"Stone Forehead? Why does he have such a name?" Then Adam's expression changed. "Oh, he's . . ." Adam stopped in mid-sentence.

"You can say it. He's half Indian."

"Is he your child?"

"Yes, he is, but we can discuss his genealogy later. I'm sure Melinda is at home, wondering about us."

"Yes, I'm sure she is."

"You're Jimmy Lee," Stone said, extending his hand. "I'm four but I think I'm about to be five."

Jimmy Lee extended his hand. "Are you really a Indian?"

"I am white, and I am Indian," Stone said.

"How can you be white and Indian?" CG asked.

"I don't know," Stone replied.

"Why don't you quit your pestering and let's go climb into the wagon?" Adam said.

The four youngsters rode in the back of the wagon and Cade was glad to hear that, very quickly, they were laughing with each other.

"They seem to be getting along well," Cade said.

"Yes, the kids are just real good about making new friends."

CHAPTER 27

THE McCALL FARM WAS LAID OUT ALONG THE EAST BANK OF the Cumberland River, about four miles southwest of Clarksville. As they turned onto the road that let up to the farm, Cade saw a side road that he didn't remember. There was an arched sign over the side road that read: "Decker Farm".

"Julius?" Cade asked, referring to the man who used to work for the McCalls.

"Forty acres," Adam said. "He's buying it himself."

"So, the farm is down to, what, 160 acres?"

Adam smiled. "Nope, now it's 310 acres. I bought 150 acres from Mr. Byrd. It's the same land you thought about buying, remember?"

"Yes, I remember," Cade said. "I thought Lloyd Botkins owned that land."

"Ha! Botkins went bankrupt and went back north. Almost all his land went into foreclosure, so Byrd got his land back. He sold it to me for a real good price."

When the wagon rolled into the old homestead they were met by a little girl.

"Daddy, did you bring me something?" she asked.

"I brought you a licorice whip," Adam said pulling the piece of candy out of a paper bag. "Susanna, this is your Uncle Cade."

"Hello," the little girl said, speaking around the licorice stick that was in her mouth.

Margaret introduced Stone, then the five children wandered away. Cade looked around the old homestead where he had been raised. He saw that the house had been enlarged, almost to double its original size, and the small house that had once belonged to Julius and Effy Decker was gone. The barn was brand new, and Cade commented on it.

"Yes, the old one burned down a couple of years ago. Fortunately, none of the animals were killed. Come on in, I know Mellie's anxious to see you."

"I'll be in, in a minute," Cade said. "I want to make a visit over here."

"Oh, yes, sure. All right, take your time. I'll take your things in and get you and the boy settled. What did you say his name was?"

"It's Stone. Stone McCall." That was the first time he had called him that and Cade liked the sound of it. He was beginning to think he had done the right thing in coming home, for both himself and for Stone.

CADE WALKED over to a large magnolia tree that stood by the little family burial plot. All four of his grandparents were buried there, as was Hazel, the sister Cade had never known. She was the first born, but she had died when she was two years old, six months before Cade had been born.

He examined the graves of his mother and father. He had been gone when both of them died. Cade ran his finger over the engraving on his mother's headstone.

Margaret Edith McCall
Born Williamsburg, Virginia, March 28, 1809
Died October 7, 1873

He was shocked to see that it had been less than a year since his mother had died, and that he hadn't been told when it happened.

"I'm sorry I didn't get back to see you, Ma," Cade said quietly.

But had he come, she wouldn't have recognized him. The war had been hard on her, what with being told her son had died, and then having her husband fall from the loft and break his neck. It was no wonder she lost her senses.

He moved to his father's grave and bent down to pull some weeds that were covering the inscription.

James McCall
Born Kirkcaldy, Scotland, August 5th, 1805
Died March 10, 1865

"Pa, I reckon that since ma's with you, you'll take care of her and she won't have to be confused anymore. It gives me comfort to know the two of you are together again."

The last time he had been here there had been another tombstone, and he saw it lying face down smothered in the fallen magnolia leaves. He waded in under the tree and turned it over.

In Memory of
Cade McCall
Sergeant, 33rd Tennessee
Born 22 November 1843
Killed in Battle, 30 November, 1864

This tombstone had been erected even though there had been no body, but everyone was convinced he had died. Cade put the stone back where it had been and got out from under the sprawling branches of the huge tree.

In effect, the headstone wasn't all that wrong. The Cade McCall who had lived the first 21 years of his life, was gone. The Cade McCall who lived now had started an entire new existence the day he left Clarksville.

"Cade?"

It was a woman's voice, a very familiar voice. Cade turned and saw Melinda standing there. Even though Adam had mentioned she was pregnant, it was a surprise to see her so pregnant.

"We all are so happy you came to see us," she said with a lilting southern accent.

"I shouldn't have stayed away so long, but first one thing and then another seemed to get in the way."

As Cade looked at her, it was as if he was greeting an old friend from long ago, not the woman he had once thought he loved. He was surprised that there were no residual feelings at all, and he almost felt guilty for not having any lingering sentiment.

"We got your letter about your wife," Melinda said. "I'm sorry she never got to meet your family."

Cade nodded his head. He didn't want to talk about Arabella, especially what she had gone through at the end of her life, and for a moment there was an awkward silence.

"I fixed chicken and dumplin's," Melinda said. "Effy told me that was your favorite when you were a little boy."

"It was, and I'm pleased that you went to the effort to make them when you are . . ."

"So big?" Melinda finished the thought. She laughed nervously.

"Yes, but I know you are proud of your children."

"They do bring Adam and me a lot of pleasure."

"You mentioned Effy," Cade said changing the subject. "Adam said that she and Julius have their own farm now."

"Oh yes, you should see how proud Julius looks when the county has a meeting of all the land holders. But you can see for yourself, because they're up at the house right now. There's no way we could keep them from seeing you when they heard you were coming home."

AFTER SUPPER that evening Cade pushed back the plate that had twice been filled with chicken and dumplings, and looked at the old black woman who had been a part of his family for as long as he could remember.

"Effie, Melinda told me she cooked these dumplin's, but there's no way I believe her. These are yours."

Effie laughed. "La'wd, child, you just paid me a big compliment 'n you don't even know it. It was me that taught that girl how to make 'em, 'n you thinkin' it was me that cooked 'em means I done a real good job of teachin'. Yes, sir, Miz Mellie, she done them dumplin's all by her ownself."

"Well, Melinda, you had a good teacher, because these were exceptional."

"I'm goin' to learn how to make 'em too," Margaret said. "Maybe next time you come you'll eat my dumplin's."

"I don't want to eat your dumplin's," CG said. "They'd be awful."

"Well, I'll be proud to eat them," Cade said.

LATER THAT NIGHT Cade sat out on the front porch, listening to the night concert provided by the crickets and the frogs.

"You were going to tell me about the boy," Adam said.

Cade told the story of finding Stone in a whiskey camp

run by two white scoundrels who were not only selling whiskey illegally to the Indians, but were also keeping some Indian women as their slaves.

"As it turns out Stone's mother was the daughter of Spotted Wolf, a chief of the Cheyenne," Cade said, and he proceeded to explain how Stone had been a 'gift he couldn't refuse.'

"But he seems to be a real good boy, and he's remarkably resilient, and adjusts quickly and to conditions." Cade continued. "He's been staying with Jeter Willis—you remember him; we were in the war together, and he got along really well with Jeter's girls."

Jeter's girls. Cade couldn't believe that was how he thought about Chantal, but she was in every way Jeter's daughter. And if he stayed in Tennessee, would it be nine years before he saw her again?

"So, what you're saying is the boy will be all right living here? He won't get homesick?" Adam asked.

"Homesick for what? So far, he's never actually known a home. I plan to give him one here."

"I think CG and Jimmy have already made friends with him," Adam said. "I think he'll get along fine."

"I hope that's true."

"Tomorrow, if you would like, I'll hitch up the buckboard and we can drive over to see Chris Dumey."

"Mr. Dumey's still around? Damn, how old is he now?"

"I think he's coming up on eighty or so. Anyway, he has two hundred acres of good bottom land that butts up against our farm. We can buy that land, and that'll give us 510 acres. That'll be plenty big enough to support two families."

"Two families?"

"Yes, Me, Mellie, and our kids, and you and Stone." Adam smiled. "And don't think there aren't enough women around here for you to find a wife. Why, Mellie 'n some of her friends will make that their special project."

"Uh, yes, well, tell them not work too hard on that," Cade said. "I'd like to at least get settled in."

"All right, you'll have plenty of time. Like I said, there are quite a few good women around here for you to choose from. Lots of young widows who lost their husbands in the war." Adam stood up, stretched, and yawned. "One thing you're going to have to learn again, in case you've forgotten. Farming means you get up early and you go to bed early, so if you don't mind, I'll be turning in, now."

"No, go ahead, I think I'll just sit out here a while longer."

After his brother left, Cade stayed out on the porch. Whippoorwills and an owl added their night calls to that of the crickets and frogs.

This was all so familiar to him, but it was like a dim memory. Could he actually come home again?

And then the next question was, is this his home?

CHAPTER 28

CHRIS DUMEY WAS A BIG MAN, AT LEAST AS TALL AS CADE, BUT without doubt, he was sixty pounds heavier. What hair he had remaining was snow white, and it stood out like little puffs over his ears. He had offered his visitors coffee and now the three of them were sitting in his parlor.

Mrs. Dumey had greeted them when they arrived, and had been the one who served the coffee, but as the men were discussing business, she kept herself busy elsewhere in the house.

"I got two hunnert acres of some of the best bottom land in Tennessee," Dumey said, "which I don't have to tell you boys nothin' about it, on account of you got land that's just as good, seein' as my property bumps into the McCall farm. Didn't always, used to be that way, seein' as the Byrd farm used to stand twixt the two farms, but since you bought the Byrd land well, now, the two of us bump into each other."

"It is good land, Mr. Dumey," Adam said agreeing with the old man. "But I must say, I'm surprised you're letting it go."

"I'm a' sellin' 'cause I'm getting too old to work it no more. But I ain't a' sellin' all of it. I'm keepin' the home place 'n the acre of land it's settin' on, so's me 'n Ethyl has us a place to live out the rest of our years. They'll be enough room for a garden, 'n for Ethyl to keep flowers and such in the yard.

"But, they's a nice little thicket o' trees on the land I'm sellin' where a feller could build hisself a right nice house 'n be in the shade in the summer, 'n protected from the cold wind in the winter."

"I know just the spot you're talking about," Adam said, "but the question is, how much are you asking?"

"I had Ethel cipher it out for me, she bein' good at that sort of thing. I figure on gettin' twenty-two dollars 'n acre, 'n that'll come to forty-four hunnert dollars."

"That's pretty steep," Adam said. "You know I bought the Byrd land for eighteen dollars an acre. And I sold Julius Decker his farm at twelve dollars an acre."

"Yes, sir, that may be. But we all know Byrd had been wantin' to sell that land for nigh on to 20 years now 'n was more 'n likely glad to get rid of it. And you can't count what you sold that land to Julius for, seein' as how he worked for you 'n you pappy, from the time he was a real young man. Why, he's most earned it just from that."

"I can't argue with that," Adam agreed. "I tell you what, Mr. Dumey, Cade and I'll talk about it, and we'll get back to you."

"Yes, sir, but don't you be waitin' too long. I've got two, maybe three others a' lookin' at it, so's I don't 'spect it to be for sale much longer."

"I'll let you know very soon whether or not I want to make an offer," Adam said.

THAT AFTERNOON CADE followed Adam through the fields. Adam was raising cotton, corn, and wheat.

"I've been thinking about putting in some tobacco," Adam said. "But I'm havin' to pay to get my cotton chopped and of course, picked. I could do a lot of the work myself for the tobacco, and the boys are getting' old enough to prime it so I wouldn't have to pay for that. I'll bet your little Stone would have a lot of fun crawling through those rows pulling off the bottom leaves. You know if you do that, it makes a better crop."

Cade nodded, only half listening to Adam. Everything Adam was saying was so foreign to him, even though Cade could remember walking behind a mule as he plowed the fields or picked the cotton or dug the potatoes. The thing he remembered most about farming was that it was hard work for not a lot of money.

But on the good side, it would be rare to ever have someone shooting at him.

After supper that evening, while the kids were out in the yard playing some sort of game which was totally inclusive of Stone, Cade and Adam were, once again, sitting on the porch. The only difference between now and last night, was that Melinda was sitting with them.

"Truth is, I know for a fact that if we made Dumey an offer of eighteen dollars an acre, he would jump on it," Adam said. "The best offer he's had so far has been from Burt Marshal, and that was for seventeen dollars an acre."

Cade nodded, but he didn't say anything.

"Thirty-six hundred dollars," Adam said.

A spontaneous laughter from the kids interrupted the flow of conversation.

Adam turned toward Melinda. "Hand it to me, Melinda."

Melinda pulled a piece of paper from the folds of her dress and gave it to Adam.

"I want to read something to you, Cade," Adam said. He cleared his throat, and began to read aloud.

"Dear Adam, you probably won't hear from me for a while, I feel the need to travel for a bit. Here is a bank draft for $3,500. I got very generous terms for the loan, which I will be able to handle myself, so there is no need for you to pay it back. This is my wedding gift for you and Melinda. Sincerely, Your brother, Cade"

Adam looked over to Cade. "Do you remember sending me that letter?"

"I remember."

"What I'm getting at, Cade, is I'll pay the $3,600, and I'll also help you put up a house. I owe that to you." He reached over and took Melinda's hand. "Hell, I owe you more than that."

"If you'll read the letter again, I said there would be no need for you to pay me back. I also said that it was a wedding present."

"All right, then don't consider this as a pay back. Consider this as me doing something for you when you need it, the way you did for me, when I needed it."

Cade was silent for a long moment. He had not told Adam that he had his half of the money he and Jacob got for selling the freighting company. He could buy the Dumey property straight out, without having to get a loan from anybody if he wanted to do it.

"Adam, I hate to say this, but I don't want to stay here, and I don't want to be a farmer. I got a taste of the West this last nine, coming up on ten years, and I like it. I thought I could come back here and make a new life for myself, but I just don't think that I can."

"You want to go back," Adam said. It wasn't a question, it was an acknowledging statement.

"Yes, I do."

Adam nodded. "I sort of had a feeling that might be the case. The way you were acting over at Dumey's place, you didn't say a word while we were there, and you haven't said anything about it since we got back either."

"I feel bad for Mr. Dumey, though. I know he's looking to sell the place and retire," Cade said.

"Don't worry about it. I was planning on buying his place anyway. Then, when we got your telegram, I just thought it might fit in well with you coming back home."

"What about Stone?" Melinda asked.

Cade sighed. "The truth is I don't have any idea what I'm going to do with him. One bad thing about the West is that people don't look too kindly on Indians. And when that Indian is a 'breed' that makes it even worse."

"Then leave him here," Adam said.

"I couldn't do that. You have four children already and another one on the way."

"Are you saying that you don't think we could handle another child?" Melinda asked. She laughed. "I'm sure Adam won't stop at five or six, or even seven or who knows how many kids we'll have."

Adam chuckled. "You might say we're raising our own hired hands. You don't know how much tobacco I can plant when they all get bigger."

"You can't take him with you, Cade. He's been through so much and you can't pull him around from pillar to post. Now you tell me what kind of life that would be for the little fellow?" Melinda pointed to the children who were playing hide and seek in the shadows of the evening. "Look at those little ones. Stone is already one of them."

"Mellie and I talked about this," Adam said. "I want you to understand, we're not telling you we're *willing* to raise him, we're telling you we *want* to raise him."

Again, Cade was silent. He had given Chantal's guardianship to Jeter and Magnolia, and now he was about to give up Stone. With Chantal, he could truthfully say it was better for her to have a mother and a father, and if he was honest, it would be better for Stone to stay here.

His only problem was his own conscience. Was he destined never to take the responsibility for any child?

"All right," he said. "If you're certain this is what you want to do, but I want to go to the magistrate and have him officially adopted. He needs to know that he belongs here."

A huge smile spread across Melinda's face. "I agree."

BY THE END OF JULY, Cade was back in Dodge City and he headed for Jeter and Magnolia's house. When the door opened, Magnolia squealed in delight.

"You're back!"

"Surprised to see me?" Cade asked.

"Surprised?" Jeter said. "Not surprised, happy. Oh, and a little bit richer."

"Richer? What do you mean, richer?"

"I have two to one odds that you'd be back by the end of the month. And let's see, by my calculations I just won $1,207.00."

"You bet I'd be back within a month? Damn, wasn't that taking quite a chance? What if I'd decided to stay and try it out for a while?"

Jeter shook his head. "I know you better than you know yourself. I said you'd be here within a month and here you are back, with almost four days to spare."

"I don't suppose Jacob's still in town. I need to figure out what I'm going to do, and I thought maybe I'd head down to Texas with him."

"He's gone, but your friend, Billy Dixon was in the saloon the other day."

"Salon," Magnolia corrected.

"All right, salon. But, you might look him up. He's got a new job and it might be something you'd be interested in."

Cade shook his head. "He's not out hunting buffalo is he? He said he'd killed his last one."

"No, he's not hunting buffalo, but he'll probably be back down along the Canadian," Jeter said. "General Nelson Miles is the new commandant at Fort Dodge, and the word is General Sheridan is hell bent to bring the Indians in to the reservations."

"So, what is Billy doing?"

"Scouting for the army. They've got some Delaware Indians with them, but they need men who know the territory."

"Well, I must say I do know the territory, but scouting for the army? I don't know about that," Cade said. "I was sort of partial to grey."

Jeter laughed. "Those days are over."

EPILOGUE

TWIN CREEK RANCH 1927

Molly had packed a lunch of fried chicken, biscuits, potato salad, and fried peach pies for Cade and Owen Wister. The two men rode their horses out to a shady, grassy knoll on the banks of Dugout Creek, one of the two creeks that gave Twin Creek Ranch its name.

"Apparently, I don't have to ask what happened to the boy," Wister said. "He became a veterinarian."

"Not just a veterinarian, a very good veterinarian. And you two share something in common, you know."

"Oh? And what is that?"

"You're both writers."

"Really. Would I have seen anything that he has written?"

Cade laughed. "I don't think so unless you've read *Eradicating Cattle Scabies* or *Every Man His Own Cattle Doctor* or *Cattle: Their Breeds and Management.*"

"You're right, those aren't on my reading list," Owen said. "But what about Billy Dixon? And Jacob, too? Did you stay in contact with either of those two?"

"Of course, I did. Billy had the job as an army scout, for

about nine or ten years. Then he filed a claim on three sections of land down in Texas. Do you know where it was?"

"I don't have any idea."

"The old Adobe Walls ruins. Yes, sir, he built his house right west of where the old stockade was. I don't know how many years he lived there, but the last time I saw him, he had diverted the water of the creek, and he put in an orchard. Probably had at least 200 fruit trees right there at the Walls."

"I would never have guessed that Billy Dixon would be content to stay in one place," Owen said.

"He didn't stay there forever. He married a good woman and eventually they moved to be near a school for their children."

"And what about Jacob? Did he get to Texas?"

"He did." Cade tossed a rock into the creek. "He died there."

"I'll have to hear about that."

"You will, someday, but I'm not ready to talk about that yet."

"Okay, that will be a story for another day."

A LOOK AT RED RIVER REVENGE BY ROBERT VAUGAN

The Name is Remington...and he's the best there is. In an untamed territory that grinds most lawmen down to blood and bone, it takes a special breed to make justice more than just a fancy word. A man gunmetal hard, as fast as desert lightning-with the brains to out think 'em and the guts to out fight 'em. Meet the law west of Stone County-Chief Territorial Marshal Ned Remington.

Remington has his hands full, keeping a beautiful hellfire from the clutches of a killer and visa versa!

AVAILABLE NOW ON AMAZON

GET YOUR FREE STARTER LIBRARY!

Join the Wolfpack Publishing mailing list for information on new releases, updates, discount offers and your FREE Wolfpack Publishing Starter Library, complete with 5 great western novels: http://wolfpackpublishing.com/receive-free-wolfpack-publishing-starter-library/

Thank you for taking the time to read Cade At The Walls. If you enjoyed it, please consider telling your friends or posting a short review. Word of mouth is an author's best friend and much appreciated.

Thank you.

Robert Vaughan

ABOUT THE AUTHOR

Robert Vaughan sold his first book when he was 19. That was 57 years and nearly 500 books ago. He wrote the novelization for the miniseries *Andersonville*. Vaughan wrote, produced, and appeared in the History Channel documentary *Vietnam Homecoming*. His books have hit the NYT bestseller list seven times. He has won the Spur Award, the PORGIE Award (Best Paperback Original), the Western Fictioneers Lifetime Achievement Award, received the Readwest President's Award for Excellence in Western Fiction, is a member of the American Writers Hall of Fame and is a Pulitzer Prize nominee. Vaughn is also a retired army officer, helicopter pilot with three tours in Vietnam. And received the Distinguished Flying Cross, the Purple Heart, The Bronze Star with three oak leaf clusters, the Air Medal for valor with 35 oak leaf clusters, the Army Commendation Medal, the Meritorious Service Medal, and the Vietnamese Cross of Gallantry.

Find more great titles by Robert Vaughan and Wolfpack Publishing, here: http://wolfpackpublishing.com/robert-vaughan/

Made in the USA
Monee, IL
21 June 2020